PLAYING THE FOOL

"All right, I'll load it," Clint said, "but remember, I warned you." Taking his time, he pulled the pistol out of his holster, broke the cylinder, and spun it. "Well, I must be gettin' forgetful. It is loaded after all." He cocked it and leveled it at Mace. "Anytime you're ready, you can go for your gun."

"What the hell . . . ?" Mace sputtered, completely confused, looking at a cocked .44 staring back at him. He looked from Curly to Blankership to the weapon trained on him again, as if expecting someone to explain what had just happened. "Put that damn gun away," he blustered after a moment. "We ain't drawed yet."

"I have," Clint said coolly. "You saw me draw. I ain't gonna show you again. That would be pretty damn stupid if I gave you another chance. I told you I was faster than you, but you just had to be shown. Let's get this thing finished. I've got to be gettin' back to work, so go on; go for your gun."

Mace stood dumbfounded, knowing that if he reached for his weapon, he was a dead man. He believed Clint was just crazy enough to shoot him down right there in the saloon.

TRIAL AT FORT KEOGH

Charles G. West

A SIGNET BOOK

SIGNET
Published by the Penguin Group
Penguin Group (USA) LLC, 375 Hudson Street,
New York, New York 10014

USA I Canada I UK I Ireland I Australia I New Zealand I India I South Africa I China
penguin.com
A Penguin Random House Company

First published by Signet, an imprint of New American Library,
a division of Penguin Group (USA) LLC

First Printing, December 2014

 REGISTERED TRADEMARK—MARCA REGISTRADA

ISBN 978-0-451-46850-5

Printed in the United States of America
10 9 8 7 6 5 4 3 2 1

For Ronda

Chapter 1

Clint Cooper squatted on his heels and picked up a piece of charred bone, which he used to poke around in the remains of a slaughtered steer. His close inspection wasn't really necessary, because it was obviously not the work of wolves or coyotes. Those predators did not usually build a fire to cook the meat. This was the second carcass he had found in the last few days, and moccasin prints around the kill told him that it was done by a small party of Indians.

The question in his mind was whether or not it was the same raiding party that hit a small ranch eight miles east of the Double-V-Bar Ranch two days before. Leonard Sample, his wife, and two sons were killed in the raid, their mutilated bodies found by their neighbor to the east of them. It was the first attack by an Indian war party in quite some time, at least since the construction of Fort Keogh. Every rancher on the south side of the Yellowstone suffered the loss of a cow now and then from small parties of Indians around this time of year when game was difficult to come by. Usually it was of no real concern as long as it wasn't allowed to get out of control. But the savage attack on the Sample Ranch was enough to cause serious worry throughout the territory.

The signs he was reading now turned up no small footprints, which indicated that the slaughter wasn't done by a party with women and children, as the first killing had been. This killing was recent—recent enough for him to be able to possibly track down the guilty parties. Clint's boss, Randolph Valentine, was not likely to miss one or two stolen cows from his herd of over fifteen hundred, so Clint had been inclined to overlook the first steer slaughtered by a party of hungry Indians. But two in a week's time was cause for concern, especially after the murder of the Sample family.

At first, Clint frowned when he thought about tracking down what he had imagined to be a small group of starving Indians, still resisting the government's orders to return to the reservation. But the winters were hard in Montana Territory. A good many of the trail-hardened longhorns from Texas were lost each year to natural predators, and it was part of Clint's responsibilities as Randolph Valentine's top hand to see that the number lost was held to a minimum.

Before these two incidents, the raiding of the herds had really not been bad, mostly because the army had built a fort on the south bank of the Yellowstone at the confluence of that river with the Tongue. Originally known as the Tongue River Barracks, Fort Keogh was only about five miles from the Double-V-Bar. Its purpose was to protect settlers from hostile Sioux raiding parties, remnants of Sitting Bull's and Crazy Horse's warriors who had escaped after the massacre at Little Big Horn.

The Texas longhorn cattle were a hardy lot and better suited than other breeds to fatten up on Montana grass over the winter before being shipped to the Chicago slaughterhouses in the spring. One thing was for sure—they were a lot easier to kill than the pronghorn antelope native to the area, especially when the hunter had nothing more than a bow.

I reckon I'd go after a cow, too, if the situation was turned around, he thought, *and I was the one needing food.*

He got to his feet when Ben Hawkins and Jody Hale appeared at the top of the ravine and came slowly down to join him. "Found another'n, didja?" Ben called out.

"Yep," Clint answered. "If I was to guess, I'd say they left here no more'n four or five hours ago, and I don't think this one was killed by the same bunch that killed that last one. Take a look."

Ben dismounted, dropped his reins to the ground, and walked over beside Clint. He squatted on his heels, as Clint had, and stirred the ashes of the small fire. "I expect you're right," he said. "Four or five hours ago, not long after daybreak." He grunted with the effort to stand up again, not being as agile as the younger man. "I reckon you're wantin' to try to track 'em."

"I expect we oughta," Clint replied. "I'm thinkin' this might be that war party that struck the Sample place. Even if they ain't, Mr. Valentine said he didn't intend to feed every starvin' Indian in the territory." He stroked his chin thoughtfully as he turned the matter over in his mind. "I'd kinda hoped, when we found that other one a few days ago, that they were just gonna kill one and move on through our range. But I reckon this is a different bunch and they're figurin' on stayin' awhile."

"Looks that way," Ben agreed. He crossed the small stream on the other side of the burned-out fire to take a look at the tracks, stepping from stone to stone to keep his boots dry. After a few moments inspecting the mixture of hoofprints and moccasin tracks, he expressed what Clint had already surmised. "'Pears to me they didn't just go after this one cow. Hell, they cut out half a dozen cows and drove 'em down here to the stream. There's cow tracks and horse tracks, and the horses weren't shod, so they was Injuns, all right."

"And they drove 'em down that side of the stream toward the river," Clint finished for him. "I figure it's that Sioux raidin' party, 'cause I couldn't find any small footprints that would mean there were women and children with 'em. I reckon they butchered this one, then just decided to take a few cattle with 'em for their food supply."

"Looks that way," Ben said again, and took another look around the edge of the water for tracks. He was thinking that if there were kids, they'd have been playing around the water. "Might be a small bunch passin' through on their way up to Canada to join up with what's left of ol' Sittin' Bull's people."

"How many you think?" Clint asked.

"I figure five, maybe six," Ben replied.

"That's about what I make it," Clint said.

It was not surprising that they agreed, since Ben Hawkins had taught Clint practically everything he knew about reading tracks. Clint was still in his teens when he left Wyoming Territory and made his way down to Texas, looking for work with one of the big ranches. With no ties to any part of the country, he was prone to wander until he found someplace that suited him. He signed on with Will Marston to drive a herd up from Texas to Ogallala. That was when he met Ben Hawkins. Ben recognized the honest, hardworking decency in the otherwise carefree young man, and unofficially took him under his wing.

It occurred to Ben that young Clint never mentioned family or home, so one day he had asked him about his home, and if there was someone there who might want to hear where he was.

"Nope," Clint answered.

Although it took some digging, Ben was finally able to learn that Clint had no idea what had happened to his mother. One day she was gone, and his father told him that she had died of pneumonia. He was about two at the time, as far as he could guess. He stayed with his father until an argument over a prostitute in a saloon turned into a gunfight and left Clint an orphan. Now at twenty, the years having softened his memories, he knew that his father's name was Clayton Cooper, and that was all he cared to know about his past. He couldn't recall his mother's name, and doubted that he ever knew it. He also had an odd, C-shaped scar on his neck but had no recollection as to how he got it.

After several years, when a natural partnership developed between them, the two friends decided to help drive a herd of Texas cattle on up to Montana for Randolph Valentine. Valentine was quick to see the potential in young Clint Cooper, and offered him a permanent job. He offered Ben a job, too, but Ben was smart enough to know that that was probably because the two were partners, and that he'd have to hire both of them to get the one he wanted. As it had turned out, however, Valentine came to appreciate the experience and the work ethic of the older partner as well. He soon came to realize that he had made a better deal than he had at first thought.

In a couple of years' time, young Clint Cooper proved to be a man capable of running the day-to-day operations of the ranch. And Valentine was aware of the steel-like strength beneath the carefree attitude he most often displayed. At any rate, Clint was physically big enough to handle objections to any orders he might issue to the crew that worked Valentine's ranch. That capability was seldom necessary, though, since Clint's orders always came in the form of suggestions, and he always seemed willing to take his share of the dirty chores. Valentine had never officially announced that Clint was foreman of his crew, but all the men knew it to be the case. It had not surprised Ben that Valentine had come to look at the young ramrod almost as a son. This was especially true in light of the fact that Randolph and Valerie Valentine had only one offspring, a daughter named Hope, who was a year younger than Clint.

"Well, I reckon we'd best go see if we can recover our stolen cattle," Clint said. He looked up at Jody Hale, who was still seated on his horse. "Jody, ride on back and tell Charley and the rest of the boys to keep moving the cattle back off that flat. I think it wouldn't be a bad idea to move 'em in closer to the ranch. Me and Ben are gonna go see if we can catch up with these Indians, and maybe get our cattle back."

Jody, the fourteen-year-old nephew of Charley Clark, nodded in reply and promptly turned his horse to ride back up the ravine.

Ben looked back over his shoulder to watch the boy

ride away. "You reckon he'll remember what you told him by the time he gets back to the herd?" he joked.

Clint laughed. "Yeah, Jody's all right. He's just got his mind on other things most of the time—not much different from any of us at fourteen." He stepped up into the saddle then, but paused for a moment. "I didn't ask you if you wanted to stick your neck out to go after a bunch of Indian warriors."

Ben waited to answer until he crossed back over the stream and stepped up on his horse. "No, you didn't, did you?" he mocked. "But then you never do. Hell, I gotta go with you anyway, to make sure you don't get yourself inta somethin' you can't get out of."

He gave his horse a kick and splashed across the stream to lead out along the opposite bank, leaving his grinning partner no choice but to follow.

It was late in the afternoon by the time they caught up with the party of Sioux raiders. From the top of a ridge a quarter of a mile from the banks of the Yellowstone, Clint and Ben scanned the band of cottonwoods that crowded the low bluffs, trying to spot the rustlers. A thin ribbon of smoke wafting up from the trees had warned them that the Indians had stopped to make an early camp, probably preferring to deal with the hassle of crossing the cattle in the morning.

"I 'spose they ain't too good at drivin' cattle," Ben speculated. "And gettin' late in the day, they're afraid they'll lose some of 'em in the river. They're hid in them trees somewhere, but I can't see 'em."

"Me, neither," Clint said, "but they've gotta be around that fire. I *would* like to see exactly how many we've gotta account for before we go walkin' in there blind."

"I'm still thinkin' six of 'em," Ben said. All the horses' hoofprints appeared to be indicatin' half a dozen and all of 'em carrying a load. "I'd like to know what kinda weapons they're totin'."

"Maybe six," Clint allowed. "But maybe just five and one of those horses is a packhorse loaded down with the meat offa that steer we found back there. We'll just have to wait till it gets a little darker, then work in a little closer."

It was a wait of a little more than an hour before the sun disappeared and deep shadows spread across the river valley to darken the narrow expanse of flat prairie approaching the trees. With their Winchester rifles loaded and ready, they walked down the ridge, leading their horses. At the edge of the cottonwoods, they tied the horses, then continued on foot, moving carefully through the trees until they spotted the fire flickering through the trees some fifty yards away. Exercising even more caution now, they worked their way in closer until they were only twenty-five or thirty yards away from the fire.

"There's our cows," Ben whispered, and pointed to half a dozen steers gathered together below the bluffs near the water. Beyond them, the Indians' ponies grazed on the brown stubble of grass covering the slope down to the bluffs.

Clint nodded, then brought his attention back to the campfire and the sleeping bodies around it. He counted four warriors, bundled in their blankets and lying like spokes of a wheel, with the fire as the hub. He had missed his guess that the party consisted of five warriors, but so had Ben, who figured there were six.

At least, they don't appear to be concerned about being attacked, he thought.

"Looks too easy, don't it?" Ben whispered. "Two apiece."

"Yeah," Clint replied. "Reckon there's a lookout hidin' somewhere?"

"If there is, he ain't stayin' close to the rest of 'em. I reckon we'll find out when we start shootin'."

Clint couldn't help harboring a small bit of reluctance to simply start firing at the sleeping bodies, but it was a good bet that they were the hostiles who had murdered the Sample family.

"Might be a good idea to split up and get a little space between us," he suggested, "in case they come outta those blankets shootin'."

"Good idea," Ben said. "Ain't no use us standin' in the same spot and givin' 'em one target for both of us. I'll work over toward the horses."

"All right," Clint said. "I'll wait for you to get where you want and take the first shot. That'll be my signal to open up on 'em."

Clint knelt down and trained his '73 model Winchester on the sleeping forms while Ben moved off into the darkness. Set to wait for Ben's first shot, Clint was surprised when it came within seconds of his departure, only to realize a split second later, when he saw the muzzle flash, that the shot had come from behind Ben.

Without taking time to think, Clint turned and pumped three shots at the spot where he had seen the flash. Unable to see a target, he quickly turned back in time to see the other four hostiles scrambling out of their blankets. Cranking out two more rounds, he was able to knock one of the warriors down before they all disappeared into the trees.

"Damn!" Clint cursed, and dived behind a sizable tree for cover when a couple of answering shots snapped through the bushes near him. "Ben! You all right?" There was no answer. "Damn," he swore again, and started running in the direction Ben had taken, dodging trees and bushes in the darkness.

Off to his left, he spotted three figures running toward the horses, but he was forced to jump behind a tree to keep from being run over by a frantic cow that had been frightened by the gunshots. When he stepped back out from behind the tree, the three he had seen had already reached their ponies. With little time to get off a shot, he drew a bead on the one closest to him and pulled the trigger. He was startled to hear another rifle shot at almost the same instant and saw one of the targets fall.

"The other two are runnin'!" Ben called out from a bank of brambles no more than thirty feet ahead of Clint. He struggled to free himself from the clutches of the berry bushes as Clint ran by him in pursuit of the two escaping hostiles.

Dodging another stampeding cow, Clint arrived at the slope where the Indian ponies had been left for the night. He was a few seconds too late to get off another clear shot, but he took the shot anyway, knowing there was little chance he would hit either of the hostiles as they galloped out of sight along the bluffs. He chambered another round but didn't fire again as Ben came huffing and puffing up behind him.

"Didja hit anything?" Ben blurted excitedly.

"No, they got away," Clint said, and eased the hammer down on his rifle, still staring into the darkness where he had last seen the fleeing Indians. He turned back to Ben then. "I thought you'd got shot back there when I yelled and you didn't answer."

"I couldn't," Ben replied. "That son of a bitch woulda shot at me again. You musta hit him when you throwed those shots at him. I wish to hell I'da knowed you got him. I wouldn'ta jumped in them damn berry bushes. They like to tore me up tryin' to get out of 'em."

"You lost your hat," Clint said.

"Well, I reckon so," Ben replied indignantly. "I'da lost more'n that if that bastard had aimed a hair lower."

"We'd better check on the ones we shot," Clint said. "It looks like those last two are long gone."

They found a hostile lying on the slope down by the river bluffs, still alive, although mortally wounded. Noticing the two wounds, Ben jokingly complained, "You shoulda told me you was aimin' at that one and I'da aimed at one of the other two."

The wounded warrior appeared to be unconscious at first, but he suddenly began to chant his death song, his voice strained and hoarse from the pain. Ben let him rasp out a few minutes of it before he silenced him with a round from his Colt handgun. "I reckon he sang enough to get him ready to meet Man Above," he said.

The next order of business was to find the one who had taken the first shot at Ben. It appeared that Clint had hit him with a lucky shot, because no more shots had come from the trees, but they didn't know that for sure. Both men were aware of the possibility that he could even then be getting in a position to fire at them again.

With that thought in mind, Ben said, "We'd better get the hell outta this clearin'." Clint quickly agreed and they went back into the trees, where they split up to approach the spot from which the first muzzle flashes were seen. They closed in on it, ready to fire if suddenly confronted, until Ben called out, "Over here! I found him." He waited for Clint beside a body lying at the base of a large cottonwood. He had apparently been killed instantly by a shot to the chest.

"Well, that was a pretty good shot, considerin' I couldn't see what I was shootin' at," Clint said.

"I don't know," Ben japed. "I counted three shots, so you missed him twice."

They then went back to the campfire, where they found the third body lying in the same spot where he had dropped when Clint shot him as he scrambled out of his blanket.

There was not enough light to see by, so they decided they might as well camp there for the night. Thinking it unwise, however, to take advantage of the fire already built, they chose a spot farther along the bluffs. They left the bodies where they were, planning to look them over in the morning. They each spent the night alternating watches while the other man tried to sleep, and guarded against the possibility of an avenging attack by the two survivors.

With dawn's light, they were able to confirm that the Indians they had killed were guilty of the Sample family's murders. A long-haired blond scalp was evidence enough for that. But there was also a Henry rifle with the initials *LS* carved into the stock. In addition, they found several items of clothing and tools obviously belonging to the family. It was enough to assuage the consciences of both men that they had not randomly murdered innocent men. Ben found his hat close to the bank of bushes where he had taken refuge. It had two neat holes near the top of the crown where the bullet passed through.

"Damn," he complained, "I just bought that hat four years ago in Ogallala. It ain't even broke in good." Looking to make the best of a bad situation, he took an eagle feather that had been braided into the locks of the

Indian who had put the holes in his hat. He inserted the feather through the two holes, held it up to look at the effect, then said, "I kinda like that. Maybe I've got his big medicine now."

"Big Chief Hawkins," Clint grunted sarcastically. "I expect we'd best round those cows up and head 'em back with the others. Charley and the boys probably wonder if the Indians got us." They had already discussed the possibility of trying to track the two surviving warriors but decided it would most likely be a waste of time and effort.

"How 'bout after we eat some breakfast?" Ben asked, reminding Clint that they had not eaten since noon the day before. "There's a load of fresh meat here already butchered that we might as well cook up. We can take the rest of it back to the boys when we drive the cows in. Cold as it is, it'll still be a while before it turns bad."

"That sounds good to me," Clint said. "I've got a little bit of coffee in my saddlebag that I didn't use yesterday."

He was short on supplies because he had planned to ride back to the ranch the previous night, before they had found the slaughtered steer. Other than the usual meeting with Randolph Valentine every Monday, Clint didn't usually check in with his boss. But now there was the matter of reporting the fight with the Sioux raiders. Clint supposed that the army should be notified and they would most likely send out a patrol to try to run down the two hostiles who got away. He decided he'd better go straight back to the ranch to talk to Valentine and let Ben drive the six head of cattle they found back to join the herd.

"What about those Injun ponies?" Ben asked. There were only two. They assumed that the missing horses had probably galloped off after the two Indians.

"We'll load that beef on the one that was totin' it,"

Clint said. "I'll take the bridle offa that other one and let him decide what he wants to do. Most likely he'll follow that one totin' the meat."

It was a little before noon when Clint rode up to the barn, dismounted, and pulled his saddle off Sam. He led the horse into the corral before taking the bridle off and letting him go free. Hank Haley walked out of the barn to greet him.

"Heard about your little set-to with them Sioux murderers," Hank said. "Heard you and Ben went after 'em."

"Is that so?" Clint replied, a little surprised. He had expected to get back to the ranch before any of the crew riding night herd.

"Yeah, Charley sent Jody on in to tell Mr. Valentine," Hank explained. "Did you catch up with 'em?"

"Yep, we caught 'em," Clint said, "but a couple of 'em got away."

"Mr. Valentine said to tell you to come straight up to the house as soon as you showed up."

"I'm on my way," Clint said, "soon as I take care of my saddle." He picked up the saddle, grabbed his bridle and saddle blanket with his free hand, and headed toward the tack room.

"I coulda took that for you," Hank volunteered, though Clint was already entering the barn. "Mr. Valentine said as soon as you got back," he reminded him.

"I won't be but a minute," Clint said. "I'll tell the boss you told me."

He continued on to the tack room. For some reason Clint could never understand, Hank, a simple soul, seemed to always think he was on the verge of being fired. He apparently never realized that, if it became necessary, Clint would most likely be the one doing the firing. If he had to guess, he would say that Hank was insecure because of his age, and the fact that he was used more around the ranch instead of working the cattle with the rest of the crew.

As far as Clint was concerned, Hank served a useful purpose. He was a helping short of a full portion of brains, and more than a little gullible, but he did his job in a willing and cheerful manner. And as long as Clint was satisfied with Hank's work, Valentine wouldn't bother to question it.

Leaving the barn, Clint headed for the kitchen door at the back of the sprawling ranch house with its wide porch that wrapped around three sides of the structure. Ben always referred to it as "the royal palace." Clint had to admit it was a bit overdone, since it housed only three people: the boss; his daughter, Hope; and a Crow cook and housekeeper named Rena. Valerie Valentine, Randolph's wife, had died the winter before last when a fever took her.

Princess Hope, as Ben referred to Valentine's daughter when she wasn't present, was the lady of the house now. Ben's title for her was not mean-spirited, for he genuinely liked the young lady. In truth, Hope was highly regarded by all the hands of the Double-V-Bar. The fact that she was also easy on the eyes gave her the look of a real princess. She was held in high regard, however, primarily because she didn't act like a princess.

At any rate, she was the apple of her father's eye and his most precious possession. Clint was not immune to the young lady's charms, and he caught himself thinking thoughts of fantasy from time to time. But he quickly stifled them, reminding himself of his station in her life. There had been occasions when he was almost convinced that she might have special feelings for him, in spite of the fact that she had entertained a young second lieutenant, recently transferred to Fort Keogh, almost every Sunday over the last four months. Thinking of it was enough to cause Clint to frown. Hope mischievously refused to give any hints of the seriousness of her interest in the young officer. Consequently Clint remained a respectful friend of his boss's daughter. She happened to be in the kitchen when he knocked on the door.

"Hello, Clint," Hope greeted him when she opened the door. "We heard about the trouble you and Ben were in last night. Thank goodness you both are all right." She paused to be sure. "You didn't get hurt, did you?"

"No, ma'am," Clint replied playfully. "You know I'm not gonna take a chance on gettin' myself shot. I let Ben take all the chances." He gave her a broad smile. "Ben's all right, but his hat got shot, two holes right through the crown."

Hope laughed with him, knowing him well enough to feel assured that he was the one more likely to take chances. "Well, I'm glad that's all. Would you like a cup of coffee? Dinner's not quite ready yet. Rena and I are still fixing it. But there's a pot of coffee on the stove."

"Ah, no, thanks," Clint replied, although the suggestion of a fresh cup of coffee sounded good to him. "Hank told me your daddy wanted to see me as soon as I got in, so I reckon I'd best see about that before I do anything else."

"Is that you, Clint?" Valentine called from the parlor. Not waiting for an answer, he strode into the kitchen. A big man, Randolph Valentine seemed to fill any room he walked into. "Tell me what happened. Did you and Ben catch up with those Indians? Charley sent Jody in to tell us you went after them. Here, let's sit down at the table here." He motioned Clint over to the kitchen table. "Rena, how 'bout pouring us a cup of coffee?" He looked back at Clint. "Maybe you need something stronger after last night."

"No, sir," Clint said when he finally got the chance. "Coffee will be just fine." He pulled a chair back and sat down.

Hope didn't wait for Rena. She got a couple of cups from the cupboard and filled them from the pot on the stove. She winked at Clint when she placed the cup before him. "I offered him a cup, but he said he didn't want it," she told her father.

"That was five minutes ago," Clint said, accustomed to her teasing. "I'd enjoy one now."

Serious again, he told Valentine what had happened the night before, the exchange of gunfire with the Sioux hostiles, and the evidence he and Ben had found indicating that the raiding party was the same one that had attacked the Sample place.

"That was a damn shame," Valentine said, referring to the Sample massacre, "and damn poor luck." Leonard Sample had only recently settled on the strip of land by the river, having moved his family from Kansas. They were not close neighbors, but Valentine had fully intended to make an effort to ride over to meet them. "Damn poor luck," he repeated, then brought his thoughts back to the incident of the previous night. "How many were in the party you caught up with last night?"

"There were five," Clint said. "We killed three of 'em. The other two got away."

"It's been a good while since we've had any sign of Indian trouble," Valentine said. "But that's been two cows now, slaughtered about a week apart. I'm just wondering if we've got a bunch of renegade Indians set on raiding along the Yellowstone again."

"I'm pretty sure the first cow was killed by a small party of hungry Indians, but I don't think they were part of the ones that hit the Sample place," Clint reminded him.

Valentine paused and nodded thoughtfully, then continued. "I want you to ride on over to Fort Keogh and tell the army what happened. I'm sure they'll wanna find out if we've got anything to worry about."

"Yes, sir, I'll head out right away," Clint said.

"You can wait till you get some dinner," Hope interjected. "It isn't that far to the fort."

"Yes, of course," her father said. "You can eat with us. I'm sure the women are fixing enough for all of us. Ain't that right, Rena?" The impassive Crow woman made no response beyond a slight nod.

It was not the first time Clint had been invited to eat at the ranch house, but he felt a little out of place at the boss's table. "Thank you just the same, but I expect Milt's cooked up dinner in the bunkhouse, so I'd best eat with the rest of the boys. I'll ride over to the fort soon as I've finished. Should be back by dark."

"Suit yourself," Hope said, still teasing, "if you're saying Milt Futch is a better cook than Rena and I."

"I'm not sayin' anything of the sort," Clint responded in kind. "I know Rena's a first-rate cook, but I don't know how much of the cookin' you did. So I don't know if I oughta risk it. I'll just go eat with the rest of the crew."

"Let the man alone, Hope," Valentine said. "He can eat where he wants to." Turning to Clint, he added, "Let me know if the army is going to do anything about those Indians."

"Yes, sir, just as soon as I get back" Clint said as he got up from the table. "Thank you for the coffee," he told Hope as he went out the door. She answered him with a smile.

She closed the door behind him and turned back to her father. "Are you ready to eat, Papa?"

"I reckon so," he replied.

"Rena's dishing you up a plate. I'll get you some more coffee."

She worried about her father. Although a powerful man, seemingly still in the prime of life despite his years, she knew that he suffered privately over the loss of her mother, his Valerie. It had been two years since her mother was taken from them, and her father still could not let her go. She knew that he talked to her mother when he was in his room, usually late at night when he thought everyone else was asleep. Hope sometimes left her bed and tiptoed to her father's door to listen. He spoke as if her mother were there with him, talking about problems with the cattle, or telling her about something she or Rena had done that pleased him. Hope knew that Rena had heard him as well, and she was sure the sullen Crow woman did not doubt that he actually *was* in contact with his late wife.

It used to worry Hope more than it now did. She had feared her father was losing his mind, but in all the time since her mother's death, he had never shown any other symptoms of irrational behavior. So Hope decided to just accept that minor idiosyncrasy as a trait her father possessed that set him apart from ordinary men.

If he did happen to start losing his grip on reality in his later years, she felt secure in the knowledge that he had Clint to rely on. Clint was special, and she thanked the good Lord that he and Ben had crossed their path. His carefree attitude could be deceiving, but he was dead serious when the situation called for it. She knew that whatever trouble might come their way, she could count on Clint to take care of it and always act in her father's best interest.

She knew that her father considered Clint as the son that maybe she was supposed to have been. She never begrudged him that position, because she also knew that she was the apple of her father's eye. In fact, she held Clint very close to her heart, mainly because of his devotion to her father. Her thoughts were interrupted then by her father's voice. "What are you concentrating so hard on?" he asked. "If you stand there holding that coffeepot much longer, it's gonna be too cold to drink."

"Sorry," she replied. "My mind was just wandering."

She filled his cup and returned the pot to the stove, where Rena stood watching her. The silent Crow woman nodded solemnly as if she could read Hope's thoughts. *You always act like you can tell what everybody's thinking,* Hope thought, *but I know it's just a damn act.*

Chapter 2

Clint guided the bay gelding past the crude structures that still remained on the original site of the cantonment, as it was called at the time they were built. Valentine had told him that General Nelson Miles didn't build the fort on the original site. He was a colonel at that time, and he decided to pick a new site one mile west of the original one to accommodate his plans.

Still, there were some enlisted men's families living in the old log huts he was passing now, who were awaiting construction of quarters at the site of newly named Fort Keogh. It was easy to imagine the hardships of living in the rough dwellings. They were constructed by digging trenches where the walls were to be. Then they cut logs, stood them on end in the trenches to make the walls, and filled the cracks between the logs with mud. The roofs were also logs with mud chinking. They made for a miserable dwelling, and in Clint's opinion, they were some sorry-looking homes. But the method was necessary because at the time of their construction there were plenty of logs, but a shortage of tools to fashion lumber. The huts sharply contrasted with the frame buildings of the new Fort Keogh.

It was around four o'clock in the afternoon when he rode up to the diamond-shaped parade ground. The bugler had just sounded Recall, which signaled the end of the evening mounted drill, and the troopers of a company of cavalry were headed toward the stables. Clint pulled up before the nearest trooper.

"Afternoon," he said. "Can you tell me where the commanding officer's headquarters is?" The soldier pointed him toward a building directly across the parade ground. "Much obliged," Clint said, and proceeded toward it. He dismounted and looped the bay's reins around a corner post.

Inside, he was met by a sergeant seated at a desk. Behind the sergeant, Clint saw two open offices, one of them empty, and an officer seated behind a desk in the other one. "Can I help you, sir?" the sergeant asked.

"I'm from the Double-V-Bar. My boss, Mr. Randolph Valentine, sent me over to tell you soldiers that we ran up on those Sioux hostiles that raided Leonard Sample's place. He figured you'd wanna know."

"I reckon we sure would," the sergeant said. "I'll let you tell the captain about it." He got up from his desk and stepped to the office door. "Fellow out here with some information about that Injun raid on those settlers back up the river."

The officer got up from his desk and came out to talk to Clint. "I'm Captain Rodgers," he said. "You say you know something about that raid?" Clint told him about the fight he and Ben had had with the Indians. "How do you know they were the same hostiles that murdered the Sample family?" Rodgers asked. Clint told him about the evidence they found that tied them to the massacre. The captain was more than interested. "A fifteen-man patrol was sent out to that farm as soon as word reached Fort Keogh, but they weren't able to pick up the hostiles' trail."

Clint didn't comment, but he was thinking that it shouldn't have taken much of a scout to pick up the trail of a war party, even one of that size. It couldn't be blamed on snow covering the tracks, because there had been no snow beyond a few flurries since then.

Rodgers paused to give Clint's report some thought before he decided what he should do. General Miles was not on the post at the present time. Neither was his second-in-command, Major Kinsey, so Rodgers was the officer in charge. After a moment, he told himself what Miles would do, and made his decision. "If I send a patrol out with you, can you take them to the spot where you had that fight?" he asked Clint.

"Yes, sir," Clint replied, "I can take you there if you want me to."

"If my memory serves me," Rodgers said, stroking his chin thoughtfully, "the Sample Farm was about a three-hour ride from here. How far would you say the place is where you had the fight with the hostiles?"

"Maybe an hour's ride short of that," Clint said.

"There's not much sense in trying to assemble a patrol to send out this evening, so we might as well wait till morning. You say there are only two of the hostiles that got away?" Clint nodded his affirmation. Rodgers continued. "No need to send a full scouting party out for two hostiles." That comment was meant more for himself, for he was wondering if it was wise to dispatch a large detail without his superior's approval. His decision made, he told Clint that a detail would leave Fort Keogh in the morning.

"Right," Clint said, and turned to leave, thinking his job was done.

Rodgers stopped him. "You are planning to lead the patrol to the place where the hostiles were killed, right?"

"Right," Clint confirmed.

"Well, then, you're probably gonna need a place to bunk tonight." He looked at a large clock on the wall. "Mess call will be sounding in about an hour. I'll send a man with you to get you something to eat. Then he can show you where you can find an empty bunk."

Clint hesitated and considered the suggestion. He hadn't planned on staying overnight at the army post when the ranch was only a little more than five miles away. "If it's all the same to you, Captain, I'll go on back to the Double-V-Bar, and I'll meet your men there in the mornin'." When Rodgers looked uncertain, Clint said, "It's on the way, so I might as well join up with your men there."

Rodgers frowned while he thought about that for a moment, but he couldn't think of any reason to object. "Well, we sure know where the Double-V-Bar is, so I guess that would be all right." Certain then, he said, "Good, they'll meet you there in the morning." He paused for a moment while he thought about it, then said, "The patrol will be under the command of Lieutenant Justin Landry."

Clint almost cringed. "Much obliged," he said, and took his leave.

Justin Landry, he thought. *Well, he sure as hell ought to know the way. He's been there often enough.* He formed a picture in his mind of Hope, all girlish and coy when the lieutenant showed up. It was a picture that always bothered him.

When Clint was gone, Rodgers told the sergeant to send a man over to the bachelor officers' quarters to find Lieutenant Landry and tell him to report to the captain. "It'll give him a chance to get a little more experience in the field. I don't expect there's much of a chance to catch up with two Sioux warriors after this amount of time, so there's not much danger to worry about."

Lieutenant Landry had recently been assigned to the Second after a temporary assignment at Fort Lincoln, having graduated from West Point with the class of seventy-six. Rodgers felt it a good opportunity to add to Landry's experience with little risk of danger to him or the men he sent with him.

Leaving the headquarters building, Clint paused to consider if he should take a few minutes to have a quick drink before starting back to the ranch. It didn't take more than a second to decide that he was justified in doing so, since it had been some time since he had last imbibed—and Ernie's place was just outside the post.

Why, hell, he told himself, *it would be downright unneighborly if I was this close and didn't stop by to say hello.*

Ernie Thigpen had built his saloon soon after the army started construction of Fort Keogh. He built it as close to the fort as the army would allow—a distance of two miles, as ordered by General Miles, who was a colonel at the time. That wasn't a great distance for a man needing a drink of whiskey, so most of his business came from the soldiers stationed at the fort.

He was not the first to open a saloon close to the fort.

A man named Mat Carroll had set up some barrels under a tarp and started selling whiskey as soon as the fort began construction. But Colonel Miles had grown tired of having his guardhouse filled with drunken soldiers, so he ordered Carroll and anybody else selling whiskey off the military reservation. Ernie built a substantial structure as close to the fort as the military allowed and, so far, had not run afoul of General Miles' patience. Even so, he often complained that it might have been better in the long run if he had been located closer in to the rising town of Miles City. At the time, the new town was little more than a few tents and a hut or two. Now it was developing into a sizable settlement. He was busying himself behind the bar when Clint walked in. "Well, I'll be damned," he exclaimed. "Clint Cooper, I ain't seen you in a while. I thought you'd forgot about us, and was doin' your drinkin' in Miles City."

"Hello, Ernie," Clint responded. "I'm a workin' man— ain't had time to do much drinkin'." He turned then to give a smile to the grinning woman approaching him from the back of the room. "You know I stop in to see you and Darcy every chance I get. I just don't get that many chances."

"Hello, stranger," Darcy Suggs greeted him cordially, her greeting genuine, unlike the manufactured one she employed for the rutty soldiers from the fort. She moved up close beside him at the bar.

"Howdy, Darcy," Clint returned. "You're just as pretty as I remembered you."

"You're so full of horse shit," Darcy said, laughing. She knew that she still looked pretty good considering the long road she had traveled, but she did not deceive herself into thinking the bloom of youth was still there. She liked Clint Cooper. He always treated her like the lady she never was. "Are you gonna stay awhile and visit a little?" she asked hopefully as Ernie filled a shot glass and slid it over to Clint.

"Not this time," Clint said. "I have to get right back to the ranch. Mr. Valentine's waitin' to hear what I found out." He told them briefly why he had come to the fort. "So I just took the time for one quick drink and a howdy, and then I'm on my way."

"That's right sorry news about the Injuns," Ernie said. "That feller that got killed, Sample, he was in here one time. Seemed like a right nice man—hate to hear I lost another customer."

"You still thinkin' about movin' your saloon to Miles City?" Clint asked him while Darcy stood beside him, her hand resting on his arm.

"No, I reckon not," Ernie said. "I don't wanna move there anymore, what with the changes and everything."

"What changes?" Clint asked.

"Ha," Ernie snorted. "You must not a' been in town for a while. The sheriff . . ."

When mention of the sheriff did not register on Clint's face as he expected, Ernie expounded. "They got a sheriff now, feller name of Simon Yeager. Sorta appointed hisself sheriff is what I hear. And he made his brother his deputy. His brother's name is Mace, and they're pretty much runnin' the town. The town ain't never had a sheriff before, so there weren't nobody to stand in their way."

Clint shrugged. "Well, maybe they'll do a good job and keep the town under control—keep the drifters from raisin'so much hell."

"Ha," Ernie snorted again, and held the bottle over Clint's empty glass, questioning.

"One more," Clint said.

Ernie filled it and continued his discourse on the Yeager brothers. "They'll keep it under control, all right. There was a feller stopped in here on his way to Bozeman. He'd heard of 'em before, said Simon Yeager wasn't nothin' but a gunman and a stagecoach bandit outta Wyomin', and his brother wasn't nothin' better. I believe him, too. Those folks in Miles City are tryin' to build a proper town, so they musta figured they needed a sheriff 'cause nobody stood up to 'em. I never seen the big stud, the one named Simon. But his brother, Mace, has been in here a couple of times, and I ain't never seen a man with a meaner streak than that one—lean as a snake and every bit as mean lookin'. Darcy can tell you."

"That son of a bitch," Darcy said in response. "He told me he needed to get his itch scratched. I wasn't too thrilled about the idea, but business is business. I found out what his pleasure was, though, and it wasn't just dippin' his pickle. He likes to play rough—slapped me so hard across the face that he left a bruise on my cheek." She paused, pleased to see the concern traced across Clint's brow. "Nobody gets a second chance to whack me across the mouth. He left here with a bruise, too—on that skinny ass of his where I jammed my hat pin halfway up to the pearl." She reached up and pulled the treacherous weapon from the bun on the back of her head to show him. "He bent it a little, too—musta hit a bone." She made a halfhearted attempt to straighten it again before replacing it in her hair.

"Homer Lewis," Ernie continued, "you know him— feller that runs the barbershop—he said some of Yeager's friends showed up in town, and they don't seem to have nothin' to do but play cards and drink likker." He shook his head, concerned.

"What about the army?" Clint asked. "Ain't it part

of their job to keep the peace? With outlaws like that runnin' the town, looks like they'd send some soldiers over there."

"I reckon ain't nobody really come to the fort to complain. The honest folks are too scared to say anything, afraid they'll end up in one of those gunfights that the Yeagers always win."

"That don't sound too good, does it?" Clint said. "I don't get into Miles City too often myself, so I hope I don't have the pleasure of makin' their acquaintance." He tossed his drink back and smacked the empty glass down forcefully. "Boy, that stuff's got a powerful burn. You must still be mixin' kerosene in it." He gave Darcy a little squeeze and a big smile. "Well, I'd best get on my way home." He started for the door.

"Don't stay away so long," Ernie said while Darcy took his arm and walked him to the door.

"Don't be a stranger," she said when she released his arm and stood watching the dark-haired young man as he deftly stepped up into the saddle. He turned to give her a smile before wheeling his horse away.

Not a chance in hell, she thought, *but it doesn't hurt to think about it.*

It was well past suppertime by the time Clint got back to the ranch. He had begun to wonder if he shouldn't have passed on the invitation to eat in the mess hall with the soldiers—either that or he should have skipped the saloon. He could feel a little gnawing in his empty stomach and figured it was Ernie's whiskey trying to eat a hole in it. It was probably not too late to grab a biscuit or two at the bunkhouse, and maybe something to go with them, if Milt hadn't fed all the scraps to the dogs. He decided, however, that he'd best report to Mr.

Valentine first, since he said that he would as soon as he returned.

He went straight to the house, even before he unsaddled the bay and turned him out to graze. He went to the kitchen door as usual. Rena was still in the kitchen, washing the dishes. When she came to the door and saw it was Clint, she opened it for him and nodded impassively as he walked in. This was as close as the stoic woman usually came to a smile, as far as Clint could determine.

"Evenin', Rena," he said. "Would you tell Mr. Valentine I'm back?" She nodded again and turned slowly on her heel to do his bidding. She returned moments later with Valentine right behind her.

"Clint," Valentine greeted him enthusiastically. "You got back in good time. I figured you might stop in one of those saloons in Miles City and forget your way home." He liked to tease Clint primarily because he was well aware of the young man's carefree nature.

"No, sir," Clint replied, and grinned, knowing his boss was japing. "I thought about it, but I didn't have enough money to buy all the whiskey that would take. Maybe I oughta ask for a raise."

"Hell, you're making more now than you're worth," Valentine came back. "You'd best settle for that." His true feeling was that Clint was worth twice what he was paying him. Joking aside then, he asked, "What did the army say?" Before Clint could answer, Valentine asked, "Did you get back in time to eat?"

"No matter, I wasn't really hungry," Clint lied.

"Pour him a cup of coffee, Rena," Valentine said.

The emotionless woman drained the last cup of coffee from the pot on the corner of the stove and handed it to Clint. Detecting the hint of alcohol on his breath, she then took a biscuit, left over from supper, sliced it in two, and placed a piece of beef between the halves. This she handed to Clint with a knowing nod. He smiled and thanked her, aware that Valentine's old hound dog had just lost a portion of his supper. Then he told Valentine what had taken place at the fort, talking between bites of his biscuit and sips of coffee that had grown as strong as horse liniment while sitting on the stove.

"So there'll be a detail of soldiers showing up here first thing in the morning?" Valentine asked. "How many did they say?"

"Don't know for sure," Clint replied, "but he said there wasn't no use to send more'n a few. I expect there won't be but about five or six of 'em."

"You'd better tell Milt that he might be feeding half a dozen soldiers in the morning." Always ready to demonstrate Western hospitality, he turned to Rena and said, "I suppose we should invite the officer to eat at the house, if they send one with 'em."

"That captain asked me if I would take 'em to the spot where we killed those Sioux," Clint said. "I told him I would. That all right with you?"

"Sure," Valentine said. "Help 'em any way you can. It's in our best interest."

"I expect I can just show 'em where to pick up the trail, then leave them to follow it, and I'll come on back."

Second Lieutenant Justin Landry stepped outside the small room he occupied in the bachelor officers' quarters and paused on the porch to check his watch when the notes of the bugle sounded Stable and Watering Call. As confirmed by the gold pocket watch presented to Landry by his father upon his graduation from West Point, the bugler was right on time at six o'clock. Without really thinking about it, he reached up with both hands to make sure his hat was sitting perfectly square with his eyebrows, a habit left over from his academy days.

Deeming himself ready, he stepped off the porch and strode smartly toward the middle of the parade ground where Sergeant Barry Cox stood before a detail of six troopers, waiting more or less in a straight line. Each man held the bridle of his horse, with the exception of the man at the end, who held his horse as well as the lieutenant's chestnut sorrel. The sergeant called the detail to attention when he saw Landry approaching from the B.O.Q.

"Good morning, Sergeant," Landry said. "You can stand at ease."

"Morning, sir," Cox returned.

"Have you drawn rations and ammunition?"

"Yes, sir," Cox replied, "rations for five days and each man a hundred rounds of ammunition, that's what I was ordered." He hesitated for a moment before asking, "It'll only be about an hour before Mess Call. Will we be eating breakfast before we go?"

"No," Landry said. "We're going to get started right away. I want to reach that ranch early. We'll take a short rest there to eat." He gave Cox a smile then and said, "Maybe the folks at the Double-V-Bar will show some hospitality and offer us some breakfast."

Cox grinned. "Maybe so," he said. It was a good sign. The sergeant had not had the occasion to serve in a detail under Landry's direct command. The lieutenant's remark might be a hint that the new officer wasn't intent upon being hard-assed, as some of the recent academy graduates tended to be.

In truth, the lieutenant felt pretty certain that they would be invited to breakfast, and that was the real reason he ordered the detail to march before mess. He took his reins from the soldier holding them.

"Let's get mounted," he said to Cox, and the patrol was under way.

"Hey, Clint," Hank Haley yelled from the hayloft, "here come your soldier boys." Clint walked out of the barn. In a few minutes, Hank joined him, and they stood watching the cavalry patrol as they approached. "Ha! Lookee yonder," Hank said. "That looks like that young rooster that's been courtin' Miss Hope. They didn't send many soldiers with him, did they?"

"Yeah, I reckon not," Clint replied. "They don't expect to have to deal with any more than the two that got away. Maybe you might better go tell Milt he could have some hungry soldiers to feed, in case they left before breakfast. I'll go up and tell Mr. Valentine."

By the time the small column of soldiers filed into the yard, Randolph Valentine had walked out to join Clint in greeting them. He was surprised to see the officer in charge was the young man who had been calling on his daughter.

"Good morning, Mr. Valentine. I've been assigned to go after those Indians Mr. Cooper encountered," Justin said as he dismounted and extended his hand. Then he turned to Clint and said, "I'm guessing you'd be Mr. Cooper." He knew Clint's name although they had never been introduced. He offered his hand to him as well.

"That's right," Clint replied.

"Glad to see you boys are gonna take a look into this Indian trouble," Valentine said. "Clint here can show you where he and one of the other men had the fight. But maybe you and your men would like a little something to eat before you get started."

"That's mighty kind of you, sir," Landry said, and turned to give Sergeant Cox a wink. "As a matter of fact, we did leave before breakfast. I certainly wouldn't want to impose on your hospitality, however. We are supplied with field rations."

"No trouble at all," Valentine insisted. "We were expecting to have breakfast for your men—give them something a little better than field rations. Hank there can take them to the bunkhouse. You, of course, will be welcome to have something with us at the house." Clint started to walk toward the bunkhouse with the soldiers, but Valentine stopped him. "Clint, why don't you come to the house with us?" he said. "I expect the lieutenant might wanna ask you some questions."

"Yes, sir," Clint said, and turned back. "I've already had my breakfast, but I reckon I could find room for another cup of coffee." He was thinking that this patrol to find renegade Indians was looking more and more like a Sunday picnic.

Like any young lieutenant fresh out of the academy, Justin Landry was eager to prove his qualifications to lead men in battle. He looked upon this assignment as an opportunity to demonstrate his ability to command, and he had no intention of wasting it. He figured that it didn't hurt to curry favor with the men in his patrol by allowing them to enjoy a good breakfast before setting out in search of the two renegade Indians. They should be more willing to respond to his orders if they thought he was fair-minded when it came to the tasks he might command them to do. Besides, hungry soldiers were reluctant soldiers, and he intended to lead an eager party after these Sioux murderers.

In spite of his desire to win the loyalty of the men in

his small patrol, however, he was not willing to waste a great deal of time enjoying the hospitality of Randolph Valentine. He was disappointed when he followed Valentine into the kitchen and Hope was not there. One of the reasons he wanted to stop at the Double-V-Bar was for the opportunity to impress her as the officer in command of the patrol. His disappointment dissolved moments later with the appearance of Valentine's daughter after he was seated at the table.

The young lieutenant jumped to his feet, almost toppling his chair, when Hope walked into the kitchen. Valentine stared at the young officer, puzzled, until he turned to see his daughter standing behind his chair. "Hope, look who's come to have breakfast with us. I believe you know the lieutenant," he teased.

"Good morning, Hope," Landry gushed, a wide smile of delight played across his handsome face. "It's always my pleasure to see you, even under circumstances such as these." He was still fairly amazed to have discovered a flower so fair in these rugged breaks of the Yellowstone.

Surprised, for Clint had not mentioned that the soldiers who would show up at the ranch would be commanded by Landry, Hope reflected his smile. "Well, good morning, Justin," she said with an almost musical lilt to her voice. "I must say I didn't expect you."

Oblivious to his daughter's staged entrance into the kitchen, and puzzled as to why Landry was still standing, Valentine motioned with his hand and said, "Sit down, Lieutenant, before your food gets cold. We don't stand on many formalities around here."

Pleased by the young man's awkwardness in her presence, Hope fairly floated by the table to help Rena, who met her with a lifeless gaze as she thrust a bowl of fried potatoes into the young girl's hands. The expressionless

Crow woman shifted her gaze to Clint, seated at the end of the table. Although her stoic countenance never showed it, she didn't miss much that happened around the ranch. And in spite of the somber indifference displayed on Clint's square-jawed face, she detected the hint of a frown on his brow. Before this occurrence she was wise enough to have recognized a certain spark in Clint when he was in Hope's presence. She could foresee heartbreak in the young man's future, however, for she knew he would never let his feelings be known.

She turned her attention to the lieutenant. His face was good, she decided. There was nothing to be read in his eyes that would indicate a lack of character. He was probably a good man. She discarded thoughts on the matter then. It was not her place to care whether Hope had any feelings for Clint beyond those of a friend or a brother.

While the lieutenant enjoyed the hardy breakfast Rena had prepared for him, he questioned Clint about the fight with the Sioux raiding party, since he had only Captain Rodgers' account of the confrontation. He paid close attention to Clint's answers, distracted only when Hope moved past the table. After he had heard the complete report, he asked, "Where do you think they headed from your range?"

"I have no idea," Clint replied bluntly. "The only thing I can do is find their trail and follow it. Maybe Ben might have a feelin' for where they're headin', but to know for sure, you have to follow their tracks."

"Who's Ben?" Landry asked.

"Ben Hawkins," Clint said. "He was the fellow with me when we jumped the Indians. He taught me everything I know about trackin'."

"Suppose we could get him to accompany us?" Justin

asked. "Sounds to me like the two of you work together pretty well. Might make our mission a little easier." He paused to smile up at Hope when she brought the coffeepot over from the stove and filled his cup.

"I reckon that's up to Mr. Valentine," Clint said, then added, "and Ben." He shrugged indifferently. "If the boss doesn't want both of us gone, you might wanna just take Ben. Can't nobody track any better'n Ben." For reasons he didn't want to admit, even to himself, he had just as soon not accompany the lieutenant.

"I'd really like to have both of you," Landry said, "if Mr. Valentine can spare you for a couple of days." He didn't express it, but he felt fairly confident that the patrol would turn back as soon as they found evidence enough to suggest the hostiles had long since left the valley.

"Oh, I expect we can survive without the two of them," Valentine joked. "Take Ben along with you, Clint."

"Good," Landry said, glancing at Hope. "I guess we'd better get started, although it's difficult to leave such pleasant company." He extended his hand to Valentine. "Thank you for the breakfast, sir. I know my men appreciated it as much as I did." On his feet then, he turned toward the door, where Hope stood holding it open, and paused to tell her, "I suppose it's you ladies I should thank for that fine breakfast."

"You're welcome," she said.

Catching Clint's somber gaze as he stood patiently by the door, she gave him a friendly smile and a wink before turning back toward the table to help Rena clear the dishes.

Always anxious to partner with Clint whenever his young friend was called upon to handle problems on or off the ranch, Ben was pleased when Clint told him to ready himself to go on the patrol. He casually introduced himself to Lieutenant Landry and gave the soldiers standing by their mounts a casual nod. "It appears you have a few scars from the encounter with the hostiles," Justin said.

Ben immediately reached up to feel a couple of deep scratches on his face. "Yes, sir, I did pick up some scratches at the time." He glanced sheepishly at Clint, who was smiling broadly and watching his reaction. Mercifully Clint did not divulge the cause for the battle scars—hand-to-hand combat with a berry bush.

Once the patrol was under way, Ben rode up beside Clint, leaving the lieutenant and his men to follow behind. A ride of two hours took them to the low ridge near the river where they had waited until dark enough to attack the hostiles' camp. They pulled up there to wait for the patrol to catch up, so they could tell them how things had happened two nights before.

"Can you show me the bodies?" Landry asked after hearing Clint's accounting of the confrontation that took place.

"Reckon so," Ben answered, pointing to half a dozen buzzards circling above the river bluffs. "Looks like they're still here."

He didn't say so, but he was somewhat surprised that the buzzards were still circling, and he wondered if there were a greater number on the ground feasting on the remains of the carcasses. Maybe, he thought, the buzzards had lost the feeding rights to wolves or coyotes. If Clint was of a like mind, he didn't say. Instead he nudged his horse and started down the ridge to see for himself.

Ben and the cavalry patrol followed along behind him as he rode through the ring of cottonwoods skirting the river. They caught up to him when he reined the bay gelding to a stop at the place where they had left the corpse of the hostile who had taken the first shot at Ben. But there was no longer a body there.

Clint didn't comment, but rode on through the trees to the clearing and the ashes of the campfire where the first of the other two had been killed. There were no buzzards or other scavengers feasting on the bodies—because there were no bodies. Clint dismounted to take a closer look around. Ben did the same.

"Looks like the buzzards had to settle for the few scraps of that cow they butchered," Ben said. "We got the best part of that cow."

"Are you sure this is the place where you had the fight?" Landry asked, still seated in the saddle.

"Yep," Clint answered. "We left them right where they fell, and that was here, back there in the trees, and on that bluff where the horses were."

"Well, there are no bodies at any of those places now," Landry pointed out needlessly. "Are you thinking that maybe buzzards ate them?"

"Hardly," Ben answered him. "Buzzards don't usually eat the rifles and moccasins and bows and arrows and skinnin' knives and everything else these bucks were wearin'. And all that stuff is gone, too." He figured it was pretty obvious what had happened, and he shouldn't have to tell Landry.

"All these bluffs look pretty much the same," Landry said, somewhat skeptical of their version of the fight now. "Maybe this isn't the right place. After all, you said the fight happened at night." He paused to emphasize his following suggestion. "Or possibly you only thought you shot the hostiles. Maybe they got away in the darkness."

"We only thought . . . ?" Ben retorted in anger before

he caught himself. He studied the lieutenant's face intently for a few moments, deciding then to chalk it up to the young officer's inexperience.

Clint, who had been concentrating on the ground where the bodies had been, almost laughed when he heard Ben's response. "If you'll climb down offa that horse and look around," he said to Landry, "you'll see where a good-sized bloodstain soaked into the dirt where this body was. You'll also see a helluva lot of tracks left by Indian ponies. I'd say twelve or fifteen. And that oughta tell you that the five we fought were only part of a bigger war party that came back to pick up their dead. So I reckon that's gonna be bad news for you and your patrol of six men." He looked at Ben then. "What do you say, partner?"

"That's about the way I see it," Ben replied. He in turn looked back at Landry and asked, "Whaddaya plannin' on doin' now, Lieutenant?"

Before Landry had a chance to answer, Sergeant Cox interjected, "I expect Captain Rodgers would want you to return to the post and report a sizable war party in the area, sir."

It was obvious to Landry that the veteran sergeant was not anxious to engage a party of superior numbers with a patrol of six troopers, but he wasn't sure what he should do. So he dismounted and stalled for time while he decided. He busied himself by examining the spots of blood and the many unshod hoof and moccasin prints on the riverbank.

After a few minutes to think of possible questions Captain Rodgers would likely ask, he made what he thought to be the proper decision. "We need to know which way this war party was heading when they left here. It's important to know if any other farms or ranches are in danger of being attacked." Turning back to Clint then, he asked, "Can you and Mr. Hawkins track them?"

"That wouldn't be hard to do," Clint said.

"Just far enough to tell us if there are innocent people in danger, or if the hostiles are heading away from Miles City, and maybe going back to their village somewhere," Landry said. "I don't want to put you or my men in danger unnecessarily."

"We can do that," Clint said, looking to get a nod from Ben. "I'd like to know for damn sure they aren't thinkin' about circlin' back toward the Double-V-Bar." He turned to Ben and said, "I'm thinkin' it was a good thing we told Charley and the boys to turn the cattle back closer to the ranch."

Chapter 3

Instead of crossing the Yellowstone to escape into the rugged hills above the river, the Sioux hostiles stayed on the south side and followed the river to the northeast. It was only for a distance of about five miles, however, before they left the river and turned due east.

"That don't look too good," Ben said. "All the tracks are headin' east," he confirmed.

He and Clint had hoped that the trail left by the hostiles would continue to follow the Yellowstone, or cross over and head directly north. If that had been the case, then they could reasonably conclude that the Indians were intent upon leaving this part of the country. With this swing back to the east, however, it indicated that the raiding party planned to remain close to the Double-V-Bar range as well as to the other ranches operating in the Yellowstone Valley.

Clint stood up in his stirrups and peered out across a seemingly endless stretch of draws and high bluffs.

"If they hold to that line, they'll strike the Powder River after about—whaddaya think—fifteen miles?"

"That's about right," Ben agreed. "The question then is, what will they do when they strike the Powder?"

There was always the chance that the raiding party would cross the Powder and continue east. But if they did not, and followed the Powder south, that could mean they intended to ride in a wide circle and possibly strike one of the ranches that grazed cattle on that prairie.

"Well, we'll find out when we get to the river," Clint said. He sat down in the saddle again and turned his horse to face Landry and the patrol, which was about half a mile behind them. "These horses are gonna be ready for a rest by the time we reach the Powder, so we can rest 'em there where there's water. Maybe we'll find out what those Indians have in mind then."

As Clint had predicted, the horses were tired and thirsty by the time the patrol reached the Powder, so named by the Indians for the powdery soil that lined its banks. Some said the soil resembled gunpowder. This analogy came to Clint's mind as he looked at the multitude of tracks left by the Sioux raiding party.

"It's damn hard to tell how many of 'em we're trailin', lookin' at this place where they camped," Ben said. "There're so many tracks."

"Looks like too damn many for a patrol of six men to engage," Sergeant Cox said, reminding the lieutenant, and obviously not too enthusiastic about continuing on.

"Maybe, maybe not," Ben said, "seein' as how you boys are all totin' Spencer repeatin' carbines, and me and Clint are totin' Winchesters. If your boys can hit anything with those carbines, we could raise a lot of hell with a party of Injuns twice our size. 'Cause I know me and Clint can shoot. It depends a lot on what kinda weapons those Injuns have. I reckon it's up to the lieutenant whether or not we try to catch up with 'em."

"I expect Ben and I will stay on their trail, if you boys decide to turn back," Clint said. "'Cause the tracks leadin' outta this camp are following the river south. And I wanna know just what a party of hostiles this size has in mind." He looked at Justin and waited for the lieutenant's decision.

"I agree with you, Cooper," Justin said, after a couple of moments. "I think it would be best to see what these hostiles have in mind. So we'll be pushing on after them as soon as the horses are rested."

Sergeant Cox's expression of disappointment was reflected in the faces of the rest of the cavalry patrol. The afternoon had turned cold and there was a hint of snow in the air, conditions that made the troopers think longingly of the stoves back in the barracks.

It was getting along in the afternoon when Justin gave the order to mount, since it was still a little early to make camp for the night. Clint and Ben rode out ahead of the column again, following tracks that headed south along the Powder River. Darkness found them four or five miles above the confluence of Mizpah Creek and the river. They made camp where a wide gully came down from the high bluffs on the western side of the river. While the soldiers searched the almost barren ravines for wood for a fire, Clint and Ben rode out to take a look around the hills on the eastern side.

"I don't know," Clint said. "I've just got a feelin'. I think I'll ride on up the river a ways, just to see what's botherin' me."

"Is that so?" Ben replied. He was familiar with Clint's occasional feelings. Sometimes they were legitimate, but most times they were not. "Most likely you're just hungry, or your bowels ain't moved today. But I'll go with you to keep you from gettin' lost."

"I appreciate it," Clint said sarcastically, and nudged Sam with his heels.

The powdery riverbank was easy to follow in the dark. Even the Indian ponies' tracks could still be seen. They moved steadily up the river in the chill night air until Clint suddenly pulled up short. "What is it?" Ben asked, coming alongside.

"There," Clint said, and pointed above the bluffs up ahead.

"Damn," Ben exhaled slowly when he saw the glow in the low clouds overhead. "That looks like a sizable camp, maybe where the creek forks off from the river, if I had to guess."

"That's what I think," Clint said. He paused to decide whether or not they should ride back right away and report their findings to Landry. "Hell, we're halfway there. We might as well go on and see how many we're dealin' with." Ben agreed, so they continued on along the river.

They found the Sioux camp at the forks of the Powder and Mizpah Creek, and as they had speculated, it was a sizable war party. They moved up as close as they dared, tied their horses in the trees, then crawled up to the top of a high bluff that paralleled the river.

"Where the hell did they come from?" Ben muttered, mystified that a party of this size was bold enough to venture back into this part of the country after Little Big Horn. "There must be forty or fifty warriors camped down there."

"Well, I reckon I've seen all I need to see," Clint

said. "We're gonna need a helluva lot more help than that patrol of six troopers back there."

"That's a sure-'nough fact," Ben replied. They remained where they were for a few minutes longer, watching the warriors moving about the campfire, before Ben said, "Let's get on back and tell the lieutenant he'd best report to his commandin' officer that he needs to send a bigger patrol to run these boys to ground. I'm thinkin' it might not be a bad idea to start back tonight."

There was no disagreement from Clint, especially since he figured the hostiles were probably armed with rifles. The five warriors he and Ben had fought on the banks of the Yellowstone had had rifles, so it was an easy assumption that there were more hostiles, maybe all of them, with rifles in the large war party.

Careful to keep a low profile, the two white men withdrew from the top of the bluff and hurried back to their horses. They returned the way they had come, holding the horses to a slow walk until they were far enough from the camp to push them to a lope. They were not halfway back to the patrol when they heard shots fired. At first thinking they had been discovered, they started to scramble for cover, only to realize that there were no shots coming their way. Clint pulled his bay to a sliding halt to listen. Ben slid up beside him. More shots were heard, sounding like a volley.

"Son of a bitch!" Ben blurted. "That's comin' from our camp!"

"They're in a fight!" Clint exclaimed. They could hear a mixture of gunshots, the solid reports of Springfield rifles telling them that the Indians were armed with captured weapons. And the distinctive snap of the Spencer carbines the troopers carried confirmed the skirmish. Adding to the mix was the sound of other rifles hard to identify.

"How the hell did they get around us?" Ben demanded, unable to understand how they could have missed a war party heading back to attack the soldiers. They would have had to circle around them. And if the Indians had already been in a position to attack the army patrol, why did they allow the two of them to continue on toward their camp at Mizpah Creek without attacking them?

"They must have seen us coming and let us pass so they wouldn't alert the soldiers they were goin' after," Clint said. "I reckon they felt sure the two of us weren't gonna attack a camp as big as theirs. And they figured on waitin' for us to come runnin' when the shootin' started at our camp." That still didn't make sense, because the question remained as to why the rest of the hostile camp wasn't in on the attack. The answer was they didn't know about it.

As if to verify that, they could now hear sounds of excitement in the Indian camp behind them. They were surprised by the gunfire, too.

"It's gotta be a different bunch," Clint exclaimed, "maybe on their way to join the camp! They probably don't even know about you and me."

That made sense as far as Ben was concerned. "We'd best get away from this river before those Injuns behind us come chargin' outta that camp to see what's goin' on." They were clearly caught between two parties of Indians. "Maybe we can circle around our camp and help the lieutenant out."

He received an agreeing nod from Clint, so without

further hesitation, he wheeled his horse and headed up into the bluffs west of the river. Clint was right behind him.

Justin Landry had never been shot at before. He wasn't aware that he had been until he was suddenly startled by the dull smack of a rifle slug into the side of the gully, followed almost immediately by the sound of the weapon that fired it.

Puzzled, he remained seated on the side of the gully until Sergeant Cox shouted, "Get down!"

Totally aware then, Justin rolled off the edge of the gully and scrambled back into the deeper part. Seconds later, the air over his head was alive with the snapping sound of bullets tattooing the earth where he had sat.

"Over there!" Cox yelled, pointing to a bank of bushes on the opposite side of the river where he had seen muzzle flashes. Hustling his troopers in position to return fire, he was thankful that they had made their camp in the cover of the deep gully. Soon his little detail of six troopers was returning fire.

"How many?" Justin exclaimed. "Can you tell?"

"Can't tell," Cox answered. "We can hold 'em off as long as we stay in this gully. The problem is they can keep us pinned down here as long as they want." After the exchange of gunfire went on for a few minutes longer, it appeared that the Indians attacking them were no more than half a dozen or so, and Cox came to the same conclusion as had Ben. "This ain't near as many as that party we've been followin'. These warriors musta been on their way to join them others and we were just unlucky enough to have 'em land right on top of us. They musta seen the smoke from our fire."

"Any way out of this gully?" Justin asked, although

he could see that the gully ran up to the bluffs above them only to end at the bottom of a steep cliff.

"Not that I can see," Cox answered between two shots aimed at the clump of foliage where he had first seen muzzle flashes. "It runs out under that cliff and then we'd have to come out in the open where they could pick us off like turkeys. We can't take the horses up there, anyway."

The situation didn't look good. Justin could see no way out of their dilemma without risking casualties. He felt he should be giving orders, but he didn't know what to do. "Don't shoot unless you have a clear target," he finally ordered. "We don't know how long we're going to be pinned down here." He stared at the foliage by the river. "I wonder what happened to our scouts."

The stalemate continued for a while longer. Justin feared that when daylight came, the rest of the Indians would join this small party attacking them now and they might be overrun. He was almost ready to order a dash for the horses, thinking that at least some of them might make it out alive and get word back to Fort Keogh. But moments before giving the order, one of the troopers exclaimed, "I see one of 'em! There's another one behind him! They're running toward that mound in the middle of the river."

Justin swung around quickly to look where the trooper pointed. He saw them. They were trying to get across the river to get to the horses. Before any of the soldiers could bring their weapons to bear, however, they heard two shots at almost the same time, and both hostiles fell. In a matter of moments, more shots were heard and the soldiers realized that the shots had come from the other side of the river.

* * *

"They're runnin' for it!" Ben blurted when two more warriors backed away from a rise they were using for cover, aware now that the shots had come from behind them.

"I see 'em," Clint said, acting quickly enough to drop one of the fleeing hostiles a fraction of a second before Ben cut the other one down. "There's another one down there somewhere."

He strained to search the dark expanse of bushes among the trees. Too late, he caught a glimpse of the Indian as he darted out of the brush and jumped on his pony. Both Ben and Clint shot at him, but both missed as the warrior galloped away, riding low on the horse's neck.

"Damn," Clint swore for missing, but there wasn't time to linger. "We've got to get the hell outta here," he exclaimed.

"You're right about that," Ben came back as they both hurried back to their horses.

Once they were in the saddle, they pulled up in the trees close to the riverbank to alert the patrol. "Lieutenant!" Ben yelled. "Hold your fire! It's me and Clint comin' across. We've got to get outta here right now, so get on your horses and get ready to ride like hell."

When there was no immediate reply from the gully on the other side, they both held up until they heard Sergeant Cox yell for them to come on. "We hear you! Come on across!"

Clint and Ben crossed over while the besieged troopers were scrambling to their horses. When they pulled up beside Justin, Clint gave him the bad news.

"There's a helluva lot more hostiles up the river than this patrol can handle, Lieutenant. So we've got to ride outta here right now. I'd guess that there's at least fifty or sixty and I expect they're on their way here to see what the shootin' was all about."

"And they ain't gonna be too tickled when they find those four we just shot," Ben added. There was no need for Justin or Cox to give the men an order to mount. They were already saddled up and ready to ride while their two guides had galloped up the gray riverbank. The troopers did not wait for Justin to give the order to ride. Led by Sergeant Cox, they rode out at once after Clint and Ben.

Since they were quite familiar with the twenty and some odd miles of rugged, hilly country between the river and Fort Keogh, they left the banks of the Powder and led the patrol to the northwest. As soon as they felt they were safely away from the open river valley, they slowed their escape down to a fast walk. The country they rode through was rough in broad daylight. In the current darkness, there was too great a risk of pushing the horses any faster, for fear of breaking a leg or worse. After a couple of miles, Clint decided to fall back behind.

"I'm gonna drop back to make sure they ain't catchin' up with us," he told Ben. "I'll catch up with you."

"It'll be pretty hard for them to trail us through this draw," Ben said. "But I reckon it ain't a bad idea to make sure."

"If you hear me fire a shot," Clint advised, "you'd better find you a place to hold 'em off, 'cause you'll know they're on our trail." He pulled his horse aside to let the line of soldiers pass him in the narrow draw.

Justin, having overheard the comments between Ben and Clint, paused before passing. "Do you think we should go ahead and pick a spot to fight, and wait for them to catch up?"

"Nope," Clint answered. "The best hope you've got is to run, and pray those Indians don't find out which gully we took offa that riverbank. If we have to hole up somewhere to hold them off, we might make it through the night. But when daylight comes, they'd most likely surround us and wipe us out. They might sing about you back at the fort, like they did for Custer, but it'd be downright stupid to try to fight those Indians. You're gonna need a troop-sized patrol to fight a bunch that big."

"Right," Justin replied. "I'll accept your opinion." He prodded his horse and continued after his men.

Clint waited until he could no longer hear the patrol disappearing into the darkness of the draw; then he slowly walked the bay back the way they had come. When he reached the head of the draw, he pulled up and listened for signs of pursuit. There was nothing but silence across the rocky ridges, broken only by the sudden flutter of a night bird's wings as it swooped over him, causing the bay to start. Then the silence returned, unbroken, and he felt confident that the Indians had been unable to determine which way they had fled. He wheeled his horse and rode after the troopers.

The first rays of sunlight penetrated the scattering of low clouds as the cavalry detail rode wearily out of the high ridges and emerged onto the gently rolling hills of the Double-V-Bar range. It was still about four miles to the ranch headquarters and another five miles beyond that to Fort Keogh. It was of paramount importance for the lieutenant and his men to get to the fort as soon as possible, of course. But unless they stopped to rest their spent horses, they were going to end up walking there.

Of additional concern now to Clint was the discovery of small groups of stray cattle that told him the main herd was not far away. With like concerns, Ben rode over next to him to confer.

"We gotta find out who's ridin' night herd and tell 'em to move the herd to hell away from here," he said. "They'll most likely be fixin' to ride back in for breakfast about now."

"I know," Clint replied. "Let's get these soldiers to that creek up ahead, so they can rest the horses, and we'll push ours a little farther and see if we can find some of the boys."

Upon reaching the creek at the southern end of a long line of low hills, the first person they saw was Charley Clark. He pulled up short when he spotted the small detail of soldiers approaching. "I swear," he called out when they rode up to the creek, "I didn't figure on seein' you boys back so soon. Did you find them Injuns?"

"Yeah," Ben answered him, "and we mighta brought 'em back here to you."

"Who's out here with you?" Clint asked.

Puzzled by Ben's comment, Charley answered, "Bobby Dees. He's circlin' around the other end, lookin' for strays." He nodded toward the troopers as they dismounted and led their horses to the water. "Looks like you fellers are plumb wore out."

Clint didn't waste much time explaining the cause for moving the herd. "You need to ride in to the ranch and get the whole crew out here. We have to move the cattle up close by the river." He figured the closer to Miles City and Fort Keogh, the better. "If our luck is holding out, that party of Indians might not wanna come this close in, but we'd best get ready in case they do."

Sufficiently alarmed, Charley responded at once.

"I'll get Bobby and we'll hightail it in to get the rest of the boys." He wheeled his horse to depart.

"And bring Ben and me fresh horses when you come back," Clint called after him. "We'll be here with the soldiers." Charley signaled with one hand that he had heard. Turning back to Justin then, Clint told him what he was going to do. "I reckon Ben and I are gonna let you go on back to the fort after you rest your horses. There ain't nothing else you need from us."

Justin was not sure that was what he wanted. "I thought you would be riding back to the post with us to report."

"What for?" Clint responded. "That war party is the army's responsibility. That's why they built Fort Keogh, to protect the settlers. I've got the ranch and Mr. Valentine's cattle to worry about, so Ben and I'll be needed here." Justin looked distressed and uncertain, so Clint tried to reassure him. "You have to report to your superiors that you ran into a war party of about sixty warriors, and it's gonna take a troop-sized patrol to go after 'em. You don't need a guide to take you back to that fork where Mizpah Creek ties into the Powder, so there ain't anything Ben or I could add. All right?"

"Right," Justin replied when he thought about it. "I won't need you anymore. We'll head straight for the post as soon as our horses have rested."

When the inexperienced lieutenant seemed to be confident in what needed to be done, Clint and Ben left the soldiers by the creek and set out to drive a small group of strays back toward the ranch.

It took most of the day to herd the cattle back close to the river, where they were left to graze. Alert to the possibility of an attack, although Clint believed the odds of that were slim now, the entire crew, including Valentine himself, rode night herd to keep an eye out for a raid on the cattle.

After the night passed with no threat to the ranch or the cattle, half the crew retired to the bunkhouse to get a few hours of sleep before relieving the others. Clint and Ben took the first rest break since it was the second night they had not had the opportunity to sleep. It was almost noon when Clint crawled out of his blanket, ready to ride again after eating some stew that Milt Futch had thrown together. He was saddling a rested Sam when a cavalry troop, already assembled, arrived on their way back to the Powder River.

B Troop, led by Captain Thomas Rodgers, rode into the ranch and came to a halt by the creek behind the barn. Numbering fifty troopers, some thirty men short of the standard cavalry troop, they dismounted to water their horses. Clint suspected the reason their line of march took them by the Double-V-Bar was to pick up a guide to help them retrace the route that Lieutenant Landry had taken the night before. He wasn't really surprised that Justin couldn't remember the way. After all, it was at night, and the country was rough between here and the Powder.

Clint walked out to meet the captain, leading his horse. There were two lieutenants talking to Rodgers. One of them was Justin Landry. He turned to greet Clint when he saw him approaching. "Mr. Cooper."

"Lieutenant," Clint returned, then nodded to Rodgers and waited for him to get down to the business he was certain he was about.

"Mr. Cooper," the captain began, "Lieutenant Landry said you told him that you weren't interested in signing on as a guide again. I'm hoping you will change your mind. I could sure use your help in finding that party of Sioux."

"Like I told the lieutenant," Clint said, "that camp was on the Powder, right where Mizpah Creek joins it. So all you have to do is head in that direction till you run into the river." He pointed toward a line of hills to the southeast.

Rodgers smiled patiently. "I believe you, but there's some awfully rugged bluffs and blind draws between here and that river. According to what Lieutenant Landry tells me, you and your partner led them straight through without a turnaround in the dark. So you could shorten the time we might take to get on those hostiles' trail. How about it? If you're worried about your place here, I doubt there's any danger this close in to the fort, and the sooner we find those Indians, the better it will be for all the ranches."

Clint shrugged. The captain was probably right. The raiding party was not likely to strike when the fort was so near, especially since they had been discovered by Landry's patrol, and they no longer had the element of surprise in their favor. He had no particular desire to ride scout for the captain, but he couldn't think of any reason not to go. Finally he said, "I'll go with you. Let me go tell my boss and pack a few things in my saddlebags, and I'll be ready to ride."

"Good man," Rodgers said.

Clint glanced at Justin, whose attention had been focused on the house for most of the time since the column arrived. He knew who the lieutenant was hoping to see, but there was no sign of Hope outside the house. Feeling a slight irritation from the thought, Clint stepped up into the saddle and pointed the bay toward the ranch house.

Rena opened the kitchen door when he knocked and held it open as he walked in. "I need to talk to Mr. Valentine," Clint said to her. She nodded and went to fetch him.

She returned in less than a minute. "Mr. Valentine coming," she said, then without asking, went to the cupboard to get Clint a cup. He took the cup of coffee from her with a nod of thanks. The stoic Crow woman was always partial toward him. He was aware of it and appreciated it, although he was puzzled by it. As soon as Valentine walked in, she left the kitchen and went to the smokehouse.

"What is it, Clint?" Valentine asked when he came in, having just then looked out the window to see a troop of cavalry down near the barn. Clint told him about the captain's request. Valentine thought it over for a few moments before deciding. "What's your feeling on it?" he asked. "You think they really need you? Hell, if they can't find the Powder River by themselves, they ought not leave the fort."

Clint laughed. "I reckon not. What the captain's after is to save some time gettin' there. He's hopin' I could keep him from backtrackin' and gettin' turned around in some of those ravines. I reckon I could go with 'em— help 'em out a little. I don't care one way or the other— whatever you say."

"Well, I guess it's in our best interest to help the army all we can, so go ahead and scout for them, but you be damn careful. You and Ben have already been in one scrape with those hostiles. Are you wanting Ben to go with you this time?"

"No, sir," Clint replied, "not this time. I don't see any reason for both of us to be gone."

"All right," Valentine said. "I'll get back to going

over my figures." He left to return to his account books as Rena came back in from the smokehouse. She was holding a cloth with slices from a salt-cured ham in one hand and a butcher knife in the other.

Clint put his empty cup on the dry sink and said, "Thanks for the coffee." He started to leave then, but she stopped him.

"Wait," she said. "I fix you some food." He realized then that the ham was for him. He stood there while she sliced some leftover biscuits and stuck the ham in them, knowing the salty, rock-hard meat would not spoil for some time.

He had planned to go to the bunkhouse to get some jerky and coffee to take with him. But what mystified him was how she knew he was going with the soldiers. He had to ask.

"How'd you know I was gonna need some food?"

She almost smiled in reply and turned away to resume her chores, leaving him mystified. He thought he could count on one hand the number of times he had actually seen her smile.

His hand was on the doorknob when Hope suddenly appeared.

"Clint, wait," she said. He paused, surprised by the note of concern in her voice. "Outside," she said, and passed by him as he held the door for her. She reached back and closed the door behind them when they were on the step. "You're going with those soldiers, aren't you?" He nodded, confused by her apparent concern. She had never expressed concern for his safety before. "If you catch up with those Indians, there's going to be some dangerous fighting." The expression on her young face told him that she was reluctant to expose her fears. Suddenly he felt his heart leap when he realized that she was on the verge of expressing something that she had kept secret, something that he could only dream about before this moment. He looked down to meet her gaze, so intense. "I'm afraid this mission you're going on will be very dangerous. I want you to promise me something." He nodded. "Will you promise?" she insisted.

"I will," he said. "I promise."

"I knew I could count on you. I can always count on you. I want you to take care of Justin. Bring him back safely. He talks so bravely, but he hasn't had time to gain any experience in warfare, and I'm afraid he'll do something foolish, just to show his bravery."

He felt as if he had taken an arrow in his chest. From the pinnacle of a dream come true, his hopes had suddenly been dashed upon the rocks of dire disappointment. He fought to hide the blow to his heart, and tried to feign a smile.

"Why, sure," he finally managed, "I'll keep an eye on him for you. As best I can," he added. "I better go now—don't wanna keep the army waitin'."

Chapter 4

It was hard to keep his mind on anything but the short conversation he had just had with Hope. But luckily it took very little concentration to lead the cavalry column through the series of game trails he had traveled before. And since there was no thought of danger before they approached the Powder River, he found it difficult to release the resentment he felt for Justin Landry. He turned it over and over in his mind, and finally decided that he could not blame Justin for his feelings for Hope. Justin was not guilty of trying to damage Clint's chances with Hope. He was merely attracted to a charming young lady who had no apparent claims upon her.

By the time the column reached the banks of the Powder, Clint had rationalized to himself that Hope would have the prospects of a much better future as the wife of a career army officer. Far better than what he could ever offer. He told himself that that was best for Hope, so it was best for him, too. But it was hard to adopt that attitude. He was glad when it came time to focus his mind on trying to find the trail left by the sizable party of hostile Sioux.

He never considered himself an expert tracker, fair maybe, but it wasn't hard to read tracks as obvious as the ones the Sioux war party had left. It was easy to read the story of their flight. They had followed the six-man patrol from the site of the fight with the five hostiles, but lost the trail when he and Ben had left the river and led the patrol into the hills. Though the tracks were easily seen in the light of day, the Sioux had missed them in the dark.

"Well," he told Captain Rodgers, "you can see here where they turned back toward their camp at the fork. I doubt they're still there today, but it wouldn't hurt for me to ride on up the river to make sure before you march your column up there."

"That sounds like a good idea to me," Rodgers said. "I'll hold back until I hear a signal from you that it's all clear." He paused, and then asked, "How will you signal?"

"I'll just ride on back and wave you on," Clint said. "If you see me comin' back at a gallop, with a bunch of arrows in my backside, you'd best find some cover and get ready to fight."

As he had anticipated, the camp near the fork had been abandoned. Examining the ashes of a couple of camp-fires, he figured they had been gone from there since early morning. The question to be answered was which way they went from there. It wasn't difficult to find the tracks of many horses leading into the water, which was what he expected. His guess was that the hostiles would head farther east to increase the distance between themselves and Fort Keogh.

He crossed over to the other side of the river to confirm his hunch. However, when he got there, he found the tracks of the war party headed back to the north, following the river toward its confluence with the Yellowstone. For some reason, they had chosen to ride down the other side of the river. He realized at once that this was not good news. There was a small settlement at that confluence, consisting of a trading post, a barn, and a couple of log dwellings. The last time Clint was there, a young couple from Omaha had just completed one of the cabins. That had been in the summer. At the time, he remembered Ben commenting to him that he sure hoped they knew how hard the winters were up in this part of the territory. Clint tried to remember their names, but he could not. Zack Bristol owned the trading post, scratching out a living with a few trappers and cutting wood to sell to the steamboats that came up the Yellowstone.

As he pictured the little settlement in his mind, it was hard for Clint to imagine it would grow into the town that Zack was hoping for. That picture was replaced with one of the settlement with a party of sixty-some-odd savage warriors bearing down on it. Wasting no more time, he started back the way he had just come, following the tracks left by the Sioux war party on the east side of the river.

When he arrived at a sandy flat across the river from the resting column of soldiers, Clint yelled to Captain Rodgers to get his men mounted and to cross over to that side. "What did you find?" Rodgers yelled back before giving the order.

"They're headin' back north, toward the Yellowstone," Clint said. "And if they don't head off in some other direction before they get there, Zack Bristol's tradin' post is gonna catch hell."

Realizing the urgency then, Rodgers got his men in the saddle at once and forded the river. When he pulled up beside him, Clint said, "It's every bit of thirty miles from here to Zack's place. I don't know if we can get there in time to help him. These horses have already done a day's work. I expect they'll play out before morning if we try to push 'em on tonight."

"I expect you're right," Rodgers said. "We'll push on as far as we can tonight." He paused while he looked up at the sky and squinted at the faint yellow ball hiding above the heavy overcast sky. "We've barely got a couple of hours of light left before dark, so we'd better use them to cover as much distance as possible."

"I reckon that's about as much as you can do," Clint said. "I'll ride on up ahead to make sure you don't run up on somebody fixin' to ambush you." He wheeled the bay and loped away. "You won't have any trouble followin' the tracks," he called back over his shoulder.

Rodgers pushed the tired mounts as hard as he thought reasonable, having the troopers dismount for short periods to walk and lead the horses. Finally, when darkness set in in earnest, he called a halt to the march. Much to Clint's disappointment, the hostiles had not veered from their course following the river. He didn't hold out much hope for the unsuspecting folks at Zack's store.

Morning brought light snow flurries and colder temperatures, made even colder by wind gusts that swept across the Powder River Valley. Captain Rodgers ordered the column under way with no time allowed for breakfast fires, planning to wait until it was time to rest the horses. In view of the fact that there were people in danger from the raiding party, he felt it was his responsibility to get to the Yellowstone as soon as he possibly could. There was no grumbling among his men, as they all understood the peril for the handful of settlers at Zack Bristol's trading post.

After conferring with Clint, who told him they were probably about an hour away from the Yellowstone, Rodgers decided to stop right where they were for a short time to make sure the horses were rested. He would have pushed on to the river, but he decided it was a good idea to arrive with horses fresh enough to give chase, if the circumstances dictated it. Of equal importance, he felt his men would be better prepared to fight if they had some food and a little hot coffee in their bellies. Soon several small fires were flickering with a group of troopers gathered around each one, vying for a space to heat a metal cup.

The breakfast stop was no longer than the captain deemed sufficient to rest his horses, and the troop was mounted and on its way again, with Clint out ahead. They had not ridden for more than half an hour when Clint spotted the smoke. Drifting almost horizontally as the brisk wind swept it along the underside of the dark clouds, it presented an ominous message that the soldiers were too late.

That message was confirmed when B Troop reached the clearing where the Powder spilled into the Yellowstone to discover the smoking ruins of all the structures that had stood there. Zack's store, his barn, and the remains of three small cabins had all been reduced to piles of charred logs, some still not quite out. A cold, eerie silence hung over the river valley, as the column of cavalry filed down into the clearing, with nothing but the sound of the horses to break the pall of death hanging over the ashes.

The mutilated bodies of Zack and his Crow wife were found outside the charred timbers of his store. Pieces of cloth, empty candle cartons, pots and pans, and other items that had been on Zack's shelves were scattered about the yard. Clint was more concerned with merchandise that he did not see. He knew that Zack carried a good supply of cartridges of several calibers, so the hostiles were more than likely well supplied now.

The bodies of the three families who had built the cabins were found near the ruins of their homes, evidence that they had tried to hold off the raiders until forced to flee their burning cabins. Captain Rodgers walked over to stand beside Clint as he stirred the ashes at the corner of the trading post.

"What do you think?" he asked, his voice grim with the helpless feeling of arriving too late to prevent the massacre. "Can you tell how long ago they were here?"

"No, sir, I can't," Clint said. "If I had to guess, I'd say they set fire to these buildin's last night sometime, but I expect they most likely camped right here, and left this mornin'. I can take a better guess after I look around a little bit."

"Make it as quick as you can," Rodgers said. "I want to run these murderers to ground." He turned away then and ordered, "Lieutenant Landry, take a squad of men and dig some graves for these poor folks."

"Yes, sir," Justin responded, a queasy look upon his face. He wasn't surprised that he got the job of digging graves since he was junior in grade to George Sawyer, the other lieutenant with the troop.

When Rodgers moved on, Sawyer hung back to needle Justin. "Make sure you dig those graves to regulation, mister."

"You go to hell," Justin replied as Sawyer rode away, laughing.

Clint could well imagine Justin's reaction to seeing such savage mutilation for the first time. He didn't blame him. It was his first time as well, and it left him with a sick feeling of anger and revolt. He went at once to search for tracks that would tell him where the war party had gone once they finished their grisly business here. A quick scout around the area soon revealed tracks that started to follow the Yellowstone eastward.

Spotting a pile of droppings, he examined the manure closely and determined that the Indians had not been gone from there for more than a couple of hours. He took that information back to Rodgers and, with the realization that they weren't that far behind the war party, the captain ordered his troop to mount and prepare to ride.

"Lieutenant Landry," he yelled. "You and your squad stay here and finish digging those graves. Catch up to us as soon as you can."

Sorry, Hope, Clint thought. *I can't keep my eye on him when he ain't with me.* He nudged his horse and started out before the troopers.

Captain Rodgers pushed his column hard, determined to overtake the raiders before they endangered more innocent victims. The Indians seemed to be in no hurry, and Clint found them late in the afternoon, already going into camp. Though it surprised him that they were stopping this early in the day, he soon saw the reason for it as he watched them from the top of a long ridge. The Indians had happened upon a herd of antelope and had taken advantage of the find to supply themselves with meat.

That's gonna cost you, he thought, and pushed back away from the ridge to return to his horse.

Rodgers was properly excited to receive the news that Clint had found the Sioux party. As quickly as possible, he urged his men forward, following Clint.

When they reached the back side of the ridge Clint had watched the Indians from before, he took Rodgers and Lieutenant Sawyer up to the top to look over the situation. Clint told them that the raiders had not posted any lookouts while they busied themselves butchering their kill. They appeared unconcerned about anyone following them. It was an ideal setup for a surprise attack. The ridge was low enough, and close enough to the edge of the river where the butchering was going on, so the soldiers could sweep down upon them before the Indians knew they were under attack.

Rodgers gathered his troopers below the ridge, forming a straight line. When all were in position, he gave the signal and the line moved up over the top of the ridge, their carbines ready, but holding their fire. They were already riding down the face of the ridge before they were spotted by the unsuspecting hostiles. Upon the captain's signal, the line of soldiers erupted in a barrage of deadly fire.

The Sioux warriors were caught totally by surprise. The first volley struck them with devastating results, and the continuous firing that followed dropped many more as they ran for their weapons. Suffering heavy losses almost immediately, those who could ran to their ponies and scattered; some drove their horses into the river, trying to escape to the other side. About half of them failed to make it across before being picked off, their bodies floating downstream like so many logs.

The battle lasted for less than half an hour, and was a

resounding victory for B Troop, accounting for twenty-eight dead on the ground, and an unknown number in the river. Obviously pleased with his successful attack, Captain Rodgers rode back and forth along the line of troopers, praising their efforts.

"That's a blow for General Custer," he exclaimed over and over. When Lieutenant Sawyer asked about pursuit of the survivors, Rodgers told him there would be none. "It's not a workable endeavor," he said. "They've scattered all over hell and back. I don't want to split my command up in that many pieces. No, I think we can say without fear of contradiction that the enemy is vanquished from our region, so our objective has been accomplished. We'll see to our wounded and prepare to return to Fort Keogh."

"Yes, sir," Lieutenant Sawyer said. Then before going to get a tally of the wounded men, he grinned wide and said, "Ol' Justin's gonna be sick about missing all the action."

Rodgers paused a moment. "Where the hell is Lieutenant Landry?" he asked. "I would have thought he'd catch up by now."

Hearing the question, Clint found it struck him odd as well. In the heat of the assault, he had not had time to think about Justin Landry. Rodgers was right. It shouldn't have taken this long for a squad of eight men with shovels to dig half a dozen shallow graves. "I'll ride on back and see if he's on the way," he volunteered. "He mighta got lost, but I don't see how."

"Very well," Rodgers said. "We'll be along as soon as we finish up here." He turned to Sergeant Cox, who happened by at that moment. "Sergeant, make sure we pick up any weapons they were using. We don't want to leave any behind."

Leaving them to police the battlefield, Clint rode back over the ridge, the sharp popping of carbines behind him as the soldiers finished off the wounded hostiles.

Riding along, chewing on a strip of beef jerky, he let his mind go back to the battle they'd just fought and pictured the scene as he had first looked down on the Indians as they skinned and butchered the antelope. He remembered thinking that he had underestimated the number of warriors when he found their camp at Mizpah Creek. Today there seemed to have been fewer in number than he remembered that night when he, Ben, Justin, and the six troopers had to run for their lives— not by many, but enough to make him question his thoroughness in scouting the camp.

"Doesn't make a helluva lot of difference," he muttered to his horse. "There were still enough to call for a full troop of cavalry." It was only a few moments later when he heard the shots.

Pulling up hard on the bay's reins, he stopped to listen. There were more shots, and from the sound, he guessed they were from at least one Springfield rifle— and maybe a Sharps or Spencer carbine.

What the hell, he wondered, *another bunch behind us?*

More than likely it was some of the survivors who had scattered from the attack at the river. Whoever it was had evidently run into Justin and the squad of grave diggers. The shots were sporadic, instead of a steady barrage. But they didn't seem to be very far away, so he nudged Sam and continued more cautiously than before.

A quarter of a mile farther brought him to a series of high bluffs, cut with draws and gullies. He remembered thinking when he had passed them riding in the opposite direction that they looked ideal for staging an ambush.

I reckon I ain't the only one thinking that, he told himself, for had he not stopped, he would have ridden right into one. He pulled the bay's reins hard to his left and rode up a narrow gully to the top of the bluff, where he left the horse and proceeded on foot. With his Winchester in one hand and a cartridge belt in the other, he made his way along the bluff until he reached a point where he could see the fight below him.

About halfway down the bluff he spotted them. He counted six warriors behind an outcropping of rock. He had a clear shot at only one of them, even though he could see enough of the others to be sure of the count. He didn't see who they were shooting at until an answering shot came from a washed-out pocket beneath the riverbank. He had let his gaze travel along the rim of the bank for several yards beyond the pocket when he detected movement along that line. For a moment, he saw a horse's head before it disappeared again, hidden by the high bank. He brought his gaze back to the pocket when one lone shot came from it, followed by a period of silence.

"That was my last round," Justin announced.

"What the hell are we gonna do?" Private Oscar Willis asked. "Ain't none of us got any more cartridges." Like the other men, he looked to the lieutenant to come up with an answer, while not really expecting him to have one.

Justin was as perplexed as the six enlisted men holed up with him in the pocket. They were all out of ammunition now, having shot it all up after taking cover in this hole beneath the bank. He should have ordered the men to conserve their cartridges, but they had all fired at the hostiles as rapidly as they could, himself included, thinking to discourage their attackers.

But the warriors had found protection in the rocks in the bluff, where they could keep the soldiers pinned down indefinitely. He had lost two men, both hit when the Indians sprang the ambush. The hole they now found themselves in had been the closest cover they could find, and it was not large enough to hold them and their horses, too. So they had had to let the horses go.

"Lieutenant," Willis pressed when Justin failed to answer his question. All of the six were suddenly aware of the hopelessness of their situation.

Groping for an answer, Justin tried to maintain some semblance of command, a task nearly impossible owing to the panic gripping him. He didn't know what to do. It would not be long, without return fire from the pocket, before their attackers concluded that the soldiers were out of ammunition.

"We're gonna hold our position," he finally said. "They don't know we're out of cartridges, and maybe they won't think it's worth the risk to charge us." He prayed with all his heart that it was true.

"Hold our position?" Willis replied incredulously. "Hold our position?" he repeated. "Not me. We don't shoot no more and they'll know damn well we ain't got no cartridges, and when they swarm all over us, we're dead men. And they'll take their own sweet time killin' us, just like those folks we just got through burying. No, sir, I ain't waitin' around for that."

Before anyone could stop him, he scrambled up over the side of the pocket and ran down the bank toward the horses, tumbling head over heels when struck almost simultaneously by two bullets from the rocks.

One of the other men had crawled to the edge of the pocket, intending to follow Willis. He sank back in fright when he saw Willis' fate. Not a word was spoken for a long moment, every man there terrified, aware of the horrific ending awaiting them.

The minutes ticked by agonizingly deliberate with no shots fired from above them. Justin crept up to the rim of the hole and peeked up at the bluff. His heart was seized by the frightful image that met his eyes. Standing above them defiantly, his feet planted solidly on the flat open surface of a rock shelf, a fierce warrior boldly challenged the soldiers to shoot him. Justin slid back down from the edge, knowing that Willis' attempt to escape had told the Indians what they wanted to know: that the soldiers had no cartridges! It would only be a matter of minutes now.

A windstorm of thoughts dashed through Justin's mind—his brief career as an officer and his father's disappointment when it would not come to pass, his home, his family, Hope Valentine. Most of all, he prayed he would face his death honorably. He didn't have to peek over the top again to know that now, one by one, the savages who had ambushed them were slipping out into the open, preparing to descend upon them.

He jumped, startled, when he heard the shot, followed by a cry of pain. The first shot was followed by more, in rapid succession, with more cries of anguish and pain. He and the five men with him would swear, when recalling this day, that the sound of that Winchester rifle was as sweet as the singing of angels.

Kneeling at the very top of the high bluff, Clint had

been unable to get a clear shot at the warriors who shot Willis. But when he saw the soldier attempt to run, he knew, as did the warriors, that Justin and his squad were out of ammunition. He also knew that his chances of saving them would depend on how patient he could be. So he held his fire when the lone warrior stepped out in the open, daring the soldiers to shoot at him. Such an easy target was hard to resist, but he waited, and soon another hostile stepped out beside the first—then another and another, until all six were standing boldly on the ledge. Clint braced himself and drew a bead on the first warrior, knowing there would be no time to take such careful aim after the first shot. His effectiveness would then depend on how rapidly he could pull the trigger, eject the empty cartridge, and fire again.

When the first warrior dropped, the second bullet was already on its way toward the next target. Instinct and reactions took complete charge of the mass execution. For a brief timeless moment, there were no conscious thoughts, only the automatic cocking of the lever and the squeezing of the trigger, as the Winchester walked down the line of warriors until four bodies dropped and slid down to the foot of the bluff. Although deadly, the rifleman was not swift enough to hit all six before two were able to dive for cover. They wanted no more of the killing machine, however, and fled. Clint sprang to his feet and worked his way down the steep bluff as quickly as he could, but he was not fast enough to get another shot off before the two survivors reached their horses and galloped away.

Confident that the two would not return, Clint went back to the foot of the bluff to make sure the other four hostiles were dead. Now that he had time to think, he realized that it had required a hell of a lot of luck for him to kill four of them. The element of surprise coupled with the confusion over where the shots were coming from had worked in his favor. But it could just as easily have resulted in a shoot-out with him outnumbered four or five to one.

I reckon it was my day to have all the luck, he told himself.

He walked back toward the water then and called out to the soldiers in the sandy pocket below the bank. "Landry, you can come out now." It was not until then that he spotted the bodies of two dead troopers lying in the path some twenty or thirty yards back.

"Mister, I'm damn glad to see you!" one of the soldiers exclaimed as they climbed up the bank. His statement was echoed by the other troopers as they abandoned their rude fortress, relieved that this was not to be their day of reckoning after all.

"That certainly goes for me, too, Cooper," Justin said. He never called Clint by his first name. "Our prospects were looking pretty slim before you showed up." Rapidly recovering his composure, he told the men to round up the horses. Turning back to Clint then, he asked, "Did Captain Rodgers send you back to find us?"

"Yeah," Clint replied. He didn't tell him that it was his idea to come back to look for him. And that the sole reason he was still alive was that Clint had promised Hope he would look after her lieutenant. He nodded toward the bodies of the two troopers. "I see you lost a couple of your men."

"That's right," Justin said, "Johnson and Martini. They caught us by surprise. We never suspected there were any hostiles around, especially since the column rode through here before." Then he looked toward the bank where the horses had gathered. "And Willis," he said, "three in all."

"It's a surprise to me, too," Clint said. He wondered if the notion he had had when seeing the main bunch, that there were not as many as before, was because this half dozen had split off. Perhaps they were not survivors of the larger fight at the river. Their conversation was interrupted by one of the soldiers, a private named Goldstein, who joined them, leading two horses. One of them was the lieutenant's. He handed the reins to Justin and paused to remark over the bodies of the hostiles.

"Mister, that was one helluva show you put on with that rifle of yours. That was some fancy shootin'. We were done for."

"I was lucky," Clint said.

"I'd say we were the ones who were lucky," Goldstein insisted. "And on behalf of my mother, I wanna thank you for saving her son."

Clint couldn't help laughing. "You're welcome, and so's your mother." Turning back to Justin then, he advised, "I expect we'd best get your men in the saddle and head back to meet the column. I don't know if there are any more Sioux parties runnin' around here or not. But it ain't a good idea to meet up with 'em with just one workin' rifle."

"I agree," Justin replied.

He instructed the men to pick up the bodies of the three dead troopers and load them across their saddles. Then they rode east along the river to join Captain Rodgers and the rest of the troop.

Chapter 5

After deciding that the raiding party had been severely damaged, and by all indications were retreating from the general area, Captain Rodgers deemed his expedition a resounding success and ordered the column back to Fort Keogh. At the captain's request, Clint went back to the fort with them to serve as a witness when Rodgers made his report to his superiors.

Although Clint felt an obligation to return to the Double-V-Bar to resume his responsibilities as Valentine's top hand, he reasoned that it would not be out of the question to stay over one night at the army post. He figured he had at least earned a drink at Ernie's saloon for his part in saving Hope Valentine's precious lieutenant.

He turned Sam out with the army's horses after the bay was served a full ration of oats. Then he was given a bedroll and shown an empty bunk he could use for the night. Since they had arrived at the post in early afternoon, the captain's report was submitted to the second-in-command, Major John Kinsey, well before mess call. Clint's part in the report was little more than corroboration of the captain's version of what had taken place on the bank of the Yellowstone.

When it was over, he saw no reason why his appearance had been necessary, but at least it gave him an opportunity to visit his friends at the saloon. As he was leaving the headquarters building, he was intercepted by Captain Rodgers. The captain extended his hand and said, "I would be remiss if I did not thank you for your service on this patrol. You did a damn good job, and the part you played in rescuing Lieutenant Landry's grave-digging detail was outstanding. Thanks to you, most of that unfortunate detail made it home."

"I'm just glad I got to those boys in time," Clint replied modestly. "I 'preciate the kind words."

He and the captain parted then, Rodgers to his quarters and Clint to the cavalry barracks, thinking Hope Valentine might be grateful as well. He was tempted to go straight to Ernie's. But knowing it would be wise to hit the saloon with some food in his belly, he waited until the mess hall was open for supper.

"Well, howdy, Clint," Ernie Thigpen called out cheerfully when Clint walked in the door of his saloon. "Didn't expect to see you back so soon."

"You know me, Ernie," Clint returned. "I get downright homesick if I stay away from you and Darcy too long."

His remark brought forth a chuckle from Ernie. "Well, I think I've got some medicine that'll fix that right up." He placed a shot glass on the counter and filled it. "This is guaranteed to cure homesickness." He paused while Clint threw the shot back and suffered the burn. "Darcy will be glad to see you. She's upstairs with one of the soldiers that just got back from fightin' those Injuns." He lowered his voice to a whisper then and said, "We're honored to have a Miles City law officer in the house tonight," he announced facetiously.

When Clint raised his eyebrows as if confused, Ernie explained, "One of those sorry gunmen that took over Miles City that I told you about—settin' back there with two of those drifters that's took to hangin' around town."

Clint turned to see the three sitting at the back corner table in a room filled with off-duty soldiers. "The sheriff you were talkin' about?" he asked.

"Yeah," Ernie whispered. "It ain't the sheriff, though. It's his brother, Mace—that one with the droopy mustache. He's as low-down a skunk as his brother." Ernie chuckled heartily then. "He ain't said no howdy-do to Darcy this time, so I reckon he remembers that hat pin of hers."

"What are they doin' out here near the fort?" Clint asked. "I thought you told me they hung out in town."

"Danged if I know," Ernie declared. "Mace just walked in two days ago. About the third time he's been here, and already he's back again, this time with his two friends." He snorted contemptuously. "Don't make no sense to me to ride all the way out here to do their drinkin'. So I expect they'll be wantin' to talk to me about payin' them to stay in business. Walt Hoffman, owner of the River House in Miles City, told 'em he didn't need no protection for his business. Night before last he got pistol-whipped and robbed when he went home for supper. Mace told me about it when he came in. Told me it might be something for me to think about, said he could arrange a little extra protection for me if I was willin' to spend a little money. I told him there's enough soldiers in here most of the time to make sure nobody jumps me."

"You might have something there, Ernie," Clint said. "He oughta have enough sense not to mess around with the soldiers' water hole." Clint wasn't in the mood to talk about Simon and Mace Yeager. He was tired from being in the saddle for the past few days. All he wanted now was a couple of drinks, a little friendly conversation, and a good night's sleep, so he was glad to see Darcy arrive at the top of the stairs. A contented-looking soldier was a few steps behind her.

She was halfway down the steps before she glanced over toward the bar and spotted Clint talking to Ernie. Her eyes brightened immediately and the bored expression she had worn a few seconds earlier dissolved into a smile. Clint returned her smile and saluted her with a tap of his finger to the brim of his hat. He only glanced at the soldier behind her, but it was enough to tell him he had seen him somewhere before. When the soldier looked toward the bar and saw Clint standing there, he at once broke out into a great big grin.

"There he is!" he exclaimed. "Mr. Sioux Killer himself." He pounded Darcy on the shoulder and said, "If it weren't for that man, I wouldn'ta been here to dip my pickle today." He pushed by Darcy and hurried down the stairs to offer his hand to Clint. Astonished by the soldier's display of appreciation, Clint shook his hand. "Mister, I'd like to buy you a drink," the soldier said. He hesitated then, remembering. "Oh hell, I ain't got no more money." He looked apologetically in Darcy's direction. "She got the last I had." He turned to Ernie then. "I'll pay you come the end of the month, Ernie. You know me. I'm good for it."

Ernie and Darcy couldn't help laughing. Clint was

still somewhat startled, but he remembered then that this was the soldier who had thanked him for saving his life before. So he quickly assured Goldstein that he appreciated the offer. "Hell, I'll buy you one," he said, "and we'll both drink to our good luck."

"How 'bout if I give you both one on the house?" Ernie offered. He had no notion what circumstances they were celebrating, but it was obvious Clint had something to do with it. "Was you with the soldiers chasin' those hostiles?" he asked Clint.

Goldstein didn't wait for Clint to answer. "I'll say he was. Me and the rest of a grave-diggin' detail was ambushed by those red devils. They had us holed up in a hollowed-out pocket under the river bank—out of ammunition, we was done for—just waitin' for the Injuns to come down and finish us off. Then all of a sudden, this feller comes along like the angel of death—Crack! Crack! Crack! And the Injuns start droppin' one by one." That was as far as he got before Clint stopped him.

"Whoa, soldier," he interrupted, already embarrassed. "We just had a little luck, that's all."

Ernie grinned at him. "Did you really do all that?"

Clint shrugged. "More or less," he said.

"Angel of death, huh?" Ernie could see Clint's discomfort with the subject. "Whaddaya think about that, Darcy?"

She favored Clint with a smile as well. "He's always been my hero," she said sweetly. "Ain't that right, honey?" She gave Clint's arm a squeeze while Ernie poured four drinks.

The celebration had gotten loud enough to be plainly heard, even in the noisy barroom, by the three men sitting at the back corner table. Mace Yeager cocked his head in the direction of the bar to listen. He had established himself among his lawless society as a gunman with no peer. He wore the reputation as if it were a badge, and never passed up an opportunity to prove it. The two hired guns seated at the table with him were not surprised when he pushed his chair back and walked casually over to the bar. The four people having a drink paid no attention to him, aware of his presence only after he spoke.

"Me, I ain't never seen no angel that I recall, and I know I damn sure ain't never seen no angel of death."

The intrusion was sufficient to halt the conversation at the bar, and they turned to look at him. No one said anything for a moment, and then Ernie spoke. "Something I can do for you, Deputy?"

"Yeah," Mace replied. "There's somethin' you can do. You can tell your hero here—what did you call him, angel of death? You can tell him he's makin' so much noise that me and my friends can't hear ourselves talk." A thin smile spread slowly beneath the drooping black mustache, barely disturbing the corners of his mouth in a face that knew no charity.

Clint took a quick moment to notice the deputy's hands hanging seemingly casually, yet poised to instantly reach for the .44 holstered at his side. His hands were narrow, with long slender fingers, almost like a woman's hands, nimble and quick. Suddenly the portion of the room close to the bar went deadly silent, so Clint's response to the blatant challenge, though softly spoken, was easily heard. "If we're disturbing you and your friends," he said to the tall, knife-thin deputy, "then we'll try to quiet down a little, so you don't hear us above all the other noise in the room."

"This is a private party," Darcy said. "We're not disturbin' you, so go on back to your table and mind your own business."

Mace's eyes narrowed immediately in angry response to her suggestion. "Shut up, bitch," he blurted. "I don't wanna hear nothin' outta the mouth of a damn whore."

Clint looked at the menacing gunman, poised like a rattlesnake ready to strike. Then he glanced at the man's two friends still seated at the table, both watching the drama intensely with grins of anticipation plastered on their rough faces.

Back to Mace again, Clint spoke. "You seem like a right friendly fellow, but you're startin' to get on my nerves a little bit now. You're probably ashamed of the way you just talked to the lady here. So we'll just let it pass this one time, figure you just didn't know any better, and you can go on back to mindin' your own business and we'll tend to ours."

Mace was not sure how to react to what he had intended to be a challenge. "You'll let it pass?" he blurted. "Well, I ain't gonna let it pass."

"I think you'd better," Private Goldstein said. And Mace became aware then of the number of soldiers who had gotten up from their tables and were now crowding around them. Though no threats were spoken, they were fairly obvious.

Furious for having to back down, but aware of his prospects if he did not, Mace growled, "This ain't over between me and you. I'll see you sometime when you ain't got the army to protect you." He started pushing his way through the uniforms that reluctantly permitted him a path to the door. "Come on, boys," he called out angrily to his two companions. "Let's get outta this damn whorehouse." There was no hesitation on their part, having seen the response of every soldier in the room.

"Ya'll come back real soon, now, you hear?" one of the soldiers nearest the door called out sarcastically to them as they left. It brought a wave of laughter over the whole room.

Back at the bar, Ernie gave Clint a serious look and said, "I'm afraid this thing might cause you some trouble if you ain't careful. That man, him and his brother, ain't nothin' but a couple of murderin' outlaws. So I'd advise you to stay outta Miles City, and watch your back everywhere else."

"Oh, I expect he was just tryin' to be friendly in his own way," Clint said in an attempt to make light of it. No one laughed. "How the hell did I get him so riled, anyway?"

"I reckon it was my fault," Goldstein said. "I shoulda kept my mouth shut—yellin' all over the room like I did."

"No such a thing," Clint said. "He's the kind of fellow that's gonna find somebody to rawhide. It just happened to be my turn this time."

"All the same," Ernie said, "you watch your back. Are you ridin' back to the Double-V-Bar tonight?"

"No, I'm stayin' right here in the cavalry barracks," Clint said.

"You can stay in my room with me," Darcy offered.

"There, you see," Clint said to Ernie. "I've got all kinds of safe places to sleep. But some of 'em are safer than others," he said to Darcy. "I might get in all kinds of trouble if I stayed with you. So I reckon I'll stay with the boys in the barracks." He laughed when she gave him a pouty face in response.

"Ain't you ever serious about anything?" Darcy said.

"Only about you, darlin'," he teased. "When you get

old and tired, and decide to quit whorin', I'm gonna marry you and make an honest woman outta you."

"You're so full of horse shit," she said, still pouty.

Curly James leaned close to Bill Blankenship as they prepared to climb into their saddles and follow Mace Yeager, who was already riding away from the saloon. "Boy, he's sure as hell hot under the collar now, ain't he?"

Blankenship grinned. "He sure is. He don't cotton to havin' to back down to nobody. I'da thought he might wanna hang around for a while to see if he could catch that feller when he came outta the saloon. It ain't like Mace to eat crow like that and let him get away with it."

"Oh, it ain't over. Ain't no way Mace is gonna let that son of a bitch live after he mouthed off at him like that."

"Maybe," Blankenship said. "But I'm damn glad he didn't decide to take on that roomful of soldiers. I didn't catch that feller's name. Did you?" Curly shook his head. "I reckon he might be ridin' scout for the army, the way that one soldier was braggin' 'bout what a hero he was." He grinned again. "That sure riled ol' Mace, didn't it?"

"I reckon," Curly said. "We'd best tiptoe around him for a while. He might decide to shoot anybody that's handy, if he don't find out who that feller is."

In the saddle then, they kicked their horses into a fast lope to catch up with Mace, who was already at the wagon track to Miles City and still fuming over the confrontation at the saloon. It didn't help to improve his disposition to have to tell his brother that Ernie Thigpen showed no sign of intimidation by the three gunmen who had sought to offer him protection. He had argued with Simon before, insisting that Ernie's saloon was so close to the fort that it might as well be considered attached to it. But Simon thought a show of three threatening gunmen would deliver a message that Ernie would be reluctant to dismiss.

Simon can get off his lazy ass and come over here himself, Mace thought.

Then his mind took him right back to the man who had caused him to have to back down in the saloon. "Damn it to hell," he cursed.

Behind him, Curly and Bill looked at each other and grinned.

After a long evening at Ernie's, during which a fair amount of time was spent making playful talk with Darcy that still didn't end the evening in the way she always hoped, Clint said good night and retired to the cavalry barracks.

Although more than ready to return to the Double-V-Bar, he delayed his departure the next morning to take advantage of breakfast in the mess hall with the troops. While he was eating, Sergeant Cox came by to tell him that Captain Rodgers would appreciate it if he stopped by to see him before he left. It turned out that the captain wanted to hire him as a scout on a more permanent basis. Clint politely thanked him for the offer, but had to decline because of his responsibilities at the ranch and his loyalty to Randolph Valentine. Rodgers understood, thanked him for his part in rescuing Lieutenant Landry and his men, and told him that the offer was still good, if he changed his mind.

"I'll think about it," Clint said, although he already had thought about it, and took his leave.

As expected, he was greeted by Hank Haley when he rode into the barnyard. "Hey-yo, Clint," Hank hailed him from the pigsty, and hurried up to the barn.

"Mornin', Hank," Clint greeted him cheerfully. "Anything goin' on?"

"Same as always," Hank replied. "Mr. Valentine told Charley he could move the cattle down to the southwest section, close to the river, since there ain't been no sign of Injuns in the last two days. Did you catch up with them Sioux?"

"Yep," Clint replied. "I doubt we'll see that bunch around here again, at least what's left of 'em."

"Ben said you'd find 'em," Hank went on. "Said he'd taught you how to track a hawk's trail in the sky." Clint grunted a chuckle. "Can a feller do that?" the simple man asked. "Charley said you can't."

"Nah," Clint said. "Charley's right. Ben Hawkins says a lot of things just to see if anybody's listenin'. It didn't take anybody special to follow that big party of Sioux. Anybody coulda found 'em. The army sure didn't need me." Hank nodded solemnly, as if giving the matter serious thought. Clint exhaled a little sigh and said, "Well, I probably oughta go up to the house and let Mr. Valentine know I'm back on the job. I'd appreciate it if you'd turn Sam out for me. Don't give him any grain. He got plenty of the army's already."

Rena answered his knock on the kitchen door and nodded her customary lifeless greeting. "Would you tell Mr. Valentine I'm back?" Clint asked her. She nodded again and left to do his bidding. In a few moments she was back with Valentine right behind her.

"Well, glad to see you got back in one piece," Valentine greeted him. "How'd it go? Have any luck?"

"Yes, sir, we found 'em all right, but not before they massacred some folks over at Zack Bristol's tradin' post."

He went on to tell his boss what they had found there, and the events that followed when they tracked the raiding party to the bluffs of the Yellowstone. Hope slipped quietly into the room while he was recounting the surprise attack the soldiers had successfully accomplished. She said nothing, but her eyes were imploring him for news of the army's casualties.

"You had to say it was a successful fight," he said, mainly for her benefit. "As far as I know, the army didn't lose but three men, privates—no officers." The relief in her eyes was obvious, causing him a painful twinge of envy. He wondered if Justin Landry knew what a lucky man he was.

To hell with it, he tried to tell himself. *I'll go down to the bunkhouse to see if Milt's got any coffee made.*

Almost as if she knew what he was thinking, Rena was standing at his elbow with a cup of coffee for him when he turned to leave. "Why, thanks, Rena," he said. "Hot coffee goes really good on a cold day like today." He turned back to Valentine. "I think I'll wait till the boys get back for supper, instead of ridin' down the river where they've got the cattle. Charley can handle anything with the herd, and he's got Ben there to help him. I need to put some new shoes on my horse, and I might as well do that today. Is that all right with you?"

"Oh, hell yeah," Valentine said at once. "Charley can handle the herd."

"Well, you got back, didja?" Ben greeted him in the bunkhouse. "I saw Sam out in the corral," he said, referring to Clint's horse. Clint had named the bay gelding Sam, short for Samson, because he was such a strong horse, like the fellow in the Bible.

"Yeah," Clint said. "I put some shoes on him. He looked like he was gettin' ready to throw one." To satisfy

Ben's curiosity, he gave him a full accounting of the fight with the Sioux.

"I reckon I shoulda gone with you," Ben said when Clint had given him all the details of the fight.

"Why?" Clint asked. "The soldiers killed more'n half of 'em and didn't have but three casualties themselves. So we figure the Indians have headed back north, and we got back safe and sound, even without you," he teased. He knew that Ben felt he should be a part of everything that happened to him. He had often teased his old friend about it, once telling him that it was the only reason he couldn't ever get married, "I don't think any respectable lady would tolerate you in the bed with us," he had japed.

Ben snorted gruffly to express his discontent, and Clint watched him, waiting for the response that was sure to come. The fact that it was slow in coming told Clint that Ben had to think hard about it. He pulled his boot off and made a show of examining a large hole in the toe of his sock. "Looks like I'm gonna have to do a little darnin' before my whole foot is stickin' out," he said. Then he raised one eyebrow as the thought came to him. "If I'd been with you, them other two Injuns wouldn'ta got away at that ambush on that grave-diggin' squad."

Clint laughed. "I reckon you're right. I hadn't thought about that, Chief Hawkins. What happened to that feather you had stuck in your hat?"

"I took it out. Somebody mighta thought I was an Injun and took a shot at me."

Peace returned to the Double-V-Bar over the next month, with no reports of Indians raiding any of the ranches in the valley. Clint figured the occurrence of a couple of heavy snows might have had a lot to do with the absence of cattle rustling—most of the cows that were lost were due to wolves and coyotes. Ben figured the recent snowstorms had caused most of the cattle to show a little more growth of their winter wool to help them make it through till spring.

For ranch hands, it was a time of year for long dreary days riding in the freezing cold. With heavy coats generally made of canvas with a blanket lining, most of Valentine's hands rode nighthawk wrapped in woolen scarves with two pairs of woolen socks. And since there was very little need for roping during the winter, they wore socks over their gloves. Some even wore mittens, since they seemed to be warmer than their gloves. Heavy coats made of bear skin or buffalo were too expensive for the average ranch hand. Only Charley Clark owned one, but he would often loan it to one of the others if he wasn't riding nighthawk.

On sunny days, when the valley was covered with a blanket of snow, there was always the danger of snow blindness. Most of the men rubbed a mixture of lampblack and coal oil on their cheeks and under their eyes to combat the painful effects of it. Ben used a section of black coat lining to wrap around his face.

It was a difficult time of year for the men who watched over Randolph Valentine's cattle, so any opportunity to go into town was welcomed when it was necessary to buy new supplies. As the unofficial foreman, Clint was responsible for taking a couple of men and a wagon into Miles City to get what supplies were needed at Horace Marshall's general store.

So early one morning Clint, Bobby Dees, and of course Ben Hawkins set out on the four-mile ride to Miles City. Bobby and Ben drove the wagon with a two-horse team while Clint rode Sam along beside them. Clint knew what to expect when they reached town, since there were two saloons open now. Of the two men with him, he figured it most likely that Bobby might possibly remain sober enough to drive the wagon back to the ranch. As the years began to add up on Ben, Clint saw that his friend couldn't consume the large amounts he did in the past. So he figured Ben would sleep all the way back.

"Look yonder, Ben," Bobby Dees exclaimed. "That place weren't here last time I was in town. Looks like another saloon to me. What's that sign say?" Bobby had never learned to read, but the appearance of the structure looked to him like a place to buy whiskey.

"Frontier Saloon," Ben responded happily.

"Hot damn," Bobby said. "Maybe since the Trail's End has some competition now, the price of a drink of likker's come down."

"Maybe," Ben replied, looking the new establishment over as the wagon rolled past.

"We're gonna take a little time to have a couple of drinks, ain't we, Clint?" Bobby asked.

"Why, sure," Clint said. "Just as soon as we get the wagon loaded up, you can go down a barrel of it as long as you get it done in time to get back to the ranch before the sun sets. You'll most likely be blind drunk by then, dependin' on how much money you've got. So that'll be trouble enough without you tryin' to drive a team of horses in the dark, too. Let's get on over to Marshall's and load up."

"Horace," Lucinda Marshall called out when Ben and Bobby walked into the store. Clint finished scraping the mud from his boots outside the door before following them. Recognizing him, Lucinda smiled and called her husband again. "It's some men from the Double-V-Bar,"

she said, "Mr. Cooper and two others." She nodded cordially to Clint. Randolph Valentine was a good customer
and always paid his bill promptly.

"Howdy, Clint," Horace said when he came from
the stockroom and saw the three men. "What can we
do for you today?"

"I got a list here of a bunch of things we need," Clint
replied. "Mr. Valentine said you'd put it on his bill as
usual."

"That I will," Marshall assured him cheerfully, and
took the list from him. "Pretty long list," he said after
perusing it for a moment. He looked up at Clint again
and said, "But I've got everything on here, and some
other things he might wanna try. Canned peaches, they
came up on the last boat that made it up the river before
that last snow." Clint showed no interest in the peaches,
so Marshall immediately started pulling the items
from the shelves, marking them off the list as he did.
"You boys can go ahead and start loading if you want
to. I've got it all right here on the bill."

When they were nearing the end of the list, Clint
told Ben, "Go ahead. I'll finish loadin' up the last of it."

There was no hesitation by Ben or Bobby, who started
for the door immediately.

"You sure you don't need no help tyin' it down?"
Ben asked as he went out the door.

"Reckon not," Clint said, laughing. "Which saloon
are you goin' to?"

Bobby looked at Ben for the answer, and Ben said,
"We might as well try the new place."

"Frontier Saloon," Horace Marshall said to Clint
after they left, "Frank Hudson's place. I woulda told you
boys to do your drinking there, instead of the Trail's End.

Hudson ain't been in it long and already's having a little trouble with the law."

"What kinda trouble?" Clint asked.

"I don't really know." Marshall quickly retreated, thinking he'd said more than he should have. "I don't have any complaints with Sheriff Yeager."

It struck Clint as a rather odd comment to make, but he shrugged it off. "Tally up the damage, and I'll sign it. Mr. Valentine said he'd be in to take care of it before the month's out."

"That'll be fine," Marshall said. "When you get back, tell him I said thank you— always appreciate his business, especially this time of year when everything's slow."

Clint loaded the last of his purchases, with a little help from Marshall, and tied a canvas tarp over them. "Don't look like snow," he said in farewell to the storekeeper, "but this time of year, you never can tell."

"That's a fact," Marshall said, and stepped out of the way while Clint tied Sam's reins to the tailgate. He climbed up into the wagon seat then, drove the team up the muddy street, and pulled up beside the Frontier Saloon, unaware of the interested spectator standing in the door of the barbershop.

"Well, I'll be damned . . . ," Curly James muttered to himself, then turned to inform Bill Blankenship, who was in the barber's chair. "You ain't gonna believe this. Guess who just drove a wagon up to the Frontier."

"Who?" Blankenship asked, not really interested, being more concerned with the trimming of his mustache at that moment.

"That feller that got ol' Mace's goat out yonder at the fort," Curly said. "You know, that jasper the soldier was callin' some kinda hero."

"You sure?" Blankenship asked, his interest piqued. He pushed the barber aside and hustled to the door to see for himself. He got there in time to see Clint climb down from the wagon and go into the saloon. "That's him, all right, bold as brass," he chortled, already anticipating Mace's reaction when he found out. "Let's go find Mace." He pulled the barber's cloth from around his neck and tossed it to him. "You can finish me up later," he said to him, and went out the door to catch up with Curly, who was already hurrying to the Trail's End Saloon.

There was no jail or sheriff's office in the fledgling town, so Simon Yeager had made his official head-quarters at Spence Snyder's drinking establishment. He could be found there most of the time, along with his deputy—his brother, Mace.

Chapter 6

By the time Clint walked into the Frontier Saloon, Ben and Bobby were already enjoying their second drink and Ben was engaged in conversation with the owner. He turned toward Clint when Hudson greeted him.

"Clint, this here's Frank Hudson. He's the owner of this fine establishment, sold the one he had in Kansas City."

"Howdy," Clint said. "Clint Cooper, pleased to meetcha. I'll have a drink of whiskey, if Ben ain't drank it all up already."

"There's a little left," Hudson said with a chuckle. "Ben here tells me you boys are with the Double-V-Bar. Horace Marshall, over at the general store, told me the Double-V-Bar was about the biggest cattle ranch close to Miles City. I hope I'll see more of your men in my place."

"I reckon you probably will," Clint said. Then, mindful of a comment that Horace Marshall had made before retreating, he asked, "How are you likin' Miles City so far?"

"All right, I guess," Hudson answered, hesitating before continuing. "The town's got some ways that take a little getting used to. But I reckon you have to allow for some things you don't particularly like in most places—especially in my business."

"Like a gawdamned crooked sheriff?" Ben asked, not beating around the bush, as was his custom.

Hudson recoiled, startled. "I didn't say anything like that," he quickly insisted, much the same reaction that Marshall had on the same subject.

"Well, I hope you have a successful business here," Clint said when it was obvious that Hudson was uncomfortable with the issue. He could see that Ernie had been right when he said the Yeager brothers were holding the town hostage. "I believe I'll have another little snort. Then I expect we'd better get that wagonload of supplies on back to the ranch." He looked at his two partners. "Is that all right with you two?"

"I reckon," Ben answered reluctantly, "although it's a while yet till dark."

They knew he was right, however, so Ben and Bobby ordered one more drink and tossed it down just as trouble walked through the door. Facing the bar, Clint was not aware of it until he saw the look in Hudson's eyes and the sudden frown. He turned to see Mace Yeager and his two yard dogs standing in the doorway. The menacing expression on the deputy's face was in sharp contrast to the gleeful countenances of Curly and Blankenship, who were standing behind him.

"Well, well, well," Mace drawled, a contemptuous grin nudging the ends of his mustache. "If it ain't the . . ."

He paused to glance at Curly. "What did they call him? The Sioux Killer?"

"That's right, Mace, the Sioux Killer," Curly said gleefully. "That's what they called him."

"Yeah," Mace said, the evil grin still on his face. "But there was another thing. What was that other thing they called him?"

"Angel of death," Blankenship piped up, eager to feed the fire of Mace's desire for vengeance. "Like an angel of death, they said."

"What the hell are they talkin' about?" Ben asked under his breath. Clint had not shared the incident that had happened in Ernie's saloon.

"I'll tell you later," Clint said. "We might be busy right now." Curly and Blankenship moved out to each side of Mace, so Clint said, "Keep your eye on those two if anything happens. You'll have to take care of them."

"Right," Ben said in a voice just above a whisper, all business now. "I'll take this one," he told Bobby, nodding toward Curly. "The other one's yours." Bobby nodded.

The situation was tense, but so far no one had reached for a gun. The reason was obviously because Mace intended to vent his anger before he provoked his antagonist into a gunfight.

"Well, Mr. Sioux Killer, you've got a helluva lot of gall showing your face in this town. Or maybe it's just a lack of sense. You ain't got no army to protect you here."

"Well, now, Mr. Yeager," Clint said. "It looks to me like you still ain't improved your disposition none. Maybe you ain't been eatin' the right kind of grub, keeps you with a sour stomach all the time. You're right, the army ain't here to protect me, but with such a fine sheriff and deputy, I don't have to worry about any trouble here in Miles City. I'd like to stay and catch up on the news with you, but we were just leavin' your beautiful town when you came in. Maybe next time we can stay and have a drink with you and your friends, but we'd best get movin' now."

Much like throwing gunpowder on an open fire, Clint's sarcasm caused a rage inside the lean gunman's head, but he managed to remain deadly calm. "That smart mouth of yours has got you in trouble one too many times, and now you're gonna pay for it." His hand moved to hover over the pistol in his holster, a Colt .44 worn high on his left hip with the handle forward. "You're wearin' a handgun, so we're gonna find out right now if you can back up that mouth of yours."

"I'm wearin' one," Clint said, "but it ain't loaded. So you're just gonna have to shoot me down, I reckon. I'm pretty sure I'm faster than you. Ain't nobody beat me yet, but it's no use pullin' it, since it ain't loaded."

Clint was not especially fast with the .44 he wore on his hip. His weapon of choice was his Winchester rifle, but it was resting in the saddle scabbard on his horse. He knew as soon as Mace walked in that he was going to have to fight, and he had hoped that his taunting would serve to confuse him. According to what Ernie had told him, Mace was lightning fast with a gun, and his style was to goad an intended victim into a gunfight.

Rising to the bait, Mace spat back, "Faster than me, my ass. You ain't never seen the day you could beat me in a fair fight."

"A fair fight?" Clint needled him. "How many times have you been in a fair fight? Back-shootin' ain't a fair fight. Hell, I can whip you with my left hand."

Mace was almost beside himself with anger. "You son of a bitch, we'll see who's the top gun hand in this

town. Load that damn pistol. Then we'll step out in the
street where we got plenty of room."

"You sure you wanna take a chance?" Clint continued to press him. "I'm pretty damn fast."

Ben was as confused as anyone. He couldn't believe
the boasting his friend continued to do, because he'd
never seen Clint demonstrate any special ability with a
handgun.

"Load your damn gun!" Mace roared. "Or I'll shoot
you down where you stand!"

"All right, I'll load it," Clint said. "but remember, I
warned you." Taking his time, he pulled the pistol out
of his holster, broke the cylinder, and spun it. "Well, I
must be gettin' forgetful. It is loaded after all." He
cocked it and leveled it at Mace. "Anytime you're
ready, you can go for your gun."

"What the hell. . . ?" Mace sputtered, completely confused, looking at a cocked .44 staring back at him. He
looked from Curly to Blankenship to the weapon trained
on him again, as if expecting someone to explain what
had just happened. "Put that damn gun away," he blustered after a moment. "We ain't drawed yet."

"I have," Clint said coolly. "You saw me draw. I ain't
gonna show you again. That would be pretty damn stupid if I gave you another chance. I told you I was faster
than you, but you just had to be shown. Let's get this
thing finished. I've got to be gettin' back to work, so go
on; go for your gun."

Mace stood dumbfounded, knowing that if he reached
for his weapon, he was a dead man. He believed Clint
was just crazy enough to shoot him down right there in
the saloon. For a long moment, the barroom fell silent
with tension that made time stand still as the standoff
between the six men continued. Finally Mace yielded.

"I ain't no damn fool. I ain't drawin'."

"Well, that decision was the first smart thing I've seen you do," Clint said. "So I'm gonna let you by this one last time, but I ain't gonna be so charitable the next time you come at me. I still ain't ready to trust you, though, so me and my friends are gonna back out the door real slowlike. And if I see you or your friends so much as wiggle your nose, I'm gonna have to cut you down. Just to make sure you understand, if either one of these two saddle bums makes a move, you're gonna get the bullet. Ben, you and Bobby ease on out now and get goin'. Untie Sam and leave him by the corner of the porch."

Clint stood in the doorway with his pistol still leveled at a fuming Mace Yeager until he heard the wagon pull away. "I don't know why I'm stickin' in your craw, Yeager. I can't think of anything I've done to cause it. So why don't you just let this be the end of it? I'm willin' to let it go if you are." He started to move out the door. "Make no mistake, men, I'll blow a hole in the first head I see stickin' out this door."

He eased out then, but as soon as he was on the porch, he ran, jumped into the saddle, and galloped away, expecting a bullet to follow him at any second. He heard one lone shot, but it was a wide miss.

As soon as they heard the sound of Sam's hooves pounding the muddy street, Mace and his two gunmen ran to the door. Outside, they saw that Clint was already too far away for the effective range of a pistol, but out of frustration and anger, Mace threw one shot after the fleeing rider.

Knowing a pistol shot was a useless endeavor, Curly quickly drew his rifle from his saddle sling and took dead aim at Clint's back. Mace grabbed the barrel of the rifle and pushed it up in the air before Curly could pull the trigger.

"What the hell. . . ?" Curly complained. "I had him!"

"He's mine, damn it," Mace snarled. "I'm gonna kill that son of a bitch. I don't want nobody else to get in the way."

"Whatever you say, Mace," Curly said, and slid his rifle back in the saddle sling. With Mace still glaring down the street after the rapidly vanishing rider, Curly turned to Blankenship and winked. Blankenship grinned and nodded.

In a matter of minutes, Clint caught up with the wagon. He reined Sam back and fell in pace beside them.

"God A'mighty," Bobby Dees exclaimed when Clint pulled even with the wagon seat. "That was startin' to get a little sticky back there, weren't it?" He threw his head back and cackled. "I swear, Clint, you sure buffaloed that deputy sheriff. He damn near filled his drawers when you had your gun on him."

Not as entertained by Clint's bluffing as Bobby, Ben took a more serious stance. "I don't know about what you done back there, partner. A man like that don't take gettin' made a fool of lightly, and you know he's gonna come after you. Only next time he ain't likely to give you a chance to bluff your way out of it."

Clint knew that Ben was genuinely concerned for him, but he didn't feel that he had had many options available to him back there in the saloon. "I hear what you're sayin', Ben, and I don't say it ain't true. But damn it, the only other choice I had was to walk out in the street like a damn jackass and try to outdraw a man that does it for a livin'. I didn't like those odds, so I decided to see if I could talk my way out of it."

Ben considered that for a moment before he replied,

"I reckon you're right. I wouldn't'ta give you a nickel for your chances in a gunfight against that killer." He shook his head, exasperated. "But dog bite it, you've got a target big as a bull's ass on your back now. You'd best stay the hell away from Miles City from now on."

"Maybe," Clint said. He didn't particularly like the idea of anybody running him out of town. "Right now, though, I'm concerned about a couple of fast horses catchin' up with this wagon before we get back to the Double-V-Bar. So I'm gonna drop off and watch our back trail when we get to the draw."

"That might be a good idea," Bobby said. He hadn't considered that very likely possibility.

When they reached the southern end of a line of low hills where the trail led up a draw between two of the taller ridges, Clint reined Sam back and guided the bay to the top of one of them. He dismounted and walked out on a ledge that gave him a view of the trail they had just traveled. There was no one in sight for as far as he could see.

After about fifteen minutes with no sign of pursuit, he began to think that he had misjudged Mace's hunger for vengeance. But he didn't want to make the mistake of dismissing the threat too soon, however, so he made himself comfortable on a rock that afforded him an overall view of the snowy valley behind him. He remained there until the sun threatened to set behind the high hills on the western side of the river. Satisfied then that no one had followed them, he got to his feet, stiff from sitting so long on the cold rock. After stamping his feet on the ledge for a minute or two, in an effort to warm them up a little, he climbed back into the saddle and loped off to catch the wagon.

When he arrived at the Double-V-Bar, Ben and

Bobby Dees were unloading the wagon with a little help from a couple of the other men. "I was beginnin' to wonder about you," Ben said. "Thought maybe you'd decided to go back to town to have a drink with your friend Mace Yeager."

"My ass was froze to a rock, and it took me a while to break it loose," Clint japed.

"Saw no sign of 'em, didja?" Ben asked.

"No, no sign," Clint replied. "I give even a jasper like Mace Yeager credit for havin' enough sense not to come on the Double-V-Bar lookin' for trouble. He needs a bigger gang than him and his brother and those two coyotes followin' him around to tangle with us." There was a decided advantage in having a year-round crew of fifteen men on average.

"I reckon you're right," Ben said. "But somethin's gonna have to be done about those outlaws runnin' that town. We get all our supplies from that general store, and if Horace Marshall finally shuts down and leaves town—or gets killed—we're gonna have to go a helluva long ways for supplies."

"I reckon you're right," Clint said. "But until something does get done about it, the army, or vigilantes, or whoever, it'd be a good idea to stay clear of the town. Hell, you can get just as drunk at Ernie's near the fort, and Ernie would appreciate the business. I think I'll take about half the crew with me next time we need supplies, though." He frowned and shook his head regretfully. "This whole thing is my fault, and I'm sorry about that. I reckon I've made it hard for all the boys on account of my little run-ins with Mace Yeager." He paused to think about it and decided that Private Goldstein should share in the blame. That was where it all had started. "I wish to hell that soldier had kept his mouth shut when he came down the stairs behind Darcy," he lamented.

"I expect it'd be best if I took some of the boys when we have to go to town for supplies again," Ben said. "You know you're stuck in that bastard's craw, and he ain't gonna quit callin' you out till you face him."

"You thinkin' I oughta strap on my .44 and stand out in the middle of the street with him?" Clint asked.

"Hell no," Ben said. "I think you'd be a damn fool to do that. I've seen you draw that pistol to kill a snake, and, partner, it wasn't like greased lightnin'. You're as fast with a rifle as any man I've ever seen, but you wouldn't have a chance against a fast gunman with a pistol. And Frank Hudson says Mace Yeager is as fast as there is." Clint shrugged indifferently. "I've known you long enough to know you ain't afraid of anything or anyone," Ben continued. "But sometimes it's just downright foolish to commit suicide just to show how brave you are."

"Is the lecture over yet?" Clint said, grinning. "I'll try to stay outta Mace Yeager's way when I can, but I'm damned if I'm gonna let him or his brother run me outta that town, or any other town."

"All right, hardhead," Ben said. "I'm just tryin' to give you a little friendly advice."

For the next few weeks, winter blasted the Yellowstone valley in earnest, and the crew spent their time trying to keep the cattle from straying from the Double-V-Bar range. There was also a constant effort to protect the cattle from the packs of wolves and coyotes that hung around the edge of the herd. It was miserable work in the penetrating cold. This was the time of year when every man earned his twenty-five dollars a month, even though the work was more demanding in the spring and summer.

But with so little time for the men to think about saloons and prostitutes, the memory of Clint's advisement to stay out of town gradually faded away. No one but Bobby Dees and Ben Hawkins had actually witnessed the confrontation with Mace Yeager, so all the hands were not as concerned with the potential for trouble as Clint and Ben were.

Two of the men, Shorty Black and Pick Pickens, were among those who doubted the necessity to avoid the saloons in Miles City. After twenty-one days in a line camp on Muskrat Creek, at the extreme western boundary of the Double-V-Bar range, they were relieved of their duties and rode back to the ranch to try to thaw out a little. When told by Clint to take the opportunity to rest and get some decent food, Shorty and Pick saw an opportunity to see to some other needs of two young cowhands.

"I don't know about you," Shorty told Pick, "but I've got a cravin' for somethin' stronger than some of Milt Futch's cookin'."

It wasn't necessary to explain his comment to Pick. For three weeks, there had been very little conversation between the two that didn't center on the topics of whiskey and women. "We ain't gotta ride back out to the line camp till tomorrow," he said. "Ain't nothin' stoppin' us from ridin' over to Ernie's to get a little drink."

"That's kinda what I was thinkin'," Shorty said. "We could start out right now before supper and get somethin' to eat at Ernie's, after we get a drink and have a little visit with Darcy."

"That suits the hell outta me," Pick said. "Let's get

goin' while Clint or Ben ain't around to try to talk us out of it."

They cut two fresh horses out of the corral with help from Hank Haley. In order to satisfy Hank's curiosity, they told him they had an errand to run for the boss, and rode away with him still wondering what it was.

When they arrived at the saloon close by the fort, they immediately satisfied their craving for a drink of whiskey, but their main objective was blocked because it happened to be a bad time of the month for Darcy. They were fully disappointed, for had they known of her "condition," they would probably not have made the ride in the cold for the whiskey alone. Dejected, they considered the cold ride back to the ranch.

"Hell," Shorty decided, "it ain't that far into town from here, and I've got an itch I need to scratch." Both young men had fueled the fire of anticipation into flames too high to be easily extinguished, so they were soon in the saddle again.

It was well into the shank of the evening when they pulled up before the Frontier Saloon, having already been warned that the Trail's End was the usual hangout for the Yeager brothers. Before entering, they decided it best not to let on that they rode for the Double-V-Bar.

"We'll let 'em think we're just two out-of-work cowhands riding the grub line," Shorty said. Generally, this time of year, there were a lot of cowhands laid off for the winter, who rode from ranch to ranch for free meals.

The Frontier was crowded, with many of the patrons no doubt riding the grub line, so the two eager men from the Double-V-Bar were satisfied that they were no more obvious than any of the thirty-odd other customers. It didn't take long before a buxom lady named Rose sidled over to wedge in beside Shorty at the bar, having noticed that he had paid for his drink and had money to put back in his pocket.

"Hey, darlin'," Rose cooed. "It'd be a shame to spend the rest of that money on whiskey when I've been waitin' for you to come in. I've got a real passion for short men."

Shorty stood up as tall as he could stretch himself, but was still no taller than she. "Well, maybe I ain't short all over," he said in defense of his lack of stature.

"Don't get cross with me, sweetie," she said as gently as she could contrive. "I figured you were a stud as soon as I saw you walk in. I didn't mean to make you mad. I was just funnin' with you. Let's go upstairs and I'll show you a good time. Whaddaya say?"

That was proof enough of the woman's sincerity for Shorty. "Maybe I'll show you a good time," he boasted. Glancing at a grinning Pick, he winked and followed Rose toward the stairs.

"Ride 'em, cowboy," Pick said, still grinning.

Wishing he had saved a little more of his last month's pay, he turned around to make small talk with Frank Hudson, who was working the bar. He figured he had enough for one more drink, so he told Frank to pour it.

We should have come here first, he thought. Had they done so, he would have had enough money to ascend the stairs to paradise that Shorty had just climbed. *What the hell?* he decided. *I'll try to save a little more next month.*

After a moment, Frank moved down to the other end of the bar to pour drinks for another patron, so Pick turned around with his back to the bar to observe the noisy bar crowd.

* * *

Down the muddy street at the Trail's End Saloon, Mace Yeager sat at a back corner table with his brother, Simon, and three other players. Bored with the game, since it didn't appear that he was going to draw any decent cards, he threw his hand in and pushed his chair back.

"Where you goin'?" Simon asked when Mace stood up.

"Aw, I ain't got no luck tonight," Mace said. "I think I'll take a little walk up the street and see what's goin' on at the Frontier."

"Take Curly and Blankenship with you. Can't hurt to let ol' Hudson think he's gettin' a lot of protection for his money," Simon told him. He glanced over at a table against the side wall where the two were sitting, drinking free whiskey. "Spence will be glad to see 'em go."

He laughed when he said it. Spence Snyder, the owner of the Trail's End, had complained that Curly and Blankenship consumed a hell of a lot of whiskey and never paid a cent for any of it. Simon had told him that the two were official sheriff's posse men and were entitled to free whiskey.

When Mace nodded to them, the two gunmen got up from the table and followed him out the door.

"What's up, Mace?" Curly asked when they got outside and started up the street, trying to avoid the deeper ruts in the mire that was Miles City's main thoroughfare.

"Nothin'," Mace replied, pulling a slim cigar out of his coat pocket. "We're just gonna go to the Frontier to remind ol' Hudson why he'd better not get outta line." He started searching his pockets for a match. When he had no luck in finding one, he asked, "One of you got a match?"

"Yes, sir," Blankenship quickly responded. "I sure do." He started digging into his pockets.

By the time he found one, they had reached the hitching rail outside the Frontier. Curly smacked a horse on its croup, causing it to step aside as they walked beside it. Blankenship paused at that moment to strike the match on his belt buckle, cupping his hands to keep the wind from blowing it out. The match flamed brightly and as Mace leaned toward it to light his cigar, he was startled by what he saw on the horse's quarters. Plainly seen in the light of the match he saw the brand *VV*. Forgetting to draw on his cigar then, he muttered, "Double-V-Bar, that son of a bitch!"

At once excited, he threw the cigar down and headed for the door of the saloon, thinking that Clint Cooper had dared to show up in town again. Blankenship followed right on his heels. Curly paused to pick up the discarded cigar and tried to clean the mud from it, but it had landed in a small pool of water, so he dropped it and hurried after them.

Inside the door, Mace paused to scan the room carefully. He had already decided that there would be no pretense of a fair fight. He had been buffaloed twice already by Randolph Valentine's top hand, so this time he intended to shoot first and dare anyone to say that Clint didn't go for his weapon. After he searched the room a second time to no avail, he walked over to the bar to question Hudson.

"Who's upstairs with the women?" he demanded.

"Hell, I don't know," Hudson said. "Some drifter's up there with Rose. There ain't nobody else right now." He was not happy to see Mace and his two outlaw posse men in the saloon. Trouble usually came in with them.

"Who is he?" Mace pressed.

"I told you, I don't know," Hudson insisted. "He came in with that fellow down at the other end of the bar, the one wearin' the 'Boss of the Range' Stetson."

Mace concentrated his gaze on Pick, leaning against the bar. "You ever see that jasper before?" he asked Curly.

"Nope," Curly answered. Mace shifted his gaze to Blankenship, who also said no.

"Somebody rode in here on a Double-V-Bar horse," Mace said. "And ain't none of us ever seen that feller before." To Mace, that meant that the man at the bar and his friend upstairs were riders for the Double-V-Bar. He walked over as casually as he could, despite the rise in temperature in his blood at the thought of a couple of Valentine's ranch hands in town.

Never having seen Mace Yeager before, Pick was not alarmed when he moved in beside him at the bar. "How do?" Mace said.

"Howdy," Pick returned.

"Was that Clint Cooper I saw goin' upstairs with Rose a little while ago?"

"Uh, no," Pick answered before thinking. "That weren't Clint. That's Shorty." He only realized that he might have said the wrong thing when his remark was met with a cynical smile.

"You know you boys from the Double-V-Bar ain't welcome to come in here and drink with honest men," Mace said, much to Curly's and Blankenship's amusement.

Pick gulped nervously as he glanced from Mace's menacing face to the two grinning bullies behind him. "Uh, no, sir," he sputtered, "we ain't from the Double-V-Bar. We're just a couple of fellers out of work, ridin' the grub line."

"Then how come you came ridin' in here on a couple of Double-V-Bar horses? Maybe you and your partner are a couple of horse thieves. I'm the law in this town, and we hang horse thieves here."

"No, sir," Pick gulped again. "We sure ain't no horse thieves. We ride for the Double-V-Bar."

"You just told me you didn't, so you're a liar, too. I hate a damn liar worst than a horse thief."

Mace was trying as hard as he could to provoke the frightened Pick into making a move to respond to his accusations, but Pick recognized a professional killer in the lean, sinister face sneering at him and he was not ready to die.

"Yes, sir," he said. "I reckon I did lie about it. I'll go get Shorty and we'll leave town right away." He turned to put his empty glass on the bar.

Disgusted with the timid man's refusal to defend his honor, Mace was not willing to let the matter be settled that easily. Clint Cooper was the man he wanted dead, but this weak-livered cowhand would temporarily satisfy his craze for satisfaction. So when Pick reached to return the glass, Mace drew his .44 and pumped two shots into his stomach, doubling him over to fall back against the bar before sliding to the floor.

"He went for his gun!" Mace exclaimed. "He went for his gun! You all saw that. The son of a bitch tried to draw on me."

"That's right!" Blankenship blurted, right on cue. "He went for his gun, Mace."

"He didn't give you no choice," Curly sang out, and looked around the crowd of spectators, nodding for emphasis. No one voluntarily voiced support for the deputy's actions. And among those close enough to have witnessed the confrontation, all were afraid to speak of what they had actually seen. The room was totally silent for a few moments, followed by whispered fearful remarks from some of the patrons near the back who had been startled by the sudden gunshots.

Also startled by the shots, Shorty Black stopped dead still at the top of the stairs, paralyzed by the sight of Pick Pickens crumpled unmoving on the floor, his back against the bar. His hand dropped automatically to rest on the handle of his pistol, but he thought better of pulling the weapon. Running seemed like a better idea, so he turned and ran back to Rose's room. Charging through the door, he almost collided with the buxom prostitute on his way to the window. She was in the process of tidying up a little after the transaction she'd just completed with him.

"What the hell?" she exclaimed. "What were those shots?"

"Nothin' good," Shorty blurted. "Lock your door!"

He went straight to the window while she watched, astonished, as he tugged on the stubborn sash. He pulled as hard as he could, but it would not open, so he drew his pistol and started to use it to smash the glass.

"Wait!" Rose yelled. "Unlock the damn thing!" She hurried to the window and turned the lock, then stepped quickly out of his way while he snatched it up and crawled through.

Outside on the narrow porch that wrapped around three-quarters of the building, Pick hurried to the short railing to evaluate his chances of dropping to the street below without breaking a leg. He hesitated, trying to decide, until he heard the sounds of pursuit through the open window, mixed with Rose's shrill screeches of indignation. That prompted him to go over the railing and hang for a brief second before letting go to land on the snow-covered ground.

Barely four or five inches deep, the snow was hardly enough to provide any cushion, causing him to sprain an ankle. Ignoring the pain, he hobbled around to the front of the saloon where his horse was tied. Almost as an afterthought, he untied Pick's horse, climbed into his own saddle, and fled, leading his dead friend's roan behind him.

Chapter 7

In the wee hours of the morning, Shorty reined an exhausted horse to a stop at the barn door. He didn't take the time to pull the saddle off either horse, but limped painfully toward the bunkhouse instead.

"Clint, Clint!" he cried out when he charged through the door. "They shot Pick!"

Shocked from a sound sleep, Clint sat up, not sure if they were being attacked, or if he was still dreaming. When he finally got his mind straight, he realized Shorty was standing by his bunk, his short, compact figure barely recognizable in the faint light of the stove.

"Who?" he asked. "Who shot Pick? Is he hurt bad?"

"He's dead!" Shorty exclaimed. "That feller, that gunman they got for a deputy, shot him down like a dog. Pick never knew it was comin'." Shorty had nothing more than his gut instincts to tell him that the shooter was Mace Yeager, but he didn't believe that the man he saw could have been anyone else.

Everyone in the bunkhouse was now awake and

gathering around Shorty. "Where did it happen?" Clint asked. When Shorty told him that it had happened in the Frontier Saloon, Clint demanded, "What the hell were you doin' in Miles City?" Before giving Shorty time to answer, he said, "Never mind that. Did you bring Pick home?"

"No, I couldn't. I just got outta there alive myself." Feeling disapproving looks, even though the room was too dark to see them, Shorty tried to defend his actions. "I was upstairs when it happened. I just came out of a room when I heard the shots, two of 'em, and I saw Pick on the floor. They came after me then, so I had to jump out of a window to get away. I think I mighta broke my ankle." The last he added in hopes of evoking some sympathy for himself, sensing that some of the men might think his actions cowardly.

Fully awake now, Clint took a moment to think about what to do. The problem between the Yeagers and the Double-V-Bar had gotten out of hand. It was no longer just bad blood between himself and Mace Yeager, and he could not help feeling that it was his fault. Now a good man had been murdered, if he could believe Shorty's version of the shooting, and Clint felt it was his responsibility to atone for Pick's death. It occurred to him that this was Mace's method of forcing him into the gunfight that he wanted so badly.

"What are you thinkin' about doin'?" Ben asked. He figured he could make a pretty good guess about what Clint was considering, and he wanted to make sure his young friend didn't go off half-cocked.

"I'm thinkin' it's time somebody held Mace Yeager responsible for his actions," Clint said. "And I damn sure owe it to Pick to settle his account with the murderin' son of a bitch."

"You know there ain't no law to go to in Miles City," Ben reminded him. "What if Shorty's accused the wrong man?" He turned to Shorty then to justify the question. "You ever see Mace Yeager before?"

"Nah, I never saw him before tonight," Shorty replied, "but it was him, all right. Couldn'ta been nobody else."

"I expect you're probably right," Ben said, and turned back to Clint to ask, "But what if it was somebody else that done the shootin'?"

Clint could see what Ben was about, but he felt fairly confident that Shorty had the right of it. "Since when did you get so particular about killin' a poisonous snake?" he asked Ben. "I'll make sure I get the right man."

"What are you figurin' on doin'?" Ben insisted. "You just gonna ride into town blazin' away with your rifle?" He was concerned for his friend, and the very real possibility that Clint would wind up getting himself shot by one of the gunmen that hung around the Yeagers. "I think maybe we'd best take half a dozen of the men into town for a necktie party."

"Ben's right," Bobby Dees said. He was standing next to Ben after having been aroused from his sleep. "Only I say more than half a dozen of us oughta go in there and clean that town out once and for all."

"No," Clint said. "I'll go in alone. There are too many decent folks tryin' to make it in that town. I don't wanna go in there with a gang to have a shootin' war with Yeager's bunch of outlaws—too big a chance of innocent people gettin' killed. Besides, we've got a herd of cattle to take care of and a ranch to look after. We've already lost one man. I don't wanna lose any more. I aim to go in to get Pick's body. Then we'll just have to see what happens after that."

"All right, then," Ben conceded. "You're still stubborn

as ever. But at least I'll ride in with you, so you don't do somethin' completely stupid."

Clint smiled and shook his head. "I need you to stay here to keep the crew workin'."

"Damn it, Clint . . . ," Ben complained, but he knew that it was the end of the discussion.

It's a nice morning for a killing, Clint thought as the first bright rays of sunlight found the snow-covered ridge to his right. It was a morbid thought to have on what appeared to be the beginning of the first clear day he had seen in a while. But he had no notion of going back to sleep after Shorty woke everybody up the night before, so he had left the ranch well before sunup. He charged Ben with the responsibility of notifying Valentine about his foreman's absence.

Behind him, he led a packhorse, carrying a canvas sheet to wrap Pick's body in for his final trip back to the Double-V-Bar. He figured he would reach Miles City at about the time most of the people would still be having breakfast. Only the saloons would be open at that early hour, since they were the only places that served food as well as alcohol. No one had opened a dining room, and there was no hotel yet, although Horace Marshall had said that there was some talk about one in the planning stages.

It occurred to Clint that there was not much chance of real growth unless the people, especially the merchants, were able to rid the town of the criminal element that had taken over law enforcement. Clint intended to take a step in that direction on this morning. An execution was what he was resolved to do, but in respect for Ben's argument, he decided to make sure of his victim's guilt before he took any action. And he figured the best way to do that was to question Frank Hudson, so his first stop was to be the Frontier Saloon.

There was very little early-morning activity in the drab little town as the lone rider, leading a packhorse, rode up its one street of frozen hoofprints and wagon ruts. Passing the stables, he nodded to Jim Duffy, one of the few souls who was up and about at that hour. Duffy made a faint nod in return and stood staring at him after he went by. Clint realized why when he saw the rough coffin propped up in front of Homer Lewis' barbershop. Instantly enraged when he rode close enough to see the display, he pulled up short to view Pick's body standing stiffly with a sign attached to it that read DOUBLE-V-BAR TROUBLEMAKER—DREW ON DEPUTY AND PAID THE PRICE.

Furious, Clint dismounted, snatched the sign off, and threw it in the street. He pulled his rifle from the saddle scabbard, and with it cocked and loaded, he tried the barbershop door. Finding it locked, he took a step back to give himself some room and kicked the door open. He stormed through the tiny shop, then through the workroom to the living quarters behind it. Homer, startled, reached for a revolver on the table beside his bed when Clint burst into the room.

"I wouldn't," Clint warned, holding the Winchester on him.

Homer immediately dropped it. Realizing who the intruder was, he immediately pleaded his innocence. "Hold on, mister; for God's sake, hold on! I didn't have no choice. Deputy Yeager told me to put your man's body out there. He said it was a warning to anybody who drew a gun on him or the sheriff."

"Are you tellin' me that Pick Pickens drew on Yeager?" Clint demanded.

"No, sir, I'm not. I wasn't there to see who drew first. I'm just telling you what Mace told me."

"Get him out of that damn box," Clint ordered. "I've got a horse out there with a canvas sheet on his back. Wrap Pick's body up real good in that canvas and load him on the horse."

"Yes, sir, I can do that," Homer replied at once. "Can I take some time to pull on my boots? It's mighty cold out there."

"Yeah, put your boots on. Leave my horse tied behind the shop. Have him ready to go when I come back."

"Yes, sir," Homer said. "He's gonna be a little hard to load on a horse—been a lot easier if you had a wagon. That body's already stiff."

"Just make sure you tie it on good, stiff or not," Clint said, "and I'll be back for him."

Clint led the extra horse around behind Homer's living quarters and tied it to a post. Then he continued on down the street to the Frontier. There were no horses tied to the hitching rail out front, causing him to wonder if Frank Hudson still opened for breakfast. But while he was tying Sam's reins to the rail, the door opened and a couple of men came out, both working toothpicks vigorously to excavate the meat between their teeth. He recognized one of them as the blacksmith, so he gave him a polite nod and received a wide-eyed stare in return.

That's the second one that's gaped slack-jawed at me this morning, he thought.

Inside, he saw Frank Hudson seated at a table near the kitchen door, eating breakfast. Pete Bender, a man who worked part-time for him, was sitting with him. There was no one else in the saloon. The table next to Frank's had dirty dishes on it, no doubt from the two men Clint had met when coming in. Hudson looked surprised when he saw Clint, but at least he didn't stare openmouthed as the others had.

"Well," he said, "I didn't expect to see you in town this morning," Hudson said in greeting.

"Oh," Clint replied. "Why is that?"

Hudson shrugged nervously. "Because of that little fracas we had in here last evening. I guess that's why you're in town." He stretched his neck in an effort to look behind Clint. "You alone?"

"Yeah, I'm alone. What's so strange about that?"

Hudson shook his head as if exasperated. "Because, damn it, Yeager's declared war on the Double-V-Bar. He's told everybody in town to no longer do business with your outfit. Hell, everybody's afraid to buck him."

"That include you?" Clint asked.

"Yeah. . . . No," he blurted, changing his mind as he replied. "No," he repeated. "You want some breakfast? Sit down here with me."

"I don't want any breakfast," Clint said. "What I want is to ask you a couple of questions, and I want straight answers. You saw that whole thing in here last night, right?" Hudson nodded solemnly. "Was the shooter Mace Yeager?" Hudson nodded again. "Did Pick go for his pistol first?"

"Your man never went for his gun at all," Hudson said. "In fact, he was trying to back away and leave the saloon."

"That's about what I figured," Clint said. "I appreciate you tellin' me the straight of it."

"Well, I expect I'd best get up from here and clear that table off," Pete Bender announced, obviously uncomfortable with his boss's honesty.

Clint waited for Pete to go into the kitchen before

asking Hudson the next question. "Where can I find Mace Yeager?"

"He and Simon both have a room upstairs over the Trail's End, so this time of day I expect that's where you'll find him," Hudson said as he studied Clint's face. "You ain't thinking about going in there after him, are you? If you do, you're gonna have Simon and those two gunmen to deal with, too."

"I reckon," Clint replied. He got up from the table. "Mace has been tryin' to call me out for a while now, so it's time I gave him a chance. Much obliged for the information." He turned and headed for the door.

Riding back up the street, he saw that Pick's body was gone from in front of the barbershop, so he continued on to the end of the muddy thoroughfare and pulled Sam up to the hitching rail at the Trail's End. As it had been at the Frontier, Spence Snyder's saloon appeared to be closed, but Clint found the door unlocked when he tried the knob. Before stepping inside, he cranked a cartridge into the chamber of his Winchester, then slowly opened the door.

Much to his satisfaction, he saw Mace sitting alone at a table eating breakfast. That was a lucky break, because it would have made his plan much more difficult if he had had to go upstairs to try to find the right room. He stepped inside, and looked the room over quickly to see if there was anyone else he should be concerned with. But there was no one else in the barroom but Spence's bartender, Floyd, who spotted him but said nothing as he stared spellbound. Clint watched him for a moment before continuing on to the center of the room. There were numerous risks in the bold plan that he had undertaken to seek justice for Pick, and he knew that he had to depend on luck to complete it successfully. One of the gambles he was forced to take was the assumption that most of the people in town felt the same about the Yeagers. He glanced back at Floyd again. The bartender had not moved a muscle, paralyzed by the scene unfolding before his eyes.

"How 'bout some more coffee, Floyd?" Mace suddenly yelled. Turning to see where the bartender had gotten to, he recoiled when he discovered Clint standing no more than ten feet behind him, his rifle before him, ready to fire. Unable to react in time, he knocked his chair over, trying to get to his feet to grab the pistol from the holster hanging on the back of the chair next to his.

"I wouldn't," Clint calmly warned him.

Mace froze, staring at the business end of the Winchester, waiting for the bullet that would claim his life. When it did not come, he recovered some of his bravado, mistakenly thinking Clint lacked the will to actually kill someone.

"You got some gall comin' in here and holdin' a gun on me," he spat. "But you ain't got the guts to do the job, have you? If you had any guts, you'd face me out in the street like a man, and we'd settle it the right way."

"Like the way you killed Pick?" Clint calmly asked.

"He went for his gun first," Mace charged.

"You're a damn liar," Clint replied.

"You son of a bitch, standin' there with a rifle pointed at me, and me unarmed, you're mighty damn brave. Why didn't you just shoot me in the back like the coward you are?"

"I thought about it," Clint said honestly. "But I'll tell you what I'm gonna do. You've been callin' me out to face you in the street, so I'm gonna give you the chance you never gave Pick. I'll be outside waitin' for you, so if you've got the guts, strap on that pistol and come out to face me."

Mace found it hard to believe his luck. *The damn fool is going to try to outdraw me,* he thought.

"I'll be there," he exclaimed as he watched Clint back out of the saloon. As soon as Clint was gone, Mace got his gun belt off the back of the chair and strapped it on. "Floyd," he yelled at the astonished man still standing behind the bar, "tell your cook to put my breakfast in the oven. I'll be back soon as I finish this little piece of business."

Outside, Clint wasted no time. He stepped up into the saddle and rode up to the barbershop, a distance of approximately fifty yards, before quickly dismounting. He dropped Sam's reins on the ground, then walked out to the middle of the street. Holding his rifle by his side, he waited. And while he waited, he thought about what he was doing. Ben would give him hell, if he knew he was standing in the street, risking a gunfight with a professional like Mace Yeager.

You shoulda shot the son of a bitch in the back while he was eatin' his breakfast, Ben would have told him.

Ben would probably never be able to understand his thinking on this. Clint wasn't sure what the ramifications of an outright murder might be, so he hoped the pretense of a face-to-face gunfight might prevent the threat of a range war. With that in mind, he decided to give Mace his fair chance. Even so, he was not willing to concede Mace's advantage of no doubt being the faster man. To offset his advantage was the reason Clint had put a distance of fifty yards between them, thereby reducing the accuracy of Mace's pistol. It was still a gamble, but it gave him a better chance of riding away from there alive.

Seeing Clint dismount outside his shop, Homer Lewis opened the door and called out, "He's loaded on your horse, just like you said. You want me to bring him around front?"

"No," Clint answered. "Leave him back there. I've got another job for you. Step outside. You can count to three, can't you?"

"Why, sure," Homer replied. "Whaddaya want me to do that for?"

"You'll see. I'll tell you when."

Eager to face the man who had caused him humiliation on two separate occasions, Mace hurried out the door of the Trail's End. Surprised when he didn't find his intended victim standing in front of the saloon, he at first thought that Clint had realized the foolishness of his challenge and fled. Then he glanced up the street to see him standing before the barbershop.

"What the hell?" he exclaimed. "Whaddaya doin' way up there? That's too far apart." He started walking toward Clint.

"It's close enough for me," Clint said. "Get ready. When Homer counts to three, you'd better draw, 'cause I'm fixin' to shoot you down whether you do or not." Mace looked confused but stopped and braced himself to draw.

"Go ahead, Homer," Clint said.

Homer sang out loud and clear, but he didn't reach "two" before Mace whipped the .44 from his side and fired. As Clint had hoped, the shot missed inches wide, but the swift gunfighter was quick enough to get off a second shot at almost the same instant Clint fired.

Though Mace's bullet tore into Clint's side, the more accurately aimed rifle slug slammed into Mace's chest, dropping him to the ground. Staggered, Clint recovered to crank another shot into Mace's body to make certain.

Watching from the door of the Frontier Saloon, Frank Hudson blurted, "He shot him! By God, he shot Mace Yeager!"

"Damned if he didn't," Pete Bender exclaimed. "But it looks like Mace got one in him, too."

Hudson wasn't sure what to do. Clint was still on his feet, but he looked to be hurt badly as he strained to step up on his horse. There was going to be hell to pay when Simon found out what had happened to his brother. It wouldn't be too healthy for anyone who tried to help the man who shot him. As much as he would have liked to thank Clint for eliminating one of the hated Yeagers, Hudson was quite relieved to see him disappear behind Homer Lewis' shop. He turned to Pete and said, "That's one less of those sons of bitches."

Seeing how badly Clint was hurt, Homer ran around the building after him and tied the lead rope to his saddle.

"Much obliged," Clint mumbled, and gave Sam his heels. The big bay gelding loped off behind the buildings, heading for the Double-V-Bar, leaving a rudely awakened town behind. Although he was every bit as happy as Frank Marshall to see the evil deputy go down, Homer couldn't help worrying about Simon Yeager's reaction when he found out.

Jim Duffy stood wide-eyed after having witnessed the duel in the street, scarcely believing what he had just seen. He had not moved from in front of his stable, having already figured there was going to be trouble when Clint rode by his place of business. It occurred to him then that Simon Yeager and the riffraff that hung around him would be on the chase as soon as they found out. So he ran to the corral and opened the gate. Then he went inside, got around behind the horses, and shooed them out.

"That'll take some time," he said as he watched the horses scatter. He would tell Simon that Clint must have opened the gate before he shot Mace.

Damn the luck, Clint thought as he held Sam to a steady lope. He wasn't sure how badly he was wounded, but it felt as if someone had driven a railroad spike into his side, and he knew he was bleeding heavily. He could feel his shirt getting soaked inside his coat, but there was no time to stop, even if he had any idea how to help himself. Simon Yeager was bound to be after him as soon as he discovered what had happened, so he knew that he had to reach the Double-V-Bar before he was overtaken.

He had faith that Sam was as stout as any horse that might give chase, and once he reached the ranch, he would be safe. The Double-V-Bar had too many men for Yeager to take on, so Clint pushed the bay hard.

"Yeah, what is it?" Simon Yeager called out when the knocking continued on his door. He had already been awakened by gunshots in the street, and he didn't like being disturbed before he was ready to rise in the morning.

"Simon, Mace's been shot!" a voice he recognized as Curly James' blurted.

"What?" Simon exclaimed when he opened the door, dressed in nothing but his long underwear. "Mace shot? Who shot Mace?"

"That Cooper feller from the Double-V-Bar," Curly said. "Shot him dead!"

"What!" Simon exclaimed, fully awake now. "Where is Cooper? Is he still alive?"

"He took off," Curly said. "But Mace put a bullet in him. He's wounded."

"You and Bill get down to the stable and get the horses saddled," Simon ordered. "Where the hell is Blankenship, anyway?" Curly said he was downstairs. "Well, get him and go saddle my horse. I'll be right behind you. I want that son of a bitch!" Curly went immediately then, and Simon turned back to get his clothes on. "Get up and get your ass outta here," he told the sleepy-eyed woman sitting up in the bed, staring at him.

It didn't take Yeager long to get dressed and run down the street to the stable, where he found Curly and Blankenship involved in an animated conversation with Jim Duffy. When Yeager arrived, all three turned to face him. "Cooper turned the horses out," Curly explained.

"I've been tryin' to round 'em up," Duffy said. "I got two of 'em back, that old pair that Frank Hudson keeps here to pull his wagon. But I ain't caught none of the others yet."

The news seemed to infuriate Yeager. "Well, don't stand here jawin' about it. Get after 'em!"

"Yes, sir," Duffy responded. "That big ol' dun you ride took off toward the creek when I tried to walk up to him."

Without waiting for Yeager to reply, he then ran in the direction he had pointed out, even though the horse, along with the others, had gone in the opposite direction.

After a considerable amount of time was spent searching for the horses near the creek, Blankenship happened to spot one of them walking back toward the stable. They returned to the corral then to find the other horses as well, gathered together behind the stables. Almost beside himself in angry frustration, Yeager frantically saddled his horse, all the while badgering Curly and Blankenship to hurry.

By the time they were in the saddle and had found Clint's tracks behind the barbershop, a considerable amount of time had been wasted. In spite of this, Yeager was determined to go after the wounded man. He charged Homer with the responsibility for taking care of his brother's body.

"I'll be back to get his things," Yeager said. "You take care of him real good."

"Yes, sir, I will," Homer said, and stood watching them gallop away from his shop after they decided the tracks indicated that Clint was running straight to the Double-V-Bar. He went then to recover Mace's body, still lying in the street in front of the Trail's End.

A fitting place for the evil son of a bitch's life to expire, Homer thought. *It's trail's end for that no-good son of a bitch.*

There was a small gathering of spectators gawking at the corpse when he walked up. Their expressions reminded Homer of the looks folks exhibited when looking at a dead rattlesnake.

"Gimme a hand, Lon," he said to Lon Bessemer, the blacksmith, who was one of the bystanders. "Take ahold of his boots and help me tote him to my shop."

"He don't look so dangerous now, does he?" Lon remarked when they had carried the body out of earshot of the other spectators.

"I reckon not," Homer replied, then glanced over his shoulder to make sure no one but Lon heard him. "He looks a lot better with those two bullet holes in him."

They carried Mace into Homer's workshop and dropped him roughly into the shabby coffin Homer had hurriedly nailed together for Pick Pickens.

There you go, Simon, all laid out with loving care, he thought sarcastically. "Come on, Lon, let's go have a drink and toast ol' Mace for a speedy journey to hell."

"Amen," Lon said.

Although Clint was not aware of it, the considerable delay behind him was enough to ensure his safe return to the Double-V-Bar. Barely able to stay in the saddle, he willed himself to remain upright, determined to return Pick's body home. He received slight encouragement by the fact that he was not spitting up blood, but the profuse oozing from his side seemed to be draining every drop of fluid from his body. He was not sure if he was going to make it all the way to the ranch until he reached the rock formation that marked the corner of the Double-V-Bar's range. It was a distinctive rock tower that they had named the Parson's Nose, and seeing it gave him the confidence he needed to make it the rest of the way.

As was usually the case, the first person to see him when the weary horses walked past the low butte one hundred yards west of the barn was Hank Haley.

"Lord have mercy," Hank gasped when he spotted Clint, who was now lying on Sam's neck. "Ben!" Hank yelled, running back toward the barn, where Ben Hawkins was in the process of preparing to ride out to relieve one of the nighthawks.

Already in the saddle, Ben rode out of the barn to see what Hank was yelling about. He spotted Clint before Hank had a chance to tell him. "Oh my Lord," Ben muttered, immediately sinking his heels in his horse's belly and charging out to meet him. He circled around the two horses and came up beside the wounded man, taking hold of Sam's bridle. Clint thankfully released the reins and let Ben lead the horses on in.

"How bad is it?" Ben asked, not encouraged by the look of his friend. "Can you talk?"

"I don't know," Clint answered in painful gasps. "I brought Pick back."

"You sure did, partner," Ben said, worried more about Clint. Pick was already dead. "Mace Yeager?" he asked.

Knowing what Ben was asking, Clint answered, "Yeah, but he won't be shootin' anybody else."

"You got him? Who shot you, the sheriff?"

"No—Mace," Clint said.

Ben was eager to hear the whole story, but he realized that he was taxing his friend with too many questions. "You can tell me all about it later," he said. "Right now we've got to get you off that horse and see what we can do to take care of you. I'll get you up to the bunkhouse and we'll take a look at that wound." He led the horses up to the barn, where he untied the lead rope from Clint's saddle and handed it to Hank. "Tie him up to that post," he told him. "We'll take care of Clint first."

Hank stood there gaping at the odd bundle on the packhorse for a long moment without responding to Ben's instructions. "Is that Pick?" he asked, as if reluctant to take the reins of a horse carrying a dead man.

"Yeah, that's Pick," Ben replied impatiently. "He

ain't gonna bite you. We're gonna have to put him in the ground later, but right now we need to take care of Clint."

The injured man appeared to be hanging on to his horse for the moment, so Ben decided it would be quicker to leave him there and let his horse carry him over to the bunkhouse. So he took the reins and led Sam slowly across the barnyard to the crew's quarters. Then, with Hank's help, he carried Clint inside and laid him on his bunk. A couple of the other hands were just leaving the bunkhouse when Clint was brought in. Alarmed, they hurried over to help.

"What happened?" Bobby Dees asked. When Ben told them the story, their first reaction was to round up the rest of the crew and ride into town.

"Ain't no need to start a war," Ben said to them. "The man that done the shootin' is dead. Clint killed him. Besides, you go into town blazing away, there's gonna be innocent people hurt. Clint told you that. That's the reason he went in to get Yeager by himself."

When they had him settled, Ben got him out of his coat and pulled the bloody shirt open to inspect the ugly hole in Clint's left side. Ben had seen a few gunshot wounds before, and he hoped that this one would have an exit wound as well, but this was not the case.

"Damn bullet's still in there," he fretted. He feared that the bullet would have to be removed, and he didn't trust his hand as steady enough to do it.

Hank stood on the other side of the bunk, watching Ben examine the wound, and made no comment until Ben said he thought the slug should be removed. It was obvious that Ben was concerned about that, so Hank said, "Rena."

Ben glanced up at the simple man and realized that he was right. Rena's firm hand and steady nerve were what was needed in the absence of a doctor.

"I expect you're right. Go up to the house and tell her what's happened." He turned to Bobby then and said, "You boys go on about your work, and one of you ride out to the line shack and tell Jody to come on in. I was gonna ride out there and tell him, but I'll stay to help look after Clint. There ain't no use in anybody out in that shack, anyway. All the cattle are down near the river now."

"What?" Hope cried in alarm when Hank told her that Clint had been shot. "Where is he?" Hearing her exclaim, Rena looked up from the pot of beans she had filled with water and put on the dry sink to soak. Hope turned from the door and said, "Ben sent Hank to get you. Clint's been shot! Go! I'll tell Papa. You go ahead."

The imperturbable woman dropped the big spoon she was holding, wiped her hands on her apron, and went immediately to the door, without taking the time to put on her coat.

Hearing the minor commotion in the kitchen, Raymond Valentine came just in time to see Rena go out the back door. "What's all the fuss?" he asked Hope.

"It's Clint," Hope said. "He's been shot. I was just coming in to tell you. Ben sent for Rena to look at his wound. I'm going to see for myself."

"I'll go with you," her father said, and grabbed his coat from a peg on the wall. "Put something over your shoulders. It's cold out there." Struggling to force his wide shoulders into the heavy coat, he asked, "How serious is it?"

"I don't know," Hope said. "Hank didn't say. He just said Ben sent for Rena." They hurried out the kitchen door to follow the cleared path to the barn and bunkhouse.

Clint's eyes were closed and Rena was bent over the wounded man when Hope and her father rushed inside the bunkhouse. Hope pushed ahead of her father to move to the other side of the bunk, anxious to get a better look at the wound.

After a few moments examining the ugly bullet hole in Clint's side, Rena looked up at Valentine and said, "I fix." Immediate relief registered on the faces of everyone gathered around the bunk, so much so that the somber Crow woman cautioned them, "I fix, but he lose much blood. It will take time." She looked around her then, shook her head, and said. "No good here. Take him my room."

Hope exchanged glances with her father. They both shrugged, unable to see any reason to object. Ben spoke up then, very much in favor. "Good idea," he said. "That way she can keep a close eye on him after she digs that bullet out of him."

That made sense to Valentine, so he told Ben to move Clint up to the house right away. While they carried the apparently unconscious patient up to the house, Ben told Valentine what he knew about what had taken place in town. It was very little beyond the fact that Mace Yeager was dead, and Mace had shot Clint. "He passed out before I could get any more out of him."

"I expect it'd be a good idea to post some of the men back at the Parson's Nose to keep an eye on the trail from town," Valentine said. "That brother of Mace's is liable to come looking for Clint."

"Yes, sir," Ben said. "I expect that would be the thing to do, although he'd better bring an army with him if he's got any ideas about gettin' Clint."

By sheer coincidence, that same thought was taking root in Simon Yeager's mind just then.

Chapter 8

Even though the three men riding after Clint had pushed their horses mercilessly in a frantic effort to overtake the wounded man, Simon Yeager gave the signal to pull up after reaching the Parson's Nose. It was apparent that they were not going to catch him before he made it to the ranch.

Simon was angry, but not to the point where he would foolishly expose himself to the rifle fire of Valentine's sizable crew. The death of his brother was eating away at his innards, and the frustration of knowing he couldn't get to Clint as long as he was holed up at the Double-V-Bar was enough to make his blood boil. Simon Yeager had never loved anyone, and that included his younger brother. But Mace's death meant Simon had lost his right-hand man as well as the fast gun that demanded the respect he needed. So he saw Mace's death as a personal injury to himself. And to have to turn back now caused bile to rise inside him, threatening to strangle him.

"Let 'em rest," he said as he stepped down from his horse and stood glaring at the trail stretching out onto the Double-V-Bar before them. Relieved to hear the order, Curly and Blankenship dismounted, both thinking it a foolish move to ride into the ranch with the idea of gunning Clint Cooper down.

"Whatcha thinkin', boss?" Blankenship asked after a few minutes with no further instructions from Yeager. "You thinkin' 'bout ridin' on in?"

Yeager paused a moment before answering, reluctant to say it. "No, damn it. You'd need a damn army to ride in there against that bunch." As soon as he said it, the idea popped into his head.

I need an army, he repeated to himself. *Maybe I can get myself an army.*

This was the reason he had always been the boss, not because he was the elder, but because he was the thinker. Mace had always been faster with a gun, but Simon was the one who called the shots. They were even physically opposite, a fact that had caused their father to accuse their mother of infidelity, resulting in more than a little abuse to the poor long-suffering woman before she died. Where Mace had been hatchet-thin with dark sunken eyes and hands almost delicate, Simon was heavyset, square framed, with a broad, round face and hands with big knuckles on stubby fingers. The only common thread between them was an evil streak and no regard for human life.

"We're goin' back," he finally announced, and started walking, leading his weary horse.

By the time the three outlaws returned to Miles City, the whole town was abuzz with the news that Mace

Yeager was dead. As they walked their horses slowly down to the stables, every window along the way had at least one pair of eyes watching and wondering. The death of Mace was looked upon as a step in the right direction by most of the town's citizens. And the question to be answered now was how it would impact their town.

As for Clint Cooper, he was an unknown factor. Would he stalk Simon? Or was his trouble only with Mace, and now that it had been settled, would that be the end of it?

"Well, one thing," Horace Marshall said to his wife as he watched the hated three ride slowly by, "they aren't leading a horse with Clint Cooper's body on it. And they would be if they had caught up with him." It was Yeager's practice to display the bodies of his victims.

The first person to find out for sure was Jim Duffy. "Did you catch up with Cooper?" he asked when they pulled up before the stable and dismounted. Yeager didn't answer right away, instead taking his time to pull the saddle off the dun.

"No," he finally answered. "The son of a bitch got away, but I'll get him. He'll pay for murderin' my brother." He fixed Jim with a chilling stare. "Nobody gets away with that."

He pulled his saddlebags and started walking toward the Trail's End. Curly and Blankenship followed along behind. Jim stood there for a few moments before returning to the stables, a smile of satisfaction on his face. One of the hated pair was dead, Clint Cooper had gotten away, and he had played a key part ensuring Clint's escape.

Not a bad day's work, he thought.

* * *

At about the same time the three outlaws reached the
front door of the saloon, the object of their pursuit was in
the care of the somber Crow woman at the Double-V-Bar.
Working silently, Rena probed deeply enough to extract
the bullet that had lodged itself in the muscle in Clint's
side. He had been mercifully unconscious for much of
the procedure, but awoke during the sewing up of the
wound in painful confusion.

Thinking that Simon Yeager had somehow caught
up with him and was torturing him, he tried to get up
from the bed. It took the strong hands of both the
Indian woman and Ben Hawkins to hold him down on
the bed.

"Easy, Clint; easy, boy," Ben said, much as he would
calm a horse he was trying to saddle-break.

Gradually Clint's brain began to come back to reality, and he looked up at the solemn woman bending
over him, working intently to finish her suturing as fast
as she could.

"Rena?" he questioned. "Where the hell am I?" She
shifted her gaze only momentarily to meet his, then,
without answering, went back to her task.

"You're in the house," Ben said to him, "in Rena's
room. She's gonna take care of you, help you heal up.
She's done took the bullet out, and now you're just gonna
have to get your strength back. You lost too much blood,
but Rena knows how to fix you up. Right, Rena?"

She tied a knot in her thread and clipped the ends
with her scissors before answering. "I make you well,"
she said, looking directly into his eyes. "In the morning, I go to river, pick plants for medicine. You heal
good, eat meat, build blood. You'll see."

Ben nodded and laughed. Clint started to but checked it when it caused him pain. Neither man had heard the stoic Indian woman say that many words at one time.

"If you're done with me, I reckon I need to get outta your room," Clint suggested weakly, knowing that he was going to have to be carried to accomplish it.

"You stay here," Rena said. "Not strong yet."

Clint tried to protest but found himself too weak to push the issue. "For a little while," he muttered painfully. "Then I can make it." He relaxed then and lay back.

Concerned, Ben asked her how long she expected Clint to occupy her bed, and what she was going to do in the meantime. She didn't seem worried about the inconvenience to herself and was about to answer when Hope suggested that she could move into her room while Clint was recovering.

"No," Rena said. "I stay here. Sleep on floor." Her expression seemed to signify that the matter was settled. Hope exchanged glances with Ben; then they both shrugged. "I go cook now," Rena said. "He need rest." She picked up the blood-soaked towels and old sheets she had cut bandages from, put them in the basin of bloody water, then went to the door and held it for them to leave. After they left, she closed the door. "He need rest," she repeated.

"It's mighty hard to argue with that woman," Ben commented to Hope when they returned to the kitchen while Rena went outside to empty the basin.

"I can't believe she wants him to stay in her room," Hope said.

"Looks to me like she wants to make sure he's took

care of good and proper," Ben said. "I reckon that's the best thing for Clint, anyway. She always favored him more'n the rest of the crew."

"How's he doing?" Raymond Valentine asked as he came into the room.

"He's gonna make it all right," Ben assured him. "He's a tough son of a gun."

"Good," Valentine said. "I want you to take charge of the men while he's healing up."

"I figured," Ben replied.

Major John Kinsey looked up when the sergeant on duty rapped lightly beside the open door to his office. "Sir, there's a fellow out here wants to see you. Says he's the sheriff in Miles City."

Kinsey frowned. "I didn't know they had a sheriff there. What's he want?"

"I don't know, sir. Somethin' about a murder in the town. He said he'd explain it to you," Wilson said.

"All right," Kinsey said. "Send him in." He got to his feet and stood behind his desk while Wilson motioned for the sheriff to come in. Yeager entered the office and the major motioned toward a chair. "I'm Major Kinsey. What is it I can do for you? You say you're the sheriff in Miles City?"

"Yes, sir," Simon replied. "I'm Sheriff Yeager. I came to see if I can get some help from the army."

"Help with what?" Kinsey asked. His first impression of the sheriff was not a particularly approving one. The man looked as rough as any road agent one might see on trial in a territorial courtroom.

I suppose it takes a pretty rough-cut individual to uphold the law in a frontier town, he conceded.

"Well, sir," Yeager said, "the town's been havin' trouble

with a wild bunch of cowhands from the Double-V-Bar, raisin' hell, threatenin' the town-folk, and such wild stuff as that. I've done the best I can to keep the peace, but yesterday one of the worst ones, feller name of Clint Cooper, came into town and shot my deputy down. Murdered him right in broad daylight, right in the middle of the street. Well, me and a couple of posse men went after him, but we couldn't catch him before he got back to the Double-V-Bar. I had to turn back, 'cause there's too many for me and my two men to fight. All I wanna do is go in there, get Cooper, and take him back to Miles City for trial. But as long as they're protectin' him, I can't do nothin' about it, and he'll get away with murder."

Kinsey took a moment to consider the sheriff's request. It would certainly fall under the army's responsibility to protect the citizens from outlaws as well as Indians. He was quite surprised to hear the fugitive's name was Clint Cooper, however. If his memory served him, Cooper was the scout that accompanied Captain Rodgers' patrol against the Sioux war party on the Powder River. Rodgers was highly complimentary of Cooper's work. This didn't sound like the sort of thing the man that Rodgers described would do. Still, he could have been on his best behavior while riding with Rodgers.

"So I assume you're asking me to send a cavalry patrol into that ranch to take your suspect into custody, and bring him in for trial?" he asked.

"Yes, sir," Yeager said. "Only he ain't no suspect. He done it, all right. There's folks that saw him do it."

"That would be up to a jury to decide, wouldn't it?" the major asked.

"Uh. . . . Why, yes, sir," Yeager hurried to amend.

"All I'm askin' is for you boys to help me take him to trial. You get him outta that place and I'll take him off your hands and take him to jail to wait for his trial." He hoped the major wasn't aware of the absence of a jail in Miles City.

Kinsey was hesitant to approve the sheriff's request. "Have you got some official papers that show you are the sheriff?" he asked.

"Well, no, sir," Yeager replied. "I ain't got no papers. I got a badge." He pulled his coat aside so that the major could see his badge. "If I ain't mistaken, I believe I've seen that sergeant out there in town a time or two. Maybe he can tell you I'm the sheriff all right."

Kinsey considered that. He also realized what a naïve request he had made, asking for official papers. Thinking about it now, he doubted that there were ever any official papers certifying sheriffs in any of a dozen frontier towns in the territory. The sheriff's appeal for help was most likely legitimate, so he decided to comply.

"All right, Sheriff, I'll give the order to assemble a fifteen-man patrol ready to depart right after breakfast in the morning. Is that satisfactory?" He didn't tell the sheriff, but without a territorial judge, he would be bringing the accused into the fort for trial, instead of taking him to Miles City. He could have been wrong, but he had a feeling that there would not likely be a trial. There would more likely be a hanging without benefit of judge or jury.

"Yes, sir," Yeager replied promptly, unable to suppress a wide smile. "What time would that be?"

"Why don't you show up here at seven and you can eat some breakfast with the troops?" Kinsey said. He paused then to be sure. "You're sure this fugitive is still at the Double-V-Bar?"

"Yes, sir, I'm sure, 'cause one of my men put a bullet in him before he got away," Yeager said confidently.

Kinsey had to ask then, "You're sure this was outright murder, and not a duel?"

"Oh no, sir, it weren't no duel. He shot my deputy when he wasn't lookin'—shot him from down the street with a rifle."

"All right, then. I'll look for you in the morning." He stood up, indicating the end of the meeting.

"I'll be here," Yeager said, and took his leave, saving his smug smile of satisfaction until outside the building.

Major Kinsey sat down again just as Lieutenant Justin Landry appeared in his doorway. "Landry?" Kinsey inquired.

"Begging your pardon, sir," Justin said, "but I couldn't help overhearing the conversation you just had with the sheriff. That fellow is pretty boisterous. I just happened to be standing by Sergeant Wilson's desk."

"Do you know something about the sheriff's charges?" Kinsey asked.

"Uh, no, sir, not about his charges. What I was going to say is I'd like to volunteer to command that patrol. I'm pretty familiar with the people at the Double-V-Bar, and maybe I'd be of some help finding the fugitive, Cooper. I rode with him on the Powder River patrol."

"That's right. You did," Kinsey replied. "Good—consider yourself in command of the patrol."

"Yes, sir. Thank you, sir." Justin walked out of the headquarters building with a devilish smile on his face. It was a chance to see Hope Valentine again, even if for just a little while. But he was somewhat surprised to hear that Clint Cooper was guilty of murdering the town's deputy sheriff. On the other hand, he had seen for himself what the man was capable of with a rifle. Still, it was ironic that Justin should now lead a patrol of troopers to find and capture a man who had saved his life.

It's not my call at any rate, he told himself. *If the man's guilty of what the sheriff charged, and there were witnesses to that fact, then he should be brought to pay for his crime.*

In fact, he was not really sympathetic toward the man for the simple reason that he believed that Hope was overly fond of him.

"Well, now, lookee yonder," Hank Haley exclaimed, although he was alone in the hayloft. The thing that had caught his eye was a column of cavalry turning onto the lane that led to the barnyard. He stood there, watching the soldiers for a moment longer, before he recognized Justin Landry at the head of the column. He scrambled down the ladder then to tell Charley Clark, who was in the tack room.

Hank and Charley walked out of the barn to meet the soldiers. "That's Hope's feller leadin' 'em, all right," Charley remarked. "Maybe he brung all them soldiers to carry her off to marry him."

Hank considered that for just a moment before realizing that Charley was joking. "Might be at that," he said then, and laughed. "Who's that other feller, ridin' beside him?"

"Son of a bitch!" Charley muttered, finding it hard to believe his eyes. "That's Simon Yeager! That's who it is!" He had never seen Simon Yeager, but from what he had heard of the man, he was betting that was who it was. "What the hell is he doin' here?"

They hurried out to the front of the barn, anxious to

learn the occasion for the visit by the army, but Justin simply nodded to them and continued on toward the house where he ordered his men to dismount. Hank and Charley followed after them.

Randolph Valentine came out the front door and walked out on the porch. "Well, Lieutenant," he greeted Justin cordially, "to what do we owe the occasion for this visit?"

"Good morning, sir," Justin said. "I'm afraid this is an official visit this time. I've been sent to take one of your men in custody."

Valentine, startled for a moment, asked, "One of my men? Who?"

"Clint Cooper," Justin replied. "He's been charged with the murder of the deputy sheriff of Miles City. I apologize for inconveniencing you, but my orders are to bring him in for trial. I'm hoping that he will come peacefully."

"Murder?" Valentine demanded. "Who the hell is charging him with murder?" At that moment, Hope walked out onto the porch.

Justin smiled warmly. "Good morning, Hope."

"Go back in the house," Valentine told her. The stern expression on his face told her not to argue. She immediately turned on her heel and went back inside. Turning back to the lieutenant, Valentine repeated his question. "Who's charging him?"

Justin, uncomfortable now with the way the confrontation was going, said, "The sheriff." He nodded to indicate the man standing to the side, watching intently.

"Simon Yeager," Charley blurted in disgust.

Valentine, his eyes narrowing under a deep frown, said, "That man's nothing but a common outlaw, and you come marching onto my land on his word? This deputy, I'm told, was the sheriff's brother, the same murdering dog that shot one of my men down in cold blood. Why in hell didn't the army do something about that?"

"I really don't know anything about that," Justin replied helplessly. "I guess the civilian authorities didn't report that."

"I guess not," Valentine roared back. "There isn't any civilian authority in Miles City." He pointed an accusing finger at Simon Yeager. "There's your civilian authority, a damn two-bit gunman who's probably wanted everywhere outside this territory."

Stung by the big man's insults, Yeager automatically dropped his hand to rest on the handle of his pistol, his palm itching with the desire to draw it.

Justin was at a loss for words. "He is the sheriff," he offered weakly as justification for his actions.

"He's a murdering outlaw," Valentine stated flatly. "How the hell did he get to be sheriff? Did the town hire him? I don't think so. He just appointed himself sheriff."

Yeager's broad face became twisted with an angry snarl as he glared at the owner of the Double-V-Bar. Itching to pull the .44 riding on his hip, he was forced to remain silent, but he promised himself that he would eventually settle with Randolph Valentine.

Justin was completely flustered at this point. What he had thought was simply another opportunity to posture before Hope had quickly turned sour, and Justin was not certain how to proceed. To his distress, he appeared to be antagonizing the man whom he anticipated would someday be his father-in-law.

"He's the sheriff, regardless of what you may think of him," he insisted.

"Clint ain't here," Charley called out then.

"I have my orders, sir," Justin began again. "So I have to take Cooper into my custody. If he's innocent of the charges, then it will no doubt be decided in his trial."

Valentine would not yield. "Trial? Where's he supposed to be tried? There's no judge that I know of in Miles City. Are you talking about a military trial at Fort Keogh?"

"I don't know," Justin confessed. It was his assumption that he would turn Clint over to civilian authorities, and that would be Sheriff Yeager.

When it was obvious that Justin wasn't really certain what was to be done with the prisoner, Valentine said, "You heard Charley. Clint's not here."

"Where is he?" Justin asked.

"I don't know," was the reply.

"Ol' Clint's long gone from here," Charley called out again.

Justin was caught in the midst of indecision, wishing at this point that he had not volunteered to lead the patrol. In his mind, he believed that Clint Cooper was, in fact, somewhere on the Double-V-Bar. The silence of the apparent standoff settled like a blanket over the snow-covered yard. A snarling self-appointed sheriff continued to glare at Valentine, who met his gaze with one of unbending defiance. The troop of fifteen soldiers stood in bored impatience, awaiting orders while Justin tried to decide what to do. Finally he decided that he had no choice; he had his orders.

"I'm really sorry, sir, but my orders are quite explicit. I'm afraid I'll have to search the premises for the fugitive."

"You cannot accept my word?" Valentine demanded.

"I'm afraid not," Justin said. "I have to report to my superiors that I conducted a search of the premises." He turned to give the order. "Sergeant Cox, search the bunkhouse. If you don't find him there, search the barn and the outbuildings. Be thorough." He glanced at the smirking Sheriff Yeager and added, "And take him with you."

"Yes, sir," Cox replied, and led thirteen of his men to the bunkhouse while the other two remained to hold the horses. Both Charley and Hank followed along behind them. Valentine, thoroughly incensed by the intrusion upon his property, promptly turned and went back inside the house, leaving Justin and his two troopers standing in the yard.

Inside, Hope and Rena went in to tell Clint what was going on, and implored him to remain quiet, fearing that he might attempt to defend himself against the soldiers. "You just be still," Hope told him. "They've gone to the bunkhouse to look for you, and when they don't find you, they'll go on and leave us alone." Then she and Rena returned to wait with her father in the kitchen, closing Rena's door behind them.

The minutes ticked slowly by, and every five or so, Hope would go to the front window to peek at the three soldiers standing, waiting, stamping their feet against the cold. Looking down toward the barn, she could see the soldiers, their weapons ready, surrounding the bunkhouse. Her father sat at the kitchen table, drinking coffee from the cup that Rena kept filled. It was an awkward situation for all three, as all were intensely concerned for the man lying wounded just beyond the door to Rena's room.

More minutes ticked by, and Hope went to the window again. She could not help feeling sorry for Justin, standing there, looking completely miserable. Surely he would have preferred not to have been in this position. As she watched him, he suddenly turned to look toward the barn. She looked beyond him to see what had caught his attention.

"They're coming back," she announced to her father and Rena.

Valentine waited until the soldiers were all back in the front yard before he walked out onto the porch again. "Well, Lieutenant?" he questioned Justin.

"Sergeant Cox said they couldn't find him," Justin said.

"I told you he wasn't here," Valentine said. "That should have been enough for you."

Knowing he would be held accountable for his actions, Justin said reluctantly, "I'm sorry, sir, but we're going to have to search the house, too."

"My hired help doesn't live in my house," Valentine replied angrily. "You ought to know that. Clint Cooper has a bunk in the bunkhouse with the rest of my crew. If he wasn't there, then he isn't on the property."

"I'm sorry," Justin repeated, then turned to Sergeant Cox. "Take three men and look in the house."

Valentine followed them inside, with Justin trailing him. Through the parlor and the dining room they walked, then back to the kitchen, where Hope and Rena waited anxiously.

"I'm really very sorry for this," Justin said to Hope. "I hope you understand that I'm only following orders."

She did not reply, as she was far too nervous to think of anything beyond getting the soldiers out of the house. He continued to look at her with eyes pleading for forgiveness. She could not meet his gaze, knowing that if the soldiers went through that one door, her father would be caught in a monstrous lie. But worse than that, Clint would be hauled off under arrest, and she feared that he was in no condition to be moved.

"The bedrooms are down the hall," Justin said then. Two of the troopers went down the hall to search.

"Where does that door lead to?" Cox asked, indicating the door to Rena's room.

Hope started, alarmed, but Rena caught her arm and held her steady. "That's just my housekeeper's room," Valentine said. "Nothing in there."

Cox did not miss Hope's sudden reaction. "Go take a look," he told the one private still in the kitchen. Hope uttered a little gasp, and Rena's hand tightened on her arm as the soldier turned the doorknob.

Inside the room, Clint could hear most of the conversation through the door. Determined not to be moved from the room, he strained to reach the Winchester that was halfway out of sight under the bed. It took every bit of strength he had to pull the rifle up from the floor, but he managed to lay it across his thighs. Biting his lip to keep from crying out, he pushed himself up to a halfway sitting position with his back against the headboard.

He saw the doorknob turning, and then the door opened. The two men locked eyes for a brief moment. The soldier was startled to see the wounded man, with the rifle across his legs, staring back at him. Nothing was said as the moment turned into eternity. Then the soldier slowly withdrew, backing out the door and carefully closing it behind him.

"Nobody in there," he reported.

"All right, Goldstein," Sergeant Cox said. "You and the other men can go on outside. We're through in here." He turned to Justin then. "We've looked in every nook and cranny on this ranch, Lieutenant. The man just ain't here."

He didn't say so, but he was glad they couldn't find him. He would have liked to remind the lieutenant that they shared a great debt to the man with the Winchester rifle.

Justin was still determined to discharge his responsibility as commander of the patrol, and he was already thinking about what would be in his report to Major Kinsey. So he suggested to Valentine that it would be the honorable thing to do to reveal Cooper's whereabouts if he knew.

"You have my word, Lieutenant," Valentine said. "If he's not here, then I have no idea where he would be."

There was little more Justin and his patrol could do. Clint could be holed up anywhere in the rugged cuts and draws between the Tongue and Powder rivers. Or possibly he could have even crossed over the Yellowstone and disappeared into the hills to the north of that river. Without a trail to follow, he couldn't know which way to start looking.

"I expect he'll show up somewhere, maybe looking for a doctor," Justin said.

Valentine seized upon his remark. "You say he's wounded? Well, how'd he get wounded, if he sneaked up on the deputy and shot him? That sounds more to me like there was a gunfight in the middle of the street, and the sheriff's brother came in second."

It caused Justin to think for a moment, and then he remembered what he had been told. "According to the reports we received, Cooper was shot by one of the sheriff's posse men when he was escaping."

"According to the reports," Valentine repeated, "reports from who, Simon Yeager?"

"I don't recall," Justin lied, for there were none from anyone but Yeager. Major Kinsey had taken the sheriff's word as fact, and no one thought to question it. Anxious to get mounted and leave the property, he said, "There will be wanted notices up and down the Yellowstone, I suppose, but I doubt the army will follow up unless he's spotted somewhere." He made his apologies once again to Valentine, and ordered his troop to mount up for the return ride to Fort Keogh. "I sincerely hope you will understand that I came here strictly because I was ordered to," he said in parting. "I would appreciate it if you would tell Hope that."

"I'll tell her, Lieutenant," Valentine replied coolly, then turned and went back inside the house.

As the column rode out of the yard, Hank asked Charley what had just happened inside the house. "How come they didn't find Clint?" he wondered.

"Beats the hell outta me," Charley replied. "He's laid up in the bed, helpless as a baby. I reckon they musta figured there weren't no use to look in Rena's room."

The same topic of discussion was under way inside the kitchen between Hope and her father. "How could that soldier not see him?" Hope asked, still finding it hard to believe.

"I don't know," her father said. "But that soldier looked like he'd seen a ghost when he came out of that room. Whatever happened in there, we'd best thank our lucky stars, because I'm afraid we would have been in for a real mess. I can't see Clint surrendering peacefully."

Equally astonished, Clint was not sure what had just happened. Contrary to what Valentine had told Hope, Clint knew that he probably would have had second thoughts and surrendered, for the simple reason that he could not have put Hope, her father, and Rena in danger. He was in no condition to take on fifteen soldiers when he had barely enough strength to lift his rifle. And had he tried to do so, there could be no guarantee that the house would suffer no damage. He was prepared for the door to be opened again, and he was expecting half a dozen soldiers the second time. But when it finally happened, it was Hope who entered the room, with her father and Rena right behind her.

"What happened?" Hope exclaimed. "What did you say to that soldier?"

"I expected to find you under the bed," her father said, shaking his head in wonder to see Clint still propped up against the headboard.

Rena went to the bedside and placed her hand on his forehead. Satisfied that she felt no fever, she stepped back while he answered their questions.

"I know that soldier," he said. "He was in a grave-diggin' detail that got ambushed by a handful of that Sioux raidin' party. I reckon he figured he owed me because of that, but I sure am surprised he took a chance and lied about seein' me."

It occurred to him that Private Goldstein could also be blamed for stirring up Mace Yeager's dislike for him with that performance he put on when coming down the stairs from Darcy's room at Ernie's.

"I think you'd better lie back down," Hope told him. "We'll have something for you to eat in a little while."

Clint let her help him lie flat again, and when he was settled, she knelt to brush a wisp of his dark hair from his forehead.

"Don't think ill of Justin," she said. "I'm sure he didn't want to lead that group of soldiers out here." She rose to her feet again. "We'll get busy and fix you some dinner."

"I'm not hungry," he said. "Don't bother yourself."

Rena stepped up beside the bed again to fix him with a stern gaze. "I cook," she said. "You eat. You need plenty meat to build blood."

He couldn't help smiling. "Yes, ma'am," he said. "You cook; I eat."

It was suppertime when Ben and the rest of the men came in from rounding up strays and driving them back to the main herd near the river. Before going to the bunkhouse, he went up to the house to check on Clint. Hope met him at the door and told him about the visit from the U.S. Army that morning. He was immediately appalled to hear that the purpose of the army's mission had been to escort Simon Yeager to the ranch to arrest Clint for murder.

"Why, that low-down, son of a . . ." He caught himself before finishing. "That murderin' snake," he continued. "How did he get the soldiers to swallow a story like that? If it was murder, how did Clint get a bullet in his side? Did anybody ask your little lieutenant that?"

"Yes, Papa did," Hope replied, rankled somewhat by Ben's reference to Justin as *her little lieutenant.* "He said he was told that one of the sheriff's men had shot Clint on his way out of town." She softened her tone slightly. "Justin only did what he was ordered to do. Don't blame him for this."

Ben snuffed, thoroughly annoyed by the farce perpetrated by the crooked sheriff. "The lieutenant oughta know Clint better'n that."

"Maybe you're right," Hope said. "Are you going in to see Clint? We're fixing him some supper."

"Yes, ma'am. I didn't mean no disrespect to your lieutenant," Ben answered meekly.

"Damn it, Ben, stop calling Justin *my lieutenant.* He's not *my lieutenant.*"

He couldn't help snickering at the tone of her voice. "Yes, ma'am," he said with a wide grin, and followed her through the kitchen into Rena's room.

"How you makin' out?" Ben asked when Clint opened his eyes to discover his old partner standing over his bed.

"I'm afraid I'm gonna live," Clint said, and gave him a smile. "Thanks to Rena. I believe that woman oughta hang up a shingle and go to doctorin' for a livin'."

Clint was interested to know if there had been any serious loss of cattle, since the winter cold seemed to be getting harder. He was told that there were no unusual losses, and that Ben was keeping the boys busy. There was little more talk about the cattle, because Ben was more interested to discuss another subject.

"Partner, we need to get you offa this ranch as soon as you can ride. That bastard, Yeager, has got you marked. He's out to get you any way he can." He snuffed, disgusted. "Goin' to the army with that tale, and the damn dumb soldiers believin' it. All they had to do was look at the man and know he was a liar."

"Hell," Clint said, "let him come. I'll be happy to do the town a favor, once I get on my feet again."

"Yeah, that'ud be just grand," Ben scoffed. "Only that ain't his style. More'n likely you'd get one in the back when you were out ridin' nighthawk or chasin' strays. And what if the army shows up out here again one day when you ain't hidin' here in Rena's room? Them fools bought Yeager's story. They think you're a murderer. This might not be the end of your trouble with them. You're liable to have Yeager and his two killers and the army, too, tryin' to hunt you down."

Clint considered what Ben was trying to tell him. It seemed absurd to him, since he was guilty only of having a gunfight with Mace, which shouldn't have involved the army at all. And since he had settled with Mace for killing Pick, that should end it, as far as he was concerned—an eye for an eye. But he knew Ben was making sense. Simon Yeager was not likely to let it go at that, and he was not alone. Maybe Clint should listen to Ben. "What you're sayin' is you think I oughta go on the run. Is that right? It don't seem to me like I've got any reason to run."

"How 'bout to keep from gettin' your ass shot off?" Ben replied. "I'm sayin' we oughta get the hell outta here as soon as you can sit on a horse. Reason ain't got nothin' to do with it. You ain't dealin' with a reasonable man. We need to go somewhere and lay low for a while till your side heals up and maybe this business with the army dies down. I'll go with you. The boss will get along all right without us till spring. There ain't that much to do in the winter, anyway. Charlie and Bobby Dees can handle the men till we get back in the spring. Hell, by then, maybe those folks over in Miles City will get together and do somethin' about Yeager and his two coyotes, instead of just talkin' about it."

It was a hard decision to make. "Maybe you're right. I don't know," Clint said. "Maybe I oughta take my trouble away from the Double-V-Bar. If it wasn't for me there wouldn't be any trouble with Yeager. We'll talk to Mr. Valentine."

Their discussion was interrupted then when Rena came into the room with a plate of food for her patient. Clint couldn't generate much interest for food at the moment. "Like I said, Rena, I 'preciate it, but I ain't really hungry."

She fixed him with her stern look and said, "You eat food." It was not a suggestion.

Ben laughed. "You better do what she tells you. I'll be back to see you later. I'm goin' to the bunkhouse before the rest of them grub-hounds eat it all up."

Chapter 9

The ride back to the fort had not been a pleasant one for Simon Yeager, since it was absent the satisfaction he had anticipated. He found it hard to accept the premise that Clint Cooper was not hiding someplace on that ranch, and they had just been unsuccessful in finding his hiding place. He was there; he had to be. The man was wounded—how badly, he wasn't sure— but he would need help from someone.

Maybe that whore at Ernie Thigpen's saloon near the fort, he thought. *He might have gone there instead of back to the ranch.* He remembered Mace saying that the whore seemed to treat Cooper like something special. *When I get shed of these damn soldiers, I think I'll pay her a little visit.*

There was also the possibility that Clint was holed up at the line camp on the northeast edge of the Double-V-Bar range. He decided he would send Curly and Blankenship out there to check on it. Bringing the army in on the search for Clint had been a good idea, but it was especially frustrating to Yeager when it produced nothing. Maybe the wanted notices that he was going to wire might make it difficult for Cooper to go to any of the settlements along the Yellowstone Valley to hide. Assuming that he would be trying to hide.

He'd damn sure better be, he thought, *because I'll be coming for him.* There was also one more on his list as well—Randolph Valentine needed to pay for his remarks.

When the column had come in sight of Fort Keogh, Yeager pulled up beside Justin. "All right, Lieutenant, I reckon I'll be cuttin' out here."

Justin was somewhat surprised, for he had assumed that Yeager would ride in with the column and report to the major. "Don't you want to talk to Major Kinsey?" Justin asked.

"There ain't nothin' to talk about," Yeager said. "We searched the damn ranch and didn't find a damn thing. That about covers it, don't it?"

Justin couldn't argue with that. It was concise, to say the least. "I guess it does," he answered. "But don't you want to see if the major plans any further action on this?"

"Nope, I'll handle it myself from now on," Yeager said as he wheeled his horse to the side and loped away from the column.

A waste of the army's resources, Justin thought, *and a damn cold ride for no purpose.*

The patrol had resulted in consequences that Justin had not anticipated as well. Thanks to the search of Randolph Valentine's house, he had created an unwanted amount of friction between himself and Hope's father. As far as the fugitive, Clint Cooper, was concerned, Justin didn't care about him one way or the other. He admitted that he was surprised when he first heard what Clint had done, but he later reminded himself of the caliber of men like Clint Cooper, who were barely civilized at best.

Ernie Thigpen glanced toward the door when the heavyset, squarely built man walked in. Ernie had never seen Simon Yeager before, but he knew at once that it was him. He stood, silently waiting, while Yeager looked the almost empty room over, as if searching for someone, before he walked up to the bar.

"Somethin' I can do for you?" Ernie asked. The badge he saw when Yeager unbuttoned his coat confirmed his identity.

"Yeah," Yeager answered. "Pour me a drink of likker. I need somethin' to warm my insides." He watched Ernie pour his drink, then he picked up the shot glass and tossed it down his throat like a dose of medicine. He made a point of paying for the whiskey, tossing the money on the bar carelessly. "I wanna see that whore that hangs out here."

"Darcy?"

"Yeah, Darcy. Where is she?"

Ernie hesitated before answering. He knew for sure that Darcy didn't want any dealings with Simon Yeager. "Darcy ain't here right now," he said, hoping that would be the end of it.

"The hell you say," Yeager replied. "She lives here." He turned to look toward the stairs leading to the second floor. "One of them rooms upstairs," he insisted. "Which one?"

Ernie couldn't think of anything to say to discourage Yeager, who seemed determined to see Darcy. "Uh, Darcy ain't feelin' too well right now. She ain't entertainin' customers."

"That right?" Yeager replied defiantly. "Well, she's seein' this one." He marched straight for the stairs.

"You can't go up there!" Ernie exclaimed. "She's got a customer with her."

Yeager spun around, his hand hovering threateningly over the .44 on his hip. "You mealy-mouthed old bastard, you can't open your trap without a lie fallin' out. You just told me she ain't seein' customers today. You just stay there behind that counter and mind your own business, and maybe you'll live to see another day."

He felt certain now that Darcy was hiding someone in her room, and that someone had to be Clint Cooper. Taking two steps at a time, he charged up the stairs. When he reached the second floor, he started down the narrow hall. With his pistol drawn, he tried the first door. It was unlocked, and he opened it slowly to find that the room was unoccupied. Moving to the next door, he stopped when he heard a woman's voice on the other side. He knew that there was only one prostitute working at Ernie's, so he stepped back against the opposite wall, not bothering to try the knob to see if it was locked. Taking two long strides, he kicked the door open, banging it against the inside wall, startling the two people on the bed.

Shocked by the sudden intrusion, they had no time to react before Yeager was upon them. With one powerful hand, he grabbed the unfortunate man by his hair and pulled him off the screaming woman and onto the floor. Still in a state of shock, the confused soldier made an attempt to defend himself from the demon who now stuck a pistol into his face.

"Clint Cooper!" Yeager roared triumphantly, lost in his insane rage. He cocked the pistol and glared into the face of the terrified soldier.

"He ain't Clint Cooper!" Darcy yelled, knowing then who the demon was. Hearing her, Yeager hesitated before pulling the trigger. "You damn fool," Darcy shouted. "He ain't Clint. You're fixin' to shoot a soldier." It was enough to keep him from pulling the trigger, but he was not totally convinced. He had never seen Clint before. "Look," she said, pointing to a pile of clothes on the floor. "Those are his clothes, an army uniform." Again Yeager hesitated. "Look at him!" Darcy yelled at him. "He's a soldier!"

Yeager finally released the frightened soldier and stepped back to try to calm his runaway rage. He looked hard at the half-naked man shivering on the cold wooden floor. The woman was right. It wasn't him. Still angry, and now frustrated, he turned to Darcy and demanded, "Where is he?"

"How the hell do I know where he is? I ain't his mama," Darcy responded, no longer afraid she was about to be shot. "You come bustin' in here like a damn buffalo. Who told you Clint Cooper was in my room? You crazy son of a bitch, you need to go stick your head in the horse trough and wake up." She got up from the bed and pulled her robe around her. "Get outta my room. Look what you've done to poor ol' Bill there. That sure as hell ain't what he was lookin' for when he paid his two dollars. Get outta here!"

"You got a mouth on you that's liable to get you shot," Yeager warned. He was caught between two emotions—whether to back out of the room defeated or to shoot the screaming woman to shut her up. There had not been a lot soldiers to concern him when he came into the saloon, but that might not be the case now. He released the hammer on his pistol, turned, and left the room. He didn't stop when he got downstairs but headed straight for the door, the second of the Yeager brothers to slink out of Ernie's saloon.

Dumbfounded, Ernie stood staring at him, unmoving, until he had gone out the door; then he turned his attention back to the stairs, where a thoroughly disheveled soldier, eyes still wide with shock, stumbled down the steps. Darcy followed close behind, trying to soothe his frazzled nerves.

"I don't think it's really fair to want all your money back," Ernie heard her say. "You know, you had a pretty good ride up until then."

"Just keep the whole two dollars," the trembling soldier said. "I think I've been broke from wantin' to take another ride for a long spell."

"All right, hon," Darcy cooed. "You take care of yourself, now, you hear?"

Seeing Ernie, gaping wide-eyed and slack-jawed at her, then, she walked over to the bar and said, "Give me a drink, Ernie, and I'll tell you all about it." It was her first encounter with the infamous sheriff, and she only hoped that he didn't catch up with Clint.

"It's time we moved you," Ben said, walking into Rena's room to visit his partner after supper.

Clint had occupied the patient woman's room for three days, during which he could not say that he noticed any real degree of improvement in his condition. Most of the pain had gone, but he was still weak, and the few times he had tried to get on his feet, he almost fell on his back. So he naturally asked why it was time to move.

"Shorty and Jody were out on the northeast section," Ben said. "They were headed to the line shack on Muskrat Creek, but when they rode up on that low mesa just shy of it, they spotted a couple of horses tied up at the shack. Well, they knew none of our boys were supposed to be there, so they figured they'd best hold up and see who it was. Turned out it was them two coyotes that hang around with Simon Yeager, Curly what's-his-name, and that other'n. They didn't stay there long, just long enough to find out you weren't there, I'm thinkin'. You know Yeager had to send 'em out there lookin' for you. Shorty had enough sense not to let 'em know him and Jody saw 'em." Ben snorted for emphasis. "I told him it's a damn good thing he didn't. Them two skunks might not be as fast as Mace was, but they're every bit as mean."

Clint guessed what Ben had in mind. "So you're thinkin' I'd be better off at the line shack," he said.

"That's what I'm thinkin', since they've already looked there," Ben said. "Day after tomorrow's Sunday, and if that pretty little lieutenant don't show up here to court Hope, it'd be the first Sunday he's missed this month." He paused to recall the lieutenant's last visit to the ranch three days before, and laughed at the thought. "He might come crawlin' in on his hands and knees after the other day. Mr. Valentine might shoot him on sight." Getting back to the subject, he continued. "Anyway, it might be a good idea for you to be gone from here when he shows up. And we need to tell Rena to leave her door open, so the lieutenant can see ain't nobody hidin' in there."

"Why don't I just move to the bunkhouse?" Clint asked. "Landry ain't likely to be down there."

"Maybe," Ben said, considering. "But if Yeager was watchin' the line shack, he's damn sure keeping an eye on the ranch, too. And now he knows you ain't at the shack, so he'll be watchin' the ranch."

Clint didn't know if it was necessary to leave or not. He was still trying to decide when he pointed out one thing. "Even if he found out I'm here, he ain't gonna risk ridin' in here. He's too far outnumbered."

Ben shook his head impatiently. "All he'll be lookin' for is a chance to catch you outside the bunkhouse or the barn, and one shot from a rifle would be all he needed."

Ben's argument was sound. Clint knew he was right; one man alone could easily slip up close enough to the barn without being seen. Then it would be a matter of waiting for the shot, and with a good rifle, it wouldn't be that difficult. Still, it riled him to think of running from the likes of the three outlaws. Ben studied his face, waiting for his decision.

When Clint continued to procrastinate, Ben said, "I expect you're thinkin' you need to go after Yeager instead of waitin' for him to come after you. That's most likely what you'll do, but not before you give yourself a chance to heal. And all I'm sayin' is to lay low till you get that chance to heal up, and I'll go with you."

"I expect you're right," Clint finally decided. "If you can help me up on my horse, we'll head out in the mornin'."

"Good," Ben said. "We'll take one packhorse with us. I'll load it up with enough to last us awhile. Rena will fix you a good breakfast, and that'll keep you from fallin' outta the saddle."

Rena was not sure she liked the decision. She said as much while she changed the bandage on his side. Hope expressed her opposition as well. "You'll freeze to death out there in that cabin," she said. "You should stay here where we can take care of you."

Her father, however, was in agreement with Ben and

Clint. "Nonsense," he told Hope. "There's a good fire-place in that cabin. He won't freeze, unless Ben's too lazy to cut firewood."

"There'd better be some cut," Clint said.

It was the rule for the last man using the cabin to leave it in good shape with plenty of wood cut so the next man could build a warm fire as soon as he arrived. After all the discussion, Clint and Ben set out for Muskrat Creek early the next morning, with Clint still pretty shaky in the saddle.

Simon Yeager sat at the back corner table in the Trail's End Saloon, a bottle of rye whiskey before him, staring at the front door, as if expecting someone to come through it. The bottle was half empty. It had been full when he first sat down. The door to the back room opened and Spence Snyder, the owner of the saloon, walked in. Yeager seemed not to notice when Snyder walked straight to the bar to confer with his bartender.

"How long's he been sittin' there like that?" Spence asked Floyd.

"'Bout half an hour," Floyd said, "settin' there like he's been knocked in the head with a limb."

It was a condition they had seen before, as if some-one or something had seized control of his brain, and it usually meant trouble for somebody. Most of the time it was one of Spence's customers, and on one occasion, it resulted in the death of a man, who supposedly drew on the sheriff. This time it could easily be speculated that the thing driving the ruthless man to his special hell was the death of his brother at the hand of Clint Cooper.

"It has to be one helluva lot of hate to take over a man's mind like that. I hope he don't let it out in here."

Spence looked around him at the few customers brave enough to patronize the Trail's End. A familiar feeling of helplessness gripped him as he thought of the loss of business he had suffered ever since Yeager had made his saloon the official sheriff's office. In fact, all of the town's business owners had drifted toward the Frontier Saloon to have their evening drink of whiskey or glass of beer. He could hardly blame them, but he was concerned about the possibility that he might have to close, if his unwanted tenant remained for very much longer.

"Has Jim Duffy been in tonight?" Spence asked.

"Nope," Floyd replied. "Ain't seen him."

"Damn," Spence murmured. Duffy had assured him that Yeager's presence wasn't going to keep him away.

"That reminds me," Floyd said, "that Reiner kid that works at the Frontier came in here earlier. Frank Hudson sent him over to see if you were here, said to tell you he'd like to talk to you about somethin' sometime tonight, if you get a chance."

Spence nodded, then unconsciously glanced in Yeager's direction. He knew what Frank wanted to talk about. "I'll run over there in a few minutes."

If Floyd wondered why his boss was having a meeting with his competition, he didn't ask, but he could guess. Simon Yeager sat in Spence's saloon like a giant infected boil, subject to bursting at any moment. It was not a question of if, but one of when. And even though business competitors, Spence Snyder and Frank Hudson realized that Yeager would soon destroy the town. It was up to the town's merchants to do something about the problem, but so far, no one else had been willing to risk confronting the violent man. "I'll be back in a little while," Spence told Floyd.

The bartender nodded. He knew how desperate his boss had become. Before this trouble with Yeager, he wouldn't give Frank Hudson the time of day. He glanced at the sullen man, still staring trancelike at the front door.

"You'd best go out the back," he suggested.

"Heard you wanted to talk to me," Spence said when Frank Hudson answered his knock at the back door of the Frontier Saloon.

"Yeah, Spence, come on in. We can sit down in my office where nobody will bother us." Frank led the way to a desk over by a window in the combination office-storeroom. There had been several meetings between the two men competing for the town's thirsty citizens. It was an unlikely situation brought about by the threat to both of them. "Can I get you a cup of coffee? Maybe something stronger?" Frank offered.

"No, no, thanks," Spence replied. "I need to get back to my place pretty soon. Floyd's gettin' to where he's a little nervous by himself."

"Yeager?" Frank asked.

"Yeah, the son of a bitch is sitting at a table, staring like he's lookin' at something that ain't really there. And he's gotten worse since his brother was shot. I'm afraid he's gonna explode one day and start shooting everything and everybody in sight." Spence shook his head slowly. "I guess I don't have to tell you that it ain't gonna be much longer before I have to close up." It pained him to admit it, but Frank already knew it to be the case.

"It doesn't bring me any satisfaction," Frank said. "We were both doing all right before Yeager and his brother landed in our little settlement. Besides, if you

close up, that devil will most likely move in here."
They exchanged worried glances. "Anyway, what I
wanted to tell you is Ed Taylor told me today that he's
thinking about moving out of town and taking his dry
goods business someplace else."

"Hell," Spence complained, "he just opened up this
summer. Where's he gonna go? He's got to know it
takes a little time for a town to develop."

"He says he can see the writing on the wall. The
town's dying. Killed by a parasite, he says, all on account
we ain't strong enough to stand up to folks like Simon
Yeager. Folks ain't gonna wanna settle around here with
the town being run by a common criminal. I tell you,
Spence, it's time we did something to save our town, and
I think our best bet is to ask the army to help us."

"Well, I reckon you're right, it's time we did it,"
Spence said. They had talked about it before in a couple of meetings with several of the other businessmen
in town. They had also discussed the possibility of
forming a vigilance committee to take care of their
outlaw problem, but there were not enough men willing to risk confronting the four gunmen. And their
courage was no stronger since the number of outlaws
had been reduced to three. "Who do you reckon we
could get to go to Fort Keogh? It'll have to be somebody who can speak for the town."

"Hell, there ain't nobody with enough sense to talk
to Major Kinsey but you or me," Frank said. "I mean
anybody who's willing to go. You know that. Horace
Marshall ain't gonna go. Neither is Lon Bessemer. The
whole damn town is afraid Yeager will find out. I'd go,
but I ain't got anybody to take care of the Frontier other
than Pete or Billy—one a drunk, the other a kid."

"It ought not take more than half a day," Spence

said. "Hell, I'll do it. Floyd won't like it, but he's used to running the place by himself. He'll be fine till I get back." He had made up his mind that his business was finished if something wasn't done to save the town right away. "I'll ride over to the fort in the morning before those three leeches drink up all my whiskey."

"Good man," Frank said, relieved that Spence had volunteered. "We'll keep this quiet so Yeager doesn't get wind of it. It's best not to tell anybody else, just in case."

"Agreed," Spence said. "I'll leave a little after sunup. Yeager doesn't like to get up till the sun's sitting high in the sky." They shook on it then and Frank wished him luck and Godspeed.

Yeah, good luck. Curly James smiled to himself, pressed against the outside wall under the window near Frank's desk. *Ol' Simon's going to be tickled to hear about this.* He hurried away from the rear wall of the saloon to be sure Spence didn't see him when he came out the back door.

Back in the Trail's End, Simon Yeager waited for Curly to return. Although Floyd was convinced that he was captured in some manner of trance, Yeager had been aware of Spence's departure through the kitchen door. It was an unlikely door to use, because it led to nothing but a weed patch, and Spence had begun to favor that point of egress lately. And to someone as devious as Simon Yeager, any departure from normal behavior triggered suspicion. Curly happened to come downstairs at about the same time Spence disappeared through the kitchen door, so Yeager had told him to find out where he went.

"You're gonna be tickled to hear who ol' Spence has

been talkin' to," Curly said as he pulled a chair back and sat down at the table with Yeager. He paused while he watched Simon pour him a drink before continuing.

Yeager listened to Curly's report on the meeting between the two saloon owners, making no comment until Curly had finished and sat back, pleased with himself. "I reckon a man's gotta do what he feels like he's gotta do," Yeager said calmly. "Right after sunup in the mornin', huh? Well, I hope he has a safe trip." He nodded to himself while he considered the prospect of perhaps going into the saloon business. "You and Blankenship best get to bed early tonight. You're gonna be gettin' up early in the mornin'."

Frank Hudson sat at one of the side tables near the kitchen door, finishing off a bowl of soup beans and ham that Pete Bender had put on the stove that morning. It was difficult to generate much enthusiasm for the beans because of the heavy thoughts on his mind. He pulled his watch from his vest pocket and checked the time. Eleven thirty-five. Spence had most likely already seen the commanding officer at the fort and might be on his way back to Miles City. He wound his watch and put it back in his pocket when he heard Pete call from the front of the saloon, where he had been sweeping dirt out the door.

"What is it?" Hudson yelled back.

"Somebody's got shot," Pete said, and waited until Hudson came to see for himself before continuing. "Down at the barbershop, looks like Orville, and he's leadin' a horse with a body hangin' across the saddle."

Hudson peered down the street to see Orville Johnson, who owned the sawmill, get off his horse in front of the barbershop. In a moment or two, Homer Lewis came out of the shop to help Orville lift the body down from the other horse. Hudson suddenly felt a chill along the length of his spine, and he felt an urgency to see who the unfortunate soul was. He got his heavy coat from behind the bar and followed Pete down the street toward a small group of gawkers already assembled before the barbershop.

"Billy," he yelled over his shoulder before leaving, "keep an eye on the bar till we get back."

Billy, who had grabbed his coat and hurried to the door after them, answered, "Yes, sir." Disappointed, he turned around. He was as eager to see the body as they.

Hudson made his way through the ring of spectators in time to see Homer and Orville lay the body gently on the walk in front of the shop. "Who is it, Orville?" he asked, concerned because of the care they exhibited in handling the corpse.

"It's Spence Snyder," Orville said. "I was over at the fort last night, and I found him on the trail this morning on my way back."

"Spence wasn't much of a rider," Arthur O'Connor, the postmaster, said. "Reckon he fell off his horse?"

"I reckon he fell off, all right," Orville answered him, "with them three bullet holes in his back."

Hudson was speechless. He heard a voice he immediately recognized as that of Simon Yeager's behind him. "What you boys got here?"

"Somebody shot Spence Snyder," Orville said. "Shot him in the back, and it musta been early this mornin', 'cause he's already stiff as a board. Ain't that right, Homer?"

"I expect you're right," Homer said. "I wonder what he was doin' up that way so early in the mornin'."

"Ain't no tellin'," Yeager answered him. He eased

over close to Frank Hudson then. "Whatever his business was, it looks like he shoulda stayed off the trail to Fort Keogh. That's a dangerous road to ride. I reckon I oughta keep a little closer eye on it from now on, else we might have some other folks gettin' shot. Homer, I reckon he's yours now." He turned to face Hudson then. "Looks like ol' Spence ain't got no family to worry about, so I reckon the best thing is for me to take over his business, just so we can keep the doors open. Don't you reckon?"

Hudson glanced at Lon Bessemer, who had joined the spectators, but Lon looked away, preferring not to meet his gaze. Yeager's comment was a warning, clear and simple. Hudson shifted his gaze toward Horace Marshall and was met with the same reaction as Lon's. Spence Snyder was dead, murdered. That was horrible enough, but even more so than that was the fact that the town's backbone had been severed as well.

"I reckon," Hudson finally answered, and turned away to return to his saloon. It was obvious that none of the other merchants were going to take a stand against the sheriff's blatant takeover of Snyder's business. And Hudson lacked the fortitude to stand up to him alone.

Chapter 10

Simon Yeager's acquisition of an established business was surprisingly easy, given the fact that no one had the courage to challenge his right to do so. Although saddled with severely declining patronage from the residents of the town, the saloon still attracted enough customers from the ranches and the fort to keep it afloat. The thought of owning and operating a legitimate business had never entered his mind before. He had never acquired anything of value before, except by means of the business end of a cocked six-shooter.

There were other things to figure out now. He would have to have money to buy whiskey and beer and all the other supplies needed to operate a saloon. The storeroom appeared to be well stocked at the present time, but he had no idea how long it would be before it would need to be restocked. Spence had to have money somewhere, and that place had to be the safe in his storeroom. That was not the only place, however. After going through Spence's living quarters at the back end of the hallway upstairs, Simon found another safe. It was smaller than the one downstairs. He decided to wait until he sent Curly and Blankenship on some errand before attempting to break into the safes. It wouldn't do for those two back-shooters to know how much money he found.

The eagerness to search for what he felt certain was a substantial sum of money was enough to temporarily slow his thirst for vengeance. He was still determined to find Clint Cooper and settle with him for his brother's death. But the childlike excitement he derived from suddenly owning a saloon caused him to think of the potential of becoming a wealthy man. He had no intention of giving up his position as sheriff, because that gave him power, and he had Curly and Blankenship to do the dirty work for him. He couldn't help smiling when it occurred to him that he owed a debt of gratitude to the late Spence Snyder for trying to get help from the army.

Simon Yeager, businessman, he thought, his smile extending across his broad, cruel face. His reverie was interrupted then by the arrival of Floyd Kelly at his elbow.

"I'm fixin' to go to the graveyard now," Floyd said. "They're gonna say a few words over Spence. Alice and Bonny said they oughta go with me, if it's all right with you." He hesitated for a moment, not certain what he should do. "After we bury Spence, I reckon you're gonna padlock the place, so you won't be needin' us around here no more."

"The hell I won't," Simon responded. He had no intention of losing his bartender and the two prostitutes. "You'd better get your ass back here right after you bury Spence. I ain't closin' this saloon. The only one that's gone is Spence, so don't go gettin' any notions about leavin', you or the women, either. I'm running this place now."

"Yes, sir," Floyd said, afraid to say anything else. He had a pretty good suspicion about what had happened to Spence on the trail to Fort Keogh, and no doubt that the same might befall anyone else who bucked the sheriff.

As an afterthought, Simon asked, "Have you got the combination to that safe in the back room?"

"No, sir," Floyd answered. "Spence didn't tell that combination to anybody." *If I knew it, I damn well wouldn't tell it to you,* he thought as he went out the door.

His mind still humming with visions of conquest, Yeager looked toward the back of the room to the two idle gunmen, who were busy killing another bottle of whiskey. He walked over to stand at their table.

"From now on, you boys are gonna do your evenin' drinkin' at the Frontier." Met with blank stares of confusion, he explained, "I want you to be regular customers at the Frontier." He couldn't help laughing as he imagined the scene. "That sure as hell oughta drive some of them customers outta there. It sure worked like a charm here."

He was already thinking about driving Frank Hudson out of business. And if the gunmen's very presence didn't send customers to look for another place to enjoy their poison, then maybe their special clandestine talents might be called upon to thin out the competition another way. He did not forget that Hudson was conspiring with Spence to ask the army for help in getting rid of him. He wondered if there were others who might be in on it. The more he thought about his unexpected opportunity to thrive, the more ambitious he became, so he would deal with anyone standing in his way the same as he had with Spence.

Yes, sir, he thought, *Simon Yeager, businessman.* He took a moment to enjoy the image. *Wonder what ol' Mace would have to say about that.* The thought caused the smile to fade from his face. *That little business ain't over yet. That son of a bitch will pay for what he did, but right now I'm gonna figure out how to open those safes.*

He felt sure that Spence would not have relied on his memory to retain the combinations to the two safes, so he probably had it written down somewhere. The question was, Where? And it would most likely be hidden somewhere in his living quarters, so he began a search of the two rooms that had been home to the late Spence Snyder. At first, it was almost like a childish game with the excitement of finding a treasure. But as he methodically destroyed Spence's living quarters without success, he became more and more enraged at the two iron guardians silently defying him. The few tools he found in the rooms were useless in trying to open the heavy boxes, and only served to add to his frustration. In desperation, he went back to his search for the combinations, tearing everything out of the one closet, snatching pictures off the walls, looking for hidden pockets, closely examining the floor, especially under the bed, all without success.

He finally gave up, and concluded that Spence had, in fact, kept the combinations in his head. In frustration, he picked up the little framed dollar bill that Spence had hung on the wall over his dresser. It had an inscription under it that read THE FIRST DOLLAR EARNED AT THE TRAIL'S END.

"You son of a bitch!" Simon roared, and smashed

the frame against the dresser until it broke and the dollar fluttered to the floor. Still gripped by his rage, he stood there, staring down at the single dollar bill. He turned to leave the room then, feeling the need for a drink of whiskey to calm himself. But on second thought, he turned back and picked up the dollar. As he folded it into his pocket, he noticed a series of numbers handwritten on the back of it, the combination to both safes.

The feeling of childish anticipation returned as he hurried to open both safes, only to be somewhat disappointed to find that there was no great fortune in the safes, but a more modest sum of just over sixteen thousand dollars. Still, he had to admit, it was a fortune to him. He decided to go downstairs and have the drink he wanted before, but now it would be in celebration instead of frustration.

For the next couple of weeks, a fragile truce fell over the little settlement known as Miles City. The self-appointed sheriff did not appear as threatening as he had in the past, although he still collected a significant payment from each business owner to pay his salary and those of his two deputies. To demonstrate his new spirit of cooperation, however, he reduced the sum slightly, since he stood to gain considerable income from the Trail's End. As he had figured, he slowly started gaining customers when it appeared a man could come in and buy a drink without fear of being pistol-whipped or shot.

Most of them came over from the Frontier, preferring not to drink with Curly and Blankenship. And Frank Hudson was afraid to ask the two unwelcome guests to leave. Simon Yeager could envision an opportunity to become a major force in the fledgling town of Miles City.

It was the first time in his life of robbery, cattle rustling, and murder that he found himself in this position. And were it not for the nagging hatred he felt for Clint Cooper, he might have considered himself content.

Clint picked up his rifle and walked out the door of the cabin when he heard the sound of a horse splashing across Muskrat Creek. He relaxed when he recognized the familiar form of Ben Hawkins. Ben was a figure easy to identify from a distance, because of his distinctive way of sitting a horse. With his hands holding the reins chest high and his elbows slightly out to the side, he looked like a sheepdog, sitting on its hind legs, begging for a bone, Clint had told him. Ben described his riding form as dignified, telling Clint that it made the red sorrel feel proud to be toting him.

Clint stood in front of the crude line shack and watched his friend ride in. "You lost?" he greeted him as Ben pulled up.

"You let me ride in awful close before you came outta that shack," Ben said. "You'd best be careful one of Yeager's boys don't come back to check this line camp again."

Clint laughed. "All right, Daddy," he teased. "I heard you comin' from about a mile away. I could hear the wind whistlin' through those bullet holes in your hat."

Ben took his time dismounting, after a glance at Sam, standing saddled near the shed that served as a stable. "You fixin' to go somewhere?"

"Yeah," Clint replied. "I thought I might take a ride around the backside of that line of bluffs yonder." He turned and pointed to a rugged line of bluffs, dotted with pines and junipers, about a mile distant. "I think it'd be a good idea to make sure there ain't no stray cattle back in there that we mighta missed when we moved the herd in closer to the river." He had no real reason to suspect that to be the case. He was just suffering from cabin fever, and felt the need to do something.

"You do, do ya?" Ben responded. "You must be feelin' pretty sassy today. Think you're all healed up, do ya?"

Clint shrugged. "Good enough to get off my ass. I'm still sore as hell when I twist too far one way or the other, but not enough to keep me from ridin'. And I'm gonna go crazy if I don't get outta this cabin for a while."

"Well, I reckon you're the only one who knows if you're ready or not," Ben said. "I brought you some more coffee beans and Rena sent you a side of bacon. I was thinkin' about havin' a cup of coffee when I got here. Are you so crazy to get outta the cabin that you can't sit still long enough to have us some coffee?"

Clint laughed. "I reckon not."

"Has your fire gone out?"

"There's still some live coals," Clint said. "I'll throw some wood on 'em." He slid his rifle into the saddle scabbard and led Ben into the cabin.

"Feels good in here," Ben said as he pulled his heavy coat off. "That little ol' fireplace heats this place up warm as a mother's womb." He watched while Clint stoked up the fire, then turned and handed the coffee-pot to him. "Damn," Ben said. "You coulda give me that before I took my coat off."

"I'da had it filled if I'd known I was gonna have

company," Clint said. "It ain't that far to the creek." When Ben went out and left the door open, he yelled, "You born in a barn?"

In a short while, Clint ground up some coffee beans and had the pot on to boil. When he thought it had boiled enough, he pulled it back from the flame and poured a couple of cups. "I was thinkin' about ridin' in to the ranch this mornin'. Figured maybe all the fuss had died down so nobody would notice," he said.

"Well, I expect it's a good thing you didn't," Ben replied, "'cause you mighta had to have coffee with Lieutenant Landry."

"What the hell was he doin' there?" Clint asked, at once concerned.

"Hell, it's Sunday," Ben snorted, "same thing he's always doin' there, courtin' Princess Hope."

"Damn," Clint swore. "I didn't know it was Sunday." He had lost track of the days while he was lying in his blankets, healing up. "I'd better mark it down so I don't make that mistake again." He paused to refill the cups, then asked, "Is there any news about what the army's thinkin' about me?"

"Well, I hate to tell you, but I reckon they're still lookin' for you. At least that's what Rena told me. And that's all I know about it, just what I hear from Rena—and what she overhears when Landry's with Hope. It don't sound like they're sendin' out any patrols to try to find you, but they might go lookin' for you if they had any idea where you were."

"You don't think Justin Landry has any idea where I am?" Clint asked.

"Nah," Ben said. "You know Hope ain't gonna let on to nobody that you're out here. Ain't nobody else at

Double-V-Bar gonna tell him, either, and he ain't likely to figure it out for hisself. That boy's dumber'n a stump."

"I hope you're right," Clint said.

They talked on about what Clint was going to do, now that he was almost recovered from his wound and was rapidly becoming fit again. He was a wanted man, and as such, he couldn't remain there on the Double-V-Bar forever, hiding out in the line shack. Sooner or later, that shack was going to be searched again. The only option for him seemed to be to set out for some other part of the territory, change his name, and perhaps start out on a new life somewhere far from here. The problem with that was Clint didn't want to leave the Double-V-Bar and the working crew he had helped develop, and the future he had with Randolph Valentine.

"Damn it, Ben," he exclaimed in frustration. "Homer Lewis saw that fight I had with Mace Yeager. Jim Duffy mighta seen it, too. They oughta be able to tell the army that it was a fair fight, and not a murder."

"Trouble is," Ben said, "they're too scared to tell the army. They're afraid the same thing'll happen to them that happened to Spence Snyder."

"Spence Snyder?" Clint replied. "What happened to him?"

"Word is, he was on the road to Fort Keogh sometime early in the mornin', and he was shot in the back three times. Orville Johnson found him. Now, would you believe who's layin' claim to Spence's saloon?"

"Simon Yeager?" Clint replied.

"That's right," Ben said. "Wasn't hard to guess, was it?" He went on to tell Clint about Yeager's takeover of the Trail's End. "He's got the whole town scared as a bunch of sheep. Ain't no doubt who shot Spence Snyder, but nobody's gonna say anything about it."

"That just ain't right," Clint said. "Somebody's gonna have to take him down. Other towns get a vigilance committee together to take care of a killer like Yeager. Hell, if they won't do it, we oughta send a bunch of our men into that town and clean it up."

"Yeah, reckon that oughta be the way of it," Ben said thoughtfully. "But there ain't enough men in town with the backbone to do it. And Mr. Valentine ain't gonna send our boys in there, 'cause he says the army might look at it as a raidin' party, set on capturin' the town." He took a quick swig of his coffee before concluding, "Mr. Valentine don't care a dump about that town, anyway. He don't need it. He figures the army has to get supplies, even if the town dries up, so he'll get our supplies from the same place they do."

"I reckon you're right," Clint said, slowly shaking his head.

"I know I'm right," Ben said, joking. "I'm not always right, but I swear, I can't remember a time when I was wrong." He emptied his cup and set it by the fireplace. "Now, if you're still thinkin' about ridin' over toward those bluffs, I'll go with you. I wanna get back to the ranch before dark, so let's get goin'." He gave him a stern look then. "You're lookin' a helluva lot better, but you ain't all the way healed up yet. So how 'bout resistin' your itch to hit the trail again for another week? Then if you're thinkin' 'bout headin' for the far country, hell, I'll go with you."

Clint couldn't help smiling at his old friend. "Shoot, Ben, you don't have to do that. You'd best stay right here on the Double-V-Bar, and I'll come back sometime when this thing blows over. The army ain't gonna spend much time lookin' for me."

"Ha," Ben grunted. "If I don't go with you to keep you outta trouble, you're liable not to find your way home. So that's settled. Don't you ride off without me. I'll hunt you down."

Clint laughed. "All right, partner. I'll be right here."

"Whaddaya think about that?" Blankenship remarked. "Looks like ol' Simon was right." He looked over at Curly and grinned. "The son of a bitch did come back to that line shack, after all."

"What if it ain't him?" Curly asked. "It might be one of the other hands." At that distance, from their position in the high bluffs—the same bluffs that Clint had pointed out to Ben—it was difficult to clearly see the features of the two men now getting on their horses.

His question caused them both to squint in an effort to identify the faces of the two men. They watched them as they turned their horses away from the cabin. "They're headin' this way," Blankenship said. They continued to watch as Clint and Ben gradually reduced the distance between themselves and the bluffs. "It's him," Blankenship declared when they were within half a mile. "They're comin' right at us. Whaddaya reckon we oughta do?"

"Hell, they're ridin' right up, happy as a couple of gophers," Curly answered him. "They ain't got no notion there's anybody around but them. A little bit closer, and we can pick 'em off easy as shootin' fish in a barrel. We can settle that little problem that's been eatin' at Simon's gut right quick."

Blankenship wasn't so sure that was the right thing

to do. "I don't know, Curly. Simon just said to see if Cooper was holed up in that shack. I ain't sure it wouldn't rile him a little if we shot that bastard for him. I think he's got a cravin' to do the job hisself. You know, 'cause it was his brother and all."

Curly considered that. Blankenship might be right. He hated to pass up an easy shot, though. Simon had been acting a little strange ever since he found himself in the saloon business. He didn't seem like the same person who would slice a man's belly open, just to see if he could hold his guts in. He'd started talking about plans to increase the business, courting the soldiers, buying supplies, things like that. It was just strange to hear him talk like that. His temper was just as quick as ever, though, so it made it hard for a simple thief and gunman like Curly to understand him. Maybe Simon did want the pleasure of cutting Clint Cooper's string himself. Still, it was a shame to pass up a sure shot.

"If we don't knock them two outta the saddle," he finally decided, "we ain't liable to get another chance like this." His mind made up then, he crept back to his horse and pulled his rifle out of the saddle sling.

"Simon might not be too happy about this," Blankenship warned, but Curly was already crawling up behind a long flat rock to use as cover.

The discussion over, he got his rifle and moved up beside Curly, raked some of the light blanket of snow away, and settled himself for the shot.

"Let 'em get a little bit closer," Curly whispered, when their targets were still over fifty yards away. A wide grin formed on his face then. "I've been wishin' I could get a clear shot at that smart-talkin' son of a bitch—give him some of the same medicine he gave ol' Mace."

Oblivious of the harm about to befall them from the deadly ambush awaiting, Clint and Ben continued their casual approach toward the bluffs. Intent upon climbing to the top by way of a narrow gully, Clint nudged Sam with his heels. The big bay horse responded quickly, then stumbled slightly when his hoof slipped on an icy rock, covered with snow.

At the same instant, a rifle shot snapped past Clint's ear, followed at once by a second, aimed at Ben behind him. "Go!" Clint yelled as he came out of the saddle and ran for the cover of the gully as more shots filled the air around them. When he heard Ben fall in behind him, he strained to see where the shots were coming from.

"Up there!" he exclaimed when he spotted a rifle barrel protruding over the edge of a long flat rock at the top of the bluff. Within seconds, his Winchester was in business, and he pumped a series of rounds at the rock, causing the rifle barrel he had spotted to retract. "Come on!" he said, and scrambled up the gully to gain a new position before there was time for return fire.

In a few seconds, he saw the rifle barrel appear at the edge of the rock again, but from his position higher up the gully, he could now see a hand and part of an arm. He took careful aim and squeezed the trigger slowly. When the rifle bucked, he heard a yelp of pain and the rifle barrel disappeared. Without hesitation, he scrambled to a new spot against the side of the gully, expecting return fire. Pressing hard against the frozen ground, ignoring the cold, he held his rifle ready, waiting for the shots to come.

When none came, he realized the bushwhackers had withdrawn. Intent upon getting a clear shot at them, he charged up the gully to the top in time to see the two gunmen scurrying to their horses. He rushed to steady himself for a shot, but missed as the two fled recklessly across the bluffs.

"Damn!" he swore, and turned to hurry back down to the horses. Only then did he realize that Ben had not been right behind him as he had assumed. At the bottom of the gully, he saw him, struggling to climb up but unable to negotiate the steep defile. "Ben!" Clint cried out in distress, and immediately clambered down the gully to reach him. "Damn, damn, damn," he kept repeating as he hustled down to reach him.

"I'm sorry, partner," Ben said when Clint knelt beside him. "I couldn't back you up. I went and got myself shot." He leaned back against the side of the gully, exhausted by the pain.

"How bad is it?" Clint asked. "Where did you get hit?" He didn't have to wait for an answer, for he saw the hole ripped in Ben's coat. He unbuttoned the coat then to discover the wide patch of blood spreading on his shirt.

"Did you get one of 'em?" Ben asked with great effort.

"I think I nicked one of 'em," Clint said, "but they got away. I ain't worried about them right now. I've got to get you back to the ranch."

"I can wait here awhile," Ben said, "if you wanna chase after 'em."

"To hell with 'em. I'm takin' you to get some help. Can you ride, if I get you on your horse?"

"I don't know," Ben groaned, and Clint knew then that he couldn't.

"I'm gonna get you back to the cabin," Clint decided, "and do what I can to help you. Then I'll go in to the ranch and get a wagon to haul you back where Rena can take care of you."

When he tried to help him back to his horse, however, he saw at once that there was no way Ben could ride. Even a slight movement caused the blood to flow more rapidly and brought gasps of pain from his lips. Clint realized then that his partner was seriously wounded and it evidently involved his internal organs. He eased him back down against the side of the gully, the only position that Ben could stand, while he tried to figure out what to do.

"You just try to rest easy," he said. "I'm goin' to the cabin to get the ax. Then I'll be right back to get you."

He had decided to make a travois to haul Ben back to the cabin, so he made him as comfortable as he could. He then took off his coat and spread it over him before jumping into the saddle and racing toward the cabin to get what he needed.

As soon as he got to the cabin, he started calling off items he had to have to fashion a travois. There was plenty of rope at the line camp, so that was no problem. He picked up the ax and a large deer hide that had been nailed to the wall. For good measure, he took a blanket from the bed to pad the deer hide, figuring the two together would be a platform strong enough to support Ben's weight.

The next critical items were the poles, so he went behind the cabin to select two young pines. The sparse growth of trees didn't offer many choices, but he picked two that would best serve his purpose, cut them down, and trimmed the smaller limbs. Crossing the two small ends in front of Ben's saddle, he went to work building the platform. When he was satisfied that he had a travois, he took some extra rope to hold Ben on and led the horse back to the gully and his wounded partner.

Alarmed when he first rode up, for Ben's eyes were

closed and he made no sound to indicate he was conscious, Clint asked anxiously, "How you holdin' out, partner?"

Ben's eyes fluttered open, and he answered, his voice weak and strained, "I think I'm done for."

"The hell you are!" Clint responded. "You're too damn ornery to die. I swear, if you kick off after all the trouble I went to just to make you a travois, I'll shoot you myself."

"You went to a helluva lot of trouble for nothin'," Ben said painfully. "You oughta leave me right here and throw some dirt over me when I'm done."

"You know, I'm considerin' that, as a matter of fact." He was encouraged somewhat, figuring that as long as Ben could be ornery, he might be able to hang on. "I'm gonna hurt you a little, while I get your sorry ass on this fine travois I made for you, so get ready."

"All right," Ben said, and tried to steel himself for the move. Try as he might, he was unable to keep from crying out when Clint pulled him to his feet and got a shoulder under him. As quickly as he possibly could, he carried Ben to the travois and laid him on the platform. Then he tied him firmly on to keep him from rolling off. "I'da cut some longer poles so it wouldn't be so steep," Clint said, "but these were the best I could find." When he was finished, he asked, "How's that? You gonna be able to stay on there awhile?"

"Not too bad," Ben rasped.

"That's good, because as long as it ain't too hard on you, I'm takin' you back to the ranch, instead of leavin' you at the cabin till I can get back here with a wagon. Think you can stand it?"

"Hell, I'll hurt just as bad a'layin' in that shack as I do on this rickety contraption."

"Let's go, then," Clint said. He was afraid he had wasted too much time as it was. He knew it was going to be one helluva rough ride for a painfully wounded man, but he felt sure it would give Ben a better chance if Rena could attend him.

They started back to the Double-V-Bar, with Clint trying to pick the easiest routes to follow, hoping the jostling didn't jar every last drop of blood out of his friend.

On the way, he gave some thought to the bush-whackers who had ambushed them. There were two of them. He had been unable to get a close enough look to be sure, but he had a pretty good idea who they were.

The two would-be assassins drove their horses merci-lessly until positive they weren't being chased. Only then did they decide to rest the weary mounts.

"Cuss the luck," Blankenship complained as he slid off his horse and hustled over to a tiny stream cutting a narrow flow of water down through the snow-covered ravine. "Bad luck, bad luck," he fussed painfully as he tried to clean the blood from his fractured wrist. "It's broke! I can't work it at all! That son of a bitch!"

"Leastways it ain't your right hand," Curly said. "You can get that barber feller to fix it up for you as soon as we get to town."

"I ain't waitin' for that," Blankenship said. "That bastard's gonna pay for breakin' my wrist. I ain't goin' back to town until I settle with him. I know where he'll be tonight. He's gonna have to hole up in that cabin and try to take care of his partner. I know his partner's shot. I saw him when he fell. What the hell did we run for, anyway? He ain't gonna be comin' after us tonight. He'll be right there in that shack." He knew that he had panicked when he got hit, and that was enough to infuriate him. He was equally as angry with Curly for his lack of courage.

"What about your wrist?" Curly asked. "Ain't you gonna take care of it?"

"I'm takin' care of it right now," Blankenship said. "I'll wrap it in my bandanna, soon as I get it cleaned up a little. That'll hold it till I settle Mr. Cooper's account. I don't need both hands to shoot a handgun, anyway."

"We've got to let these horses rest a little while," Curly said. "But I reckon it's just as well. I don't wanna go back to that cabin till it's dark, no how. That bastard's too good with that rifle. Look at your hand. You couldn'ta had much more'n that showin' and he hit it. That was one helluva shot." He was reluctant to admit that he would have preferred to keep on running, thinking of the shoot-out that Mace had lost to the rangy rifleman. "I wish we'da hit him, instead of the other feller," he lamented.

"Well, we didn't, but I aim to settle his hash just as soon as we can get back to that line shack," Blankenship promised as he wrapped his bandanna around his throbbing wrist.

"What about Simon?" Curly asked.

"What about him?" Blankenship came back. "I ain't waitin' around for Simon to get a shot at that son of a bitch." He held his wounded wrist up to examine it as the throbbing continued. "I ain't got time to wait for Simon," he said.

Chapter 11

Darkness was approaching by the time Clint led the travois between the barn and the bunkhouse. He was met by an astonished Jody Hale and Charley Clark, who came running from the barn as he pulled the horses to a stop. "Lord a' mercy," Charley gasped when he saw Ben. "What happened?"

Clint quickly dismounted. "He got shot, and it looks pretty bad. Help me carry him into the bunkhouse," he said as he started untying the ropes. "You still with me, partner?" he directed at the wounded man as he hurried to free him.

Ben peered at him through eyes barely open. "Hell . . . ," he started to reply, before his voice trailed off and his face twisted up in pain.

"You're gonna make it," Clint tried to assure him. "We'll get you inside on a bed and you'll feel a helluva lot better." He reached down and patted his hand. It felt like a block of ice. He was afraid Ben was half frozen from the long ride on the travois, but on second thought, maybe that was a good thing. He turned to Charley. "You two take him inside and warm him up. I'm goin' to get Rena." Without waiting for a reply, he ran toward the house.

"Wait, Clint!" Charley exclaimed. "Let me get her!" But it was too late; Clint was already halfway across the yard.

Thinking only of getting help for his longtime friend, Clint took the three steps up to the kitchen door in one stride. In his anxiety, he didn't take time to knock and burst into the kitchen to confront Hope, her eyes wide in shock.

"Where's Rena?" he implored. "Ben's been shot!"

Only then did he see the startled image of Justin Landry seated at the table, his face reflecting the shock in Hope's eyes. Too late, he remembered that it was Sunday, and that meant the lieutenant was there to see Hope. Time stood still for one long frozen moment, while all parties seemed paralyzed by the unexpected confrontation. It was only for that moment, however, and then Clint repeated his plea, ignoring the young officer. "Where's Rena?"

"I am here," Rena answered, standing in the doorway to her room.

"Ben's been wounded," Clint said, continuing to ignore the startled lieutenant. "It looks pretty bad. Will you take a look at him?"

"I help," Rena said, and went to get her shawl right away.

"Clint . . . ," Hope stammered, unable to say more, still shocked by his sudden appearance and the awkwardness it created.

Equally confused, Justin was speechless for a few moments, not knowing what to do. Finally his brain started working again, and he realized that he should take action of some kind, but he wasn't sure what. He carried no weapon, and Clint was armed, a .44 Colt on his hip. The authority of the U.S. Army was the only thing he had, so he attempted to use it. "Cooper, you are wanted for the murder of the deputy sheriff of Miles City. I'll have to ask you to hand over your weapon. You're under arrest."

Clint was in no mood to spar with the lieutenant. His concern was to get help for Ben as quickly as possible. "Now, wouldn't I be a damn fool to hand you my gun?" he said. "I don't have the time or the patience to fight with you. I didn't murder anybody. Mace Yeager faced me and we shot it out. He shot me, and I shot him, but my shot was a better one, and he lost. Those are the facts, and there were witnesses who saw the whole thing. Right now there's a man who needs help, and that's the most important thing. So don't get in my way and make me do something I don't wanna do." He opened the door, held it for Rena, then followed her outside, leaving Justin in a state of total confusion.

Quick to recover her composure, Hope sought to calm Justin, since it was obvious that her young suitor was struggling with indecision. "Justin," she said as calmly as she could manage, "Clint is not a murderer. Simon Yeager lied to your commanding officer. You've got to believe that. Like Clint just said, there were people who saw the fight between him and Mace Yeager. If they tell the truth, they'll prove that it was not murder."

Somewhat recovered, Justin tried to think rationally about the situation he found himself in, so he could decide what action he should take. "It's not for me to say if he's guilty or not," he pleaded, trying to make her understand his position. "He's a wanted man, and I'm obligated to arrest him."

"You're liable to get yourself killed if you try." The statement came from Randolph Valentine, who walked into the kitchen at that moment. He had heard enough of the conversation from the parlor to know what had been said. "Right now the best thing for you to do is to let him be while he's seeing about getting some help for Ben. Once that's taken care of, we can sort this whole thing out."

Justin was not alone in having critical decisions to make. Valentine was forced to take actions that might or might not put him on uncertain ground with the army. There could well be retribution for harboring a felon. He was sure of one thing, however: it would not do for the lieutenant to force Clint's hand right now. Ben Hawkins was more than a fellow worker to Clint. He was more like an uncle, and Clint was likely to react violently to any interference with his attempt to take care of him.

A bit calmer now, yet still uncertain, Justin responded to Valentine's advice. "I understand what you're telling me, sir, but I don't see that I have any choice but to do my duty as an officer."

Valentine's brain was working hard to arrive at the best way to handle the dilemma that Ben's wound had created. He couldn't help thinking that it would solve the immediate problem if Clint jumped on his horse and hightailed it out of there. But he knew that wasn't going to happen until Clint was sure Ben was going to be all right.

On the other hand, these charges against Clint would have to be resolved. Otherwise he would be condemned to a life as a wanted man, and the only way that was not going to happen was to clear his name. And for that to occur, it was going to take a fair trial. His mind made up now, he responded to Justin's statement.

"I appreciate your sense of duty, son. But I don't want to see you get yourself killed. I'm agreeing with your position that Clint's wanted, and should be arrested. And I'll argue that with Clint for you, if you'll guarantee me that he'll be arrested by the army, tried by army judges, and not turned over to Simon Yeager and that town of cowards that he's got buffaloed. Think you can do that?"

Justin thought it over for a moment before responding. It gave him a way out of his immediate problem, but he could only hope to persuade his superiors to agree. "I think Major Kinsey might agree to do that," he said, "but I can't say for sure." Thinking to make a show of bravado for Hope's benefit, he added a comment. "I'm not sure, but what I should take him into custody right now, though."

The remark caused Valentine to flare up in agitation. "Boy!" he scolded. "I'm not worried about Clint right now. I'm worried about you, and what would happen to you if you pushed Clint too hard right now." He fixed the nervous young officer with a steel-like expression. "The way this thing would have to work is for you to go back to the fort and tell them what the deal is. Then come back here with a detail of troopers to escort Clint back to the fort for trial. I'll try to convince Clint that it's the best thing to do to clear his name. Can you do that?"

"Yes, sir," Justin answered. "I expect we would agree to that."

"Good," Valentine said. "Now you and Hope sit back down and finish your coffee and cake, or whatever

it was you were doing, and I'll go talk to Clint." He
went out the back door, knowing he had another argument to win, this one maybe harder than the one just
finished.

When Valentine got to the bunkhouse, Ben was unconscious and Rena was working over him, using a
long, sharp skinning knife. Clint, Charley, Jody, and
Hank stood on one side of the bunk, watching the crude
surgery.

"Is he gonna make it?" Valentine asked after he
watched for a few minutes.

"Maybe, not sure," the always somber woman said,
and continued probing in the hole in Ben's abdomen as
his blood flowed freely, soaking the straw tick mattress. When finally she removed the lead slug, she held
it up for Clint to see. "Bad," she said. "Have to see how
strong he is now."

"He'll make it," Clint told her. "He's too ornery to
die from one little ol' bullet." She looked at him, smiled,
and nodded. He moved closer to the bunk while Rena
cleaned up some of the blood.

"Who shot him?" Valentine asked.

"Like I told Charley, I'm pretty sure it was those two
deputies of Yeager's that bushwhacked us," Clint said.
"I'll know for sure when I find 'em." He didn't say how
he'd know, but he felt certain that he had nicked one of
them before they ran.

"We've got something we've got to talk over," Valentine said.

Clint could easily guess what that was. "You mean
your daughter's pretty little lieutenant?" he asked sarcastically. "As long as he stays up there at the house,

there won't be any problem. I'll ride on out as soon as
Ben looks like he's all right. I've got a little chore I've
got to tend to."

"That's what we need to talk about," Valentine said.
"Let's walk outside for a minute."

Clint followed him out the door, wondering what the
old man had in mind. They walked around the end of
the bunkhouse to get out of the wind before Valentine
continued. "I know what you're thinking, but before
you tangle with any more of that crowd in town, I think
it would be best for you to surrender to the army."

Clint's reaction was just as Valentine expected. He
physically recoiled, and Valentine quickly pleaded, "Hear
me out, before you go off half-cocked."

He went on to relate the agreement he had reached
with Justin and explained why Clint should consider it.
"You've got a good chance of being found not guilty, if
those people who saw the fight you had with Mace
Yeager will come forward and testify truthfully. And
damn it, Clint, you don't want to go through the rest of
your life as a wanted man, riding off to some other
remote wilderness every time civilization gets a little
too close for comfort." He paused for a moment before
continuing, wondering if it was the right time to share
his thoughts regarding another matter. "There's another
reason I want you to clear your name. I need you here.
I'm very much aware of the fact that I'm getting older
every day. I've worked hard to build the Double-V-Bar
to the working ranch it is today, but I'm tired. Two,
maybe three, more years are about all I've got left
before I'm ready for the rocking chair, and I don't want
to see all my work go for nothing. I need a man I can
trust to take over the management of this ranch, one

who'll take care of Hope and Rena, too. You're that man, but you won't be much good to me if you're hiding out somewhere on the other side of the divide."

It was a mouthful, and one that threatened to overload Clint's brain. He knew that he was Valentine's top hand, but he never suspected he was held in such high regard by his boss. He had actually never given any thought toward the future beyond next spring's roundup and making it through the winter without losing too many head of cattle. The prospects of managing the total operation of the ranch were certainly incentive enough to make him think carefully about what he was about to do.

Things could change, however. When her father died, the Double-V-Bar would surely go to Hope, and she might see things differently than the old man did. If Hope went on to marry Justin Landry, which seemed to be the way things were headed, she and her new husband might not want him to be the main decision-maker. There was certainly no bond of friendship between the two young men. In fact, there was a constant state of competition between them that Clint was sure Hope knew nothing about.

On the other hand, there might be the possibility that Hope was not interested in running the Double-V-Bar, and could be attracted more by the prospect of being the wife of a career army officer. And Justin most likely had a bright future, since he was a West Point man, whose father was a West Point man. They might be content to let Clint run the ranch while they climbed the military ladder to the top. All these thoughts ran through his mind in a matter of seconds, as Valentine studied his face anxiously, waiting for his decision.

"I expect it would be the smart thing to do, in the long run," Clint finally decided, although he had a strong need to punish Yeager's two henchmen for wounding Ben.

"Then you'll do it?" Valentine asked, needing assurance.

"Yes, sir," Clint said. "I reckon you know best, but I've got to know that Ben's gonna be all right before I do."

"Let's see what Rena says," Valentine said. "But I think the sooner we get this thing done, the better. I thought it best for the army to send an escort of soldiers to take you in to Fort Keogh, but maybe it would be better if you ride back to the fort with Justin tonight. He can make sure they understand that you're surrendering for trial on your own accord because you're innocent."

"I'll think about it," Clint said, "after I talk to Rena." They went back inside the bunkhouse then to find that Ben was awake. "How you doin', partner?" Clint asked.

Ben looked at him with eyes only half-open, a painful frown on his weathered face. "I don't know," he murmured. "I thought I was dead and gone to hell, 'cause I felt the devil's hellfire. It was so hot it woke me up."

Clint glanced at Rena. She nodded and said, "I pour whiskey in wound."

Clint nodded back, understanding. "How is he, Rena?"

"He make it. Long time, though," she replied.

That was enough to ease Clint's immediate concern. He was not sure why, but he always trusted the Crow woman's instincts. He turned to his boss, then. "All right, let's go up to the house and talk to Landry."

It was a shaky truce between the two men, but both agreed to abide by the agreement as put forth by Randolph Valentine. The person who seemed the most concerned, understandably, was Hope Valentine, for she genuinely cared for both of them, although in different degrees of intensity. In one way or another, these two men, along with her father, were the most important men in her life.

When all was settled, it was already after dark, and a later hour than Justin would normally have said his good-byes to Hope and headed back to Fort Keogh.

"Well, let's get goin', if we're gonna," Clint said.

"Right," Justin replied. "I'll ask you to turn your weapons over to me now."

"And I'll ask you to go to hell," Clint responded curtly.

"Do I have to remind you that you're under arrest?" Justin said.

"Like hell I am," Clint replied. "I just agreed to go back with you. I'm not under arrest until we get on the post, and that's when I'll turn my weapons over."

At once flustered, Justin looked to Valentine for help. Valentine shook his head, perplexed. They hadn't even left the ranch and already they were pecking away at each other like a couple of roosters.

With a tired sigh, he again assured Justin that he could trust Clint to keep his word. "Remember, Clint is volunteering to go with you, so you need to make a few exceptions for his attitude." He turned to Clint then. "And you need to realize the position Justin's in. He's a soldier and subject to follow his orders. He's agreeing to help you get the true story to his superiors so your name can be cleared. So, damn it, Clint, don't be so hardheaded."

Clint couldn't suppress a chuckle. It was the first time Valentine had spoken to him like a father to a rambunctious son. "Yes, sir," he said. "I'll go along with it, and hope I get a fair hearin'." He offered his hand to

Justin, who accepted it after a slight hesitation. There was still the issue of Hope's feelings for the tall, dark rifleman. Justin was not comfortable with Hope's apparent fondness for her father's top hand. "I don't need an army escort," Clint said. "I'll ride back with you tonight, since Rena thinks Ben's gonna make it."

Clint walked outside with Valentine while Justin took a moment to say good night to Hope. "You're doing the right thing," Valentine said to him while he checked Sam to make sure the big bay was ready to ride.

"I reckon," Clint replied, "if you think so." They paused then when Justin and Hope came outside.

When the lieutenant walked to the hitching rail to untie his horse, Hope moved close to Clint and placed her hand on his arm.

"Take care of him," she whispered, then said, "Take care of yourself, too. I hope everything works out like it's supposed to."

"Huh." A grunt was his only response. *That's the second time she's asked me to take care of him,* he thought, and the request didn't sit very well with him the first time. He climbed up on Sam then and turned to wait for Justin to come alongside.

"I'll be over to see the commanding officer tomorrow," Valentine said to Clint. "I intend to see that you get a fair hearing." He stepped back then and watched the two young men ride out to the Miles City trail.

"They're fixin' to ride out," Blankenship said, gritting his teeth against the constant throbbing of his left wrist. "It's him, all right, but it looks like a soldier with him. Now where the hell's he goin'?"

It was a clear, starry night, and the two outlaws could plainly see the two riders from the low ridge north of the ranch. They had followed their prey to this point after returning to the line shack only to find it abandoned. The tracks of two horses and the distinct ruts left by a travois in the snow were easy enough to follow, however, and led them to the Double-V-Bar. Now, as they watched the two riding out toward the trail that led into town, it was tempting to take the shot, but they were not anxious to stir up the whole ranch crew to get on their tails.

"They're headin' to Fort Keogh," Curly said, after a few moments. "We need to get on out ahead of 'em and wait for 'em to get a little piece from the ranch so we don't have the whole Double-V-Bar after our asses."

There were many places to wait in ambush along the five-mile trail to the fort. It would be an easy thing to shoot Cooper and the soldier and be long gone before anyone could come from the ranch, even if they heard the shots.

"Let's go!" Blankenship snapped, and they hustled back down the slope to get to their horses.

The spot they both agreed to be perfect was at a point where the trail followed a narrow ravine between the ends of two ridges before opening up to a flat stretch of prairie. There was a tall rock tower standing a couple of dozen yards or so from the mouth of the ravine. After they left their horses behind a thin stand of scrubby pine trees, they hurried back to the top at one end of the ridge. Not willing to test his accuracy with a pistol at a range more suited to a rifle, Blankenship pulled his Spencer from the saddle scabbard. He was sure he could be accurate enough, even with his injured left hand, if he lay flat on the ground and rested the barrel across his forearm.

It was not long before Clint and Justin approached

the narrow entrance to the rocky ravine, guarded by the rock formation named the Parson's Nose, with Clint leading. Riding at a comfortable gait, he guided Sam to the steeper side where the darker shadows cloaked the floor. There was no particular reason to hold close to the side. It was more habit than conscious thought. He always rode close to that side when going to the fort. The footing was better for his horse. There was no sound other than the creaking of the saddle leather until Sam's ears pricked and he suddenly snorted. Immediately alert to signals from the horse, Clint reined back hard. Then he heard an answering neigh from the direction of a small clump of pines. His first thought was another Sioux raiding party.

Justin pulled up beside him. "What is it? Why did you stop?"

"Something ain't right," Clint said softly. "There's a horse over in those pines somewhere."

"How do you know that?" Justin asked.

"I just heard him answer Sam," Clint said. "Didn't you hear it?"

"No, I didn't hear anything. You must be a little jumpy. I'll lead." He nudged his horse and pushed ahead of Clint.

"Wait, damn it!" Clint blurted at almost the same time the first shot was fired from the top of the ridge. He didn't hesitate but rolled out of the saddle to land on the ground between his horse and the steep side of the ravine. "Get down!" he yelled to Justin, who was still in the saddle, too startled to react. Clint ran up beside Justin's horse, grabbed the confused lieutenant by the tail of his coat, and jerked him off the horse, just as a second shot hit the chestnut gelding, causing it to scream and rear up on its back legs.

"I'm getting' damn tired of savin' your ass for Hope," Clint muttered angrily. "Hug the side of that slope!" he ordered as Justin's horse tried to run but collapsed after a few yards and crumpled to the ground.

Clint ran back to Sam to pull his rifle from the saddle sling. Then to keep his horse from getting hit, too, he grabbed his bridle and turned him around. With a sound smack on his croup, he chased him away to gallop a short distance from the narrow ravine before stopping. With little choice to avoid the many shots being fired from above them, Justin and Clint pressed hard up against the steep side of the ravine. They were protected as long as they remained where they were, but they were pinned down, unable to chance retreating to a better spot.

"We're not in a very good spot," Justin declared breathlessly. "Who do you think it is, Indians?"

"I think it's my two good friends, Yeager's yard dogs," Clint said, "and you're right—this ain't a good spot."

"They got my horse," Justin complained. "What are we gonna do?"

Clint was busy trying to assess the options available to them. They were few, but he knew they couldn't stay where they were, so he settled on a desperate plan. "You stay tight up against that hill. I'm gonna try to crawl back the way we came and see if I can get up behind them."

"They'll see you when you crawl out of this shadow," Justin protested, not confident of Clint's chances.

"You got a better idea?" Clint came back. "If you have, I'd like to hear it."

Not waiting for a response from Justin, he dropped

to his hands and knees and began crawling along the base of the dark wall.

"Stay in that shadow," he reminded Justin, knowing that he didn't have much time before the moon rose higher and the shadow diminished. The same thought must have occurred to the two snipers on the ridge, because the firing stopped. The void caused Clint to crawl faster.

In a few more seconds, he reached the mouth of the ravine and the end of any real cover. His objective now would be to reach the Parson's Nose, and there were about twenty yards of open ground between it and the point where he was now paused. He waited, hesitating to expose himself to the rifle fire above while the seconds ticked off. It seemed like a foolish gamble. The only option, however, was to turn around and crawl back to huddle up against the side of the ravine with Justin.

Hell, he thought, *nobody lives forever.*

Then before he had time to think about it further, he sprang up and sprinted toward the rocks as hard as he could go. When he reached the cover of the rocks, breathing desperately from the short sprint, he was scarcely able to believe he had made it without hearing a shot from the snipers.

Fifty feet above him, Curly and Blankenship had left their ambush position, having decided they could work their way closer to the edge of the steep side wall of the ravine. The targets of their assault were hiding in the shadow of the hill, and they wanted to be in a position to take advantage of that fact when the moon rose high enough to shrink the shadow. Moving as cautiously as they possibly could, they were careful to watch where each foot was placed. One false step might start a slide of rocks and give away the surprise they intended.

With their concentration so absorbed, they failed to notice the figure that suddenly sprinted across the open space to disappear behind the rock tower.

Pressing ever tighter against the wall, as the narrow band of shadow grew smaller and smaller, Justin cautiously pulled his feet up closer to his body when the toe of his boot was suddenly illuminated by the moonlight. He held his pistol up flat against his chest, ready to fire, not sure if he was even going to see a target before his whole body was exposed and fired upon. Clint had crawled away, saying that he intended to get behind them.

Maybe he was intent only upon saving his skin and to hell with me, Justin could not help thinking.

Little more than ten feet above the frightened lieutenant, Curly suddenly caught sight of a small protrusion on the otherwise constant edge line of the shadow cast on the floor of the ravine. When it moved slightly, he took a harder look and realized it was made by the brim of a hat. He raised his hand and signaled Blankenship, a few steps behind him. Blankenship acknowledged the signal with a nod of his head. Curly inched forward, closer and closer to the edge of the steep wall, until he could make out the entire form of Justin below him. He knelt on one knee and steadied himself to raise the Spencer carbine he carried and aim it at the unsuspecting soldier.

"Where's Cooper?" he asked the startled lieutenant seconds before pulling the trigger.

"I'm here," the answer came back. Curly turned at once, but not quickly enough to stop the rifle slug that caught him in the shoulder, spun him around, and dropped him on the steep slope. His body slid on the snow-covered shale and dropped off the edge to land at Justin's feet.

Startled, Blankenship tried to react, but in that instant of confusion, without thinking, he grabbed the forearm of his rifle with his injured hand, causing him to recoil in pain and jerk the weapon when he pulled the trigger. The result was a wide miss, moments before a slug from Clint's Winchester slammed him in the chest. Killed instantly, he slid over the edge of the short precipice to land next to Curly, who was staring into the business end of the Colt Justin held, aimed at his face.

Clint hurried back the way he had come up the slope, which took him a couple of minutes. When he reached Justin, the lieutenant was still standing over Curly, his army single-action Colt .44 still pointed at the wounded man's face.

"Why didn't you tell me what you were gonna do?" Justin complained. "This bastard almost shot me! What are we gonna do with him?"

"Yeah, but he didn't," Clint said calmly. "Almost gettin' shot ain't ever hurt nobody, so no harm done, right?"

"Right, my ass!" Justin responded. The sensation of having looked up to see a rifle muzzle pointed at him from only a few feet away had jangled his nerves, and now that it was over, he didn't appreciate the close call. "If you had been a few seconds later, I would be lying there dead like that man."

"Yeah, but I wasn't, so quit your bellyaching," Clint said. He looked at Blankenship to make sure he was dead, then slipped the toe of his boot under Blankenship's left arm and lifted it a few inches. "I knew I had nicked one of these jaspers back at the line shack." He turned back to Justin and nodded toward Curly. "Don't you reckon you oughta pull that pistol outta his holster? He ain't shot so bad he can't use it."

"I was just going to do that," Justin lied, having been too shaken to think of it before. "We have to decide what we're going to do with him."

"To hell with him," Clint said. "What about your horse? Is he dead?"

"I'm not sure," Justin replied.

His answer irritated Clint, and he let him know it. "Well, for God's sake, man, look at him and put him out of his misery if he ain't dead."

He had no use for a man who neglected to take care of his horse. He was further irritated when Justin went to the wounded horse and put his pistol to its head and shot it. *Damn,* he thought, knowing the animal had not been dead, and had been suffering all that time.

Clint took a look at the wounded man, whose eyes were wide in uncertain desperation as the discussion returned regarding his fate. "Well, we could blow his brains out and make him a helluva lot less trouble," he said. "But I expect you'd wanna take him and his friend there in to Fort Keogh and throw this one in the guardhouse."

Curly nodded vigorously and gasped, "Yes, sir. I won't give you no trouble. I surrender. Take me to see the doctor. I'm hurt bad."

"You ain't hurt that bad," Clint said. "And that's my fault. I meant to kill your sorry ass. That's what you deserve for shootin' Ben Hawkins, and I might change my mind about botherin' with you. You need some doctorin'?" He pulled his skinning knife from his belt. "I'll dig that bullet outta you."

"No, don't do that," Curly pleaded. "It weren't me that shot that other feller. It was Blankenship that done that—and you shot him deader'n hell, so everythin's all square on that account. I'm goin' peaceful. I surrender."

"Damn right you do," Clint said. "You ain't got no choice, you piece of shit. I'm still thinkin' about shootin' you." He couldn't help badgering the frightened assassin, because of the trouble the man and his partner had caused him.

"I'll be the one making that decision," Justin stated flatly, having suddenly regained control of his sense of authority. Looking at Curly then, he said, "I hereby place you under arrest for attempted murder," He glanced briefly at Clint before adding, "You will be taken, unharmed, to be incarcerated in the guardhouse to await trial." It was clearly a warning to Clint that the prisoner was not to be harmed.

"Well, let's get movin', then," Clint said. He grabbed Curly by the lapels of his coat and jerked him roughly to his feet. "Keep your gun on him," he directed Justin; then he whistled for Sam. The horse plodded obediently up beside him and stopped. Clint cut off a short piece of rope from his saddle and bound Curly's hands behind his back, ignoring the grunt of pain that Curly uttered. "Watch him," Clint said. "I'm goin' to get his horse." He stepped up on Sam, wheeled him around, and rode back toward the mouth of the ravine.

When Clint rode out of sight, Curly took the opportunity to play on the lieutenant's pride, hoping to ensure his own safety. "It's a mighty honorable thing you're doin' here, Lieutenant. I mean, standin' up to that killer, lettin' him know whose boss. He's liable to take over if you don't keep him on a short rope."

Already rankled by Clint's attitude, Justin was in no

mood to hear any comments from Curly. "Make no mistake, mister, you're a prisoner of the U.S. Army— my prisoner—and it'll be my discretion as to how you are treated."

"Oh yes, sir," Curly quickly acknowledged. "You're the boss—ain't no doubt about that."

In a few minutes, Clint returned, leading two horses. He dismounted and walked over to Blankenship's body. "Give me a hand and we'll throw this one over that horse's rump." He paused then while Justin hesitated. "Take hold of his feet." Justin finally moved to do as Clint instructed, and they hefted Blankenship to lay him behind the saddle, across the horse's croup. "Now let's help ol' Curly here up in the saddle." He paused again to ask, "You are the one called Curly, ain't you?" Curly didn't answer but allowed himself to be hoisted up into the saddle. "Well, that leaves the other horse for you, Lieutenant," Clint went on. "What are you gonna do about the saddle? You wanna take that army saddle offa your horse, or use the one that's on his partner's horse? It's a helluva lot better saddle than that army saddle." He waited again for Justin to speak. "While you're decidin', I'll tie Curly's reins to this bush. He just might take a notion to go for a ride while you're makin' up your mind."

Justin hesitated before going to collect his saddle-bags from the dead horse. The resentment for Clint Cooper was building inside him to the point of anger, especially since Clint seemed to be giving the orders when it was clearly not his authority. He didn't like Clint to begin with because of his close relationship with Hope Valentine. It didn't sit well with him, either, that Clint had probably saved him from being shot when he jerked him off his horse, then again when he killed Blankenship.

He thinks he's some kind of hero, ever since he supposedly saved me and my men on that grave-digging detail, he thought. *Damn him, he treats me like I haven't the sense to get out of the rain.*

Suddenly he had had all of Clint Cooper that he felt he could take without restitution.

"What's it gonna be, Lieutenant?" Clint asked, after tying Curly's horse to the bush. "This saddle, or the army's?"

"I'll let you know," Justin replied curtly. "First, I want an answer from you. What did you mean back there when you said something about being tired of taking care of me for Hope's sake?"

The question surprised Clint. He didn't even remember saying it in the chaos of being fired upon. "Well, I don't know, Lieutenant. I reckon I did tell Hope that I'd try to keep you from doin' something dumb and gettin' yourself shot. It sure as hell ain't been easy. I'll admit it ain't something I wanna do, but since Hope's sweet on you, I told her I would."

"I don't need a guardian angel," Justin said sarcastically. "And if I did, it sure as hell wouldn't be you."

"So you say," Clint replied, somewhat amused by Justin's attitude. "But you sure as hell woulda been dead a couple of times without somebody there to save your ass."

It was the wrong thing to say.

"Why, you insolent bastard," Justin fumed. "I ought to give you a thrashing for that."

Clint smiled, enjoying the snit Justin had worked himself into. "You oughta try," he said. Again, it was the wrong thing to say.

To Clint's complete surprise, Justin hauled off and smacked him full on the nose with his fist. Never expecting the angry reaction from the usually proper young officer, Clint staggered back a couple of steps before recovering. When he realized what had just happened, he felt a sense of satisfaction for being given the opportunity to plant one on Hope's pompous suitor. He set his feet solidly and wiped a trickle of blood away from his upper lip. Then he threw a solid right hand that caught Justin flush on the cheek, driving him backward against Curly's horse, which kept him from going down.

Too angry to be intimidated by the taller man, Justin stepped up and delivered another right that landed on Clint's forehead. He received a solid left in return, and the two adversaries stood toe-to-toe exchanging punches to the absolute astonishment of Curly James, who watched the contest, scarcely able to believe his eyes.

In his estimation, the lieutenant gave a good accounting of himself, but he was clearly overmatched. Justin remained on his feet longer than Curly, or Clint, had expected, but it was inevitable that he would go down when one too many of Clint's haymakers collided with his jaw. The brief fight was over then as Justin dropped to his knees and could not get up, much to Clint's relief. He wasn't sure how much fight he had left in him, since he was still recovering from a serious bullet wound that had left him weak.

Clint walked over to his horse and took his extra bandanna from his saddlebag. He pulled off the one around his neck and wet them both with water from his canteen. Then he walked back to Justin, who was still on his knees, and handed him one of the wet cloths. Justin looked up at him with eyes still trying to focus.

"Thanks," he said, and took the bandanna.

While the two combatants cleaned the blood from their faces, Curly shook his head, amazed. "I tell you the truth," he said. "I thought about jerkin' them reins offa that bush and makin' a run for it. But I wouldn'ta wanted to miss that fight."

Clint gave him a bored glance and said, "I'da shot you."

It was difficult to explain by either man, but the tension between them seemed to have been cleared away. Neither man could have foreseen the ensuing fight, but it was something that had to occur eventually. And now that it had, both men were ready to forget about it.

"I think I should take my saddle back, if we can get it off the horse," Justin said. "It's army property, but I'll leave the other saddle on."

"All right," Clint said. "I'll help you get the girth strap out from under him."

Chapter 12

They were challenged by a sentry when they rode into
Fort Keogh, and Justin asked who the officer of the day
was. He was told that Lieutenant Grant was the O.D.
and that he had just made his rounds of the guard posts.

"He'll be at the headquarters office now," Justin
said, and led the way. "We'll drop Mr. James off at the
guardhouse on the way over. They can get the surgeon
to treat that wound."

After turning Curly over to Sergeant O'Brien at the
guardhouse, Justin and Clint proceeded to the post
headquarters, where First Lieutenant Lawrence Grant
was on duty as officer of the day. Grant looked up in
surprise when Justin walked in with Clint.

"Hello there, Justin. Back from visiting your lady
friend?" he greeted him before Justin walked fully into
the light of the lamp on Grant's desk. He recoiled, startled, when he saw the lump beside Justin's eye and the
swelling on his jaw. "What the hell happened to you?"

Then before Justin answered, he noticed the marks on Clint's face and his swollen nose. "Damn," he blurted.

"Lawrence," Justin replied. "Yep, I'm back. This is Clint Cooper. He works for Randolph Valentine. We ran into a little trouble on the way back from the Double-V-Bar."

He went on to tell him about the ambush they had encountered at the Parson's Nose, and the prisoner he had delivered to the guardhouse.

"There's a body of one of the men that tried to ambush us on a horse outside. I wasn't sure whether I should bring it back or not. I guess we can detail a couple of men to dig a grave and bury him, if there's no need for the provost marshal to see him."

"I wouldn't think so," Grant said. He turned to a sergeant standing by, who had been listening to the exchange between the two lieutenants. "Roper, detail a couple of men to take care of it." The sergeant did as he was ordered. "I'd guess you two had a helluva time of it, from the looks of both of you," Grant continued.

Justin unconsciously reached up to touch his swollen jaw. "Yes, we did have quite a tussle of it before we took control of the attack. Nothing serious, though, just a few bumps and scratches. The worst part is I had my horse shot out from under me, and if it hadn't been for Clint's quick thinking, I might have been shot myself. But the important thing is we were able to kill one of the outlaws and capture the other one. We brought him in to be tried for attempted murder."

"Well, for Pete's sake," Grant said. "That was a helluva lot more than you expected when you just went for a Sunday visit with your young lady, wasn't it? What can we do for Mr. Cooper here?" He frowned as soon as he said it, thinking something about the name was familiar, but he couldn't remember from where.

"Well, that's another thing," Justin said, giving Clint a quick glance before continuing. "We have a rather unusual situation here that I'd like to handle with consideration for the special circumstances." Grant looked from Justin to Clint, and back again, clearly curious. "Mr. Cooper has come with me, voluntarily, to turn himself in for trial regarding a charge of murder."

"Cooper!" Grant exclaimed then. "I knew I'd heard that name somewhere. He's wanted for the murder of a deputy sheriff in Miles City." He paid Clint a closer scrutiny then. "And you captured him!"

"No," Justin was quick to correct him. "Mr. Cooper came with me voluntarily, so this false charge of murder could be resolved. And I've assured him that he would be treated as a friend of the court and get a special hearing."

"I see," Grant said, although it seemed a strange situation, and certainly one he had no experience in. "So, what are you suggesting we do with him? We would normally lock a prisoner up in the guardhouse who's awaiting trial."

"I was hoping we wouldn't have to do that," Justin said. "These are unusual circumstances, and I have Mr. Cooper's word that he willingly turns himself over to the court." He glanced at Clint again.

Clint, who had been silent to that point, confirmed it. "That's a fact. You have my word on it."

"And you have my word that Clint's word is good," Justin said. "So I suggest we give him a cot in the cavalry barracks, and he can stay there while awaiting the preparation of trial by court-martial. He's no criminal, and witnesses in Miles City can attest to his innocence of the charges."

Grant shook his head and uttered a little chuckle, still amazed by the situation. "Well, I guess that'll be all right, since you're vouching for his word. I notice he's wearing a sidearm. I assume he knows he'll have to turn that, and any other weapons, over to the provost. I would suggest he turn them over to me now, and I'll turn them over to the provost in the morning."

Justin looked quickly at Clint, knowing how reluctant he was to surrender his weapons, but Clint, expecting as much, unbuckled his gun belt without protest and handed it to Justin, who in turn placed it on the desk. Justin looked back at Grant.

"Thanks, Lawrence. I appreciate your cooperation on this. Is General Miles back on post yet?" When Grant said that he wasn't, Justin turned to Clint and said, "So Major Kinsey will likely head your hearing. I'll volunteer to act as your counsel."

He didn't tell Clint as much, but Justin had hoped General Miles would be the one to conduct the hearing. The general was a much more compassionate man than Major Kinsey and might be more sympathetic to a man who had served as a scout.

After leaving Clint's Winchester with Lieutenant Grant, Justin took him to the stables, where they left their horses and saddles. Then they went to the cavalry barracks and Justin told the barracks sergeant that Clint would be using a cot and would be eating in the mess hall with the men.

"You should be all right," Justin said to Clint. "I'll be by to see you sometime in the morning and let you know what's going to happen, just as soon as I report to Major Kinsey."

"I'll be fine," Clint said. "It'll be just like stayin' in a hotel." Noticing Justin studying him rather intensely, he said, "Don't worry. I'll still be here in the mornin'."

"I know you will," Justin told him, then hesitated for a moment. "Listen, I think maybe I owe you an—"

"No such a thing," Clint interrupted. "That's done and forgotten. Fact of the matter is, I think I owe you one, too."

Justin nodded, and they shook on it. He left then while Clint unrolled the mattress on his cot and made his bed.

After the bugler sounded tattoo and final roll call, the soldiers filed into the barracks, and there was a jovial reunion with some of the troopers who had ridden with Clint in the fight with the Sioux on the Yellowstone. Since some of them had been on the detail assigned to take him into custody at the Double-V-Bar, however, they were especially surprised to see him. He was in the midst of explaining his presence there when Private Goldstein walked in. He was startled to see the rangy scout, and stopped in his tracks to gape in disbelief.

"I'm surprised they ain't fit you with a pair of spectacles, as bad as your eyes are," Clint joked when Goldstein appeared to be speechless. Goldstein laughed but made no remarks about the occasion when he had confronted Clint in Renn's room. Clint understood why the private wouldn't want the word to get out that he had purposely abetted a wanted man. "I want you to know I appreciate it," Clint said.

Goldstein nodded, then asked why Clint was bunking in with the soldiers. "Are you going to do some more scouting for the company? What about that other thing?"

"Nope, I ain't gonna do no scoutin' for you boys. I'm here to try to straighten out that other thing, that little misunderstandin' about the charges the army posted about me. Lieutenant Landry is gonna help me tell the truth of it."

"I thought you'd be long gone from here," Goldstein said. "You say Lieutenant Landry is gonna help you?" Clint nodded. "Well, I sure hope it all works out for you."

The sound of reveille woke him the next morning after a sound night's sleep in the barracks. Goldstein walked by and told him the next call he would hear would be the Stable and Watering Call. Mess Call would not sound until seven. It seemed like a long time to wait, since he had had no supper the night before, so he went out with the soldiers to check on Sam to pass the time. The bay seemed content enough, and was watered and fed with the army horses.

With no notion what he should do after he went to the mess hall for breakfast, he returned to the barracks to await word from Justin, or someone, about his meeting with Major Kinsey. The word came a short time after the bugle signaled assembly and roll call, but it was not in the form Clint expected.

On the other side of the diamond-shaped parade ground, Major John Kinsey was informed that the fugitive who had eluded the detail he had sent to capture him was even then sitting in the cavalry barracks.

"What?" Kinsey demanded. "Are you telling me that Clint Cooper is sitting in one of the barracks right now, after having spent the night there, and having breakfast in the mess hall? Whose brilliant idea was that? The man's a wanted criminal. He should be in the guardhouse instead of being treated like a visiting dignitary," he fumed. "How was he captured?"

"That's just it, sir," Justin tried to explain. "He wasn't captured. He came in voluntarily, requesting a hearing, so he could prove his innocence. He rode in with me last night, and were it not for his presence of mind and quick reflexes, I would not be standing here before you this morning." He went on to relate the circumstances that led to their encounter with the would-be assassins, James and Blankenship. "One of them is at present in the guardhouse. The other man is dead. Both men are wanted criminals."

Still in a state of disbelief, Kinsey bolted to his feet, glaring at Justin. "Damn it, Landry, the man's wanted for murder! I want him locked up before he decides to run for it again." He turned to First Sergeant Paul Weaver. "Sergeant, take a couple of men from the guard detail, go over to that barracks, and place Cooper under arrest. Turn him over to Sergeant O'Brien at the guardhouse."

"Yes, sir," Weaver said, drolly, finding the situation amusing. A soldier for more than twenty years, he was not surprised by anything that happened in the army. With a slight shake of his head, and the beginnings of a grin on his face, he left to obey the major's orders.

"Sir, I gave him my word," Justin protested, "He's here of his own accord."

"You gave him your word?" Kinsey replied. "I believe you acted a little beyond your authority, Lieutenant. We don't negotiate with criminals." He sat back down hard, his anger draining somewhat. "It doesn't matter if you give your word to a murdering outlaw, anyway. It's not the same as giving it to an honest man."

"I sincerely believe the charges made against him are false," Justin insisted. "I think he deserves his day in court."

"Oh, he'll get his trial, all right. I wouldn't deny even the lowest form of humanity that privilege, and it'll be right away, so the proper sentence can be pronounced."

It was later in the morning when Clint saw Justin again. He was accompanied by Randolph Valentine. Clint's accommodations were decidedly different from those of the previous night.

"I'm sorry about this," Justin apologized at once, when he greeted him through the bars of the one large cell room. "I protested your treatment to Major Kinsey, but he insisted that you be held here until your trial is over."

Clint was none too happy about the turn of events, having been rudely escorted out of the cavalry barracks by a sergeant and two armed guards. But he maintained a patient disposition, thinking that in the end, everything would land right side up.

"It kinda sounds to me like they ain't too interested in my version of what happened to Mace Yeager," he said to Valentine.

"We've been talking to Major Kinsey this morning," Valentine said. "That arrogant fool talks like he believes Simon Yeager's version of the killing. He said it was highly unlikely that the sheriff would seek the army's help if he was not certain of the charges." His comment caused Justin to glance nervously at Sergeant O'Brien, but Valentine seemed unconcerned that the sergeant might report his comments to Kinsey. "I told the son of a bitch that there were witnesses to the shooting that would back your side of the story. But he babbled something about army regulations saying you had to be under arrest until they have a hearing."

That wasn't good news to Clint. The few hours he had spent in the guardhouse with seven soldiers, incarcerated mainly for drunk and disorderly charges, were already more than he cared for. He was separated from the other prisoners by a partition of bars across one end of the open cell room, since the charges against him were of a more serious nature.

"Hell," he said, "they treated that back-shooter, Curly James, better than me. They carried him over to the hospital." He looked directly at Justin, but the lieutenant could only shrug apologetically. "What about the hearin' they're supposed to give me?" Clint asked. "How soon are they gonna have that?"

"In three days," Justin said.

"I've already given Kinsey the names of the two witnesses who saw the fight," Valentine was quick to assure him. "I told him Homer Lewis and Jim Duffy. Was there anyone else who might have seen it?"

"They're the only ones I know of for sure," Clint said.

"Well, they ought to be enough," Valentine said. "And Kinsey assured me that they will be notified to testify. So you just keep cool here for a spell. I'll be back for the trial. Justin here is going to act as your lawyer. That panel of judges can't help seeing you're in the clear."

Arthur O'Connor, postmaster for Miles City, looked up from the paper he was reading when Simon Yeager walked in the door. "Can I help you, Sheriff?"

"Yeah," Yeager replied. He unfolded a piece of paper, put it on the counter, and slid it under O'Connor's face.

"Read this." Arthur started reading the paper, and couldn't help recoiling when he saw what it was about. "Read it to me, damn it!" Yeager roared.

O'Connor realized then that Yeager couldn't read. "Sorry," he said, and looked at the message again. "It's from Major Kinsey, over at the fort."

"I know that," Yeager said impatiently. "A soldier brung it to me this mornin'. What does he want?"

Arthur looked over the short text again and decided to give Yeager the gist of it without reciting word for word. "He's telling you that the army is trying Clint Cooper for the murder of your brother, and says you might want to come to the trial, since you're the one pressin' the charges."

"They caught the son of a bitch!" Yeager exclaimed. "Hell yeah, I wanna go to the trial. When is it?"

"Day after tomorrow, nine o'clock in the morning, at the post headquarters." Arthur shook his head slowly.

They ought to be pinning a medal on him, instead of trying him for shooting that worthless piece of trash, he thought.

This was sad news, indeed. He knew that Clint killed Mace Yeager in a fair fight. Both Homer and Jim had seen the shooting. This whole mess with the wanted poster and all was ridiculous, all instigated by their self-appointed sheriff, and it chafed Arthur that Yeager was going to get the chance to gloat over his evil work.

Yeager snatched the paper off the counter and stuffed it in his coat pocket. With no word of thanks or anything else, he turned and left the post office, his mind already churning with what the army might need for a trial. The first thing that came to mind were witnesses, so he decided he'd best make some calls on the merchants in town, especially Jim Duffy and Homer Lewis.

Homer Lewis was in his workroom behind the barber-shop when he heard the tiny bell on his front door. Assuming someone wanted a haircut, he took off his shop apron, hung it on the hall tree, and put on his barbering apron in exchange. He was met by Simon Yeager almost before he went through to the front room. Never happy to see the bullying sheriff, he nevertheless tried to be polite, assuming he wanted a free haircut or shave as usual.

"What can I do for you, Sheriff?"

"Why, nothin' right now," Yeager said, attempting a smile. "Just thought I'd pay you a friendly little visit to see how things are goin' with you. It's been a little spell since we've had us a little talk, and I like to make sure you ain't had no problems that the law needs to take care of." He paused to look all around him, as if taking everything in. "Yes, sir, you've built yourself a fine little business here, and I'm right proud to know I'm here to keep an eye on it for you. I make it my job to protect merchants like you. When you think about it, if a fire got started in the back part of your building, it could burn this place to the ground before anybody had a chance to spit. That's why I make it my business to know everything that's goin' on in this town. Now, you take that murderin' dog that shot my brother down—poor Mace never had a chance. I'll settle with him if the army don't. Everybody knows he was hidin' beside a buildin' when he shot Mace. Ain't that right?"

"I suppose," Homer replied cautiously, afraid to disagree.

"Sure you do," Yeager said. "And it's important that everybody remembers that murderer bushwhacked my brother right on the street of our town. I always say that if everybody don't stick together, then trouble's bound to happen. I don't know if you heard about it, but the army's fixin' to try Clint Cooper for what he done to this town, and I'm gonna be there watchin' every bit of it." He looked back at the stove in the center of the room. "Well, I'd best be gettin' along now to keep my eye on the town. You be careful in this cold weather we're havin', and don't get that stove burnin' too hot. You hear?"

"Yeah, I will," Homer said.

"I'll see you at the Trail's End tonight," Yeager said.

Homer stood at the door for several moments after Yeager left. "That son of a bitch knows I was called as a witness," he muttered, recognizing the none-too-subtle threat.

Homer was standing at the bar in the Trail's End Saloon, talking to Floyd Kelly, when Jim Duffy walked in for an evening drink. There was a totally different atmosphere in the Trail's End since Spence Snyder's death and Simon Yeager's takeover. Most of the customers frequented the saloon out of fear that Yeager would retaliate. Some stopped in only briefly for just one drink and then went up the street to the Frontier to relax and make small talk over a couple of drinks with friends.

Orville Johnson summed up the situation the best. "The bastard's got his hands on one of the only two saloons, and that's the same as havin' 'em on the town's throat. Makes a man think about quittin' drinkin', or ridin' all the way out to the fort to Ernie's to keep Simon from finding out he'd been to the Frontier. And if he did go to Ernie's, he'd have to worry about the ride back home in the dark."

"You're just the man I wanna see," Jim said to Homer when Floyd moved to the other end of the bar to pour a drink.

"Yeah?" Homer replied. "I'll bet I know what's on your mind." He glanced toward Floyd to make sure he was out of earshot in the noisy saloon. "You get a visit from our noble sheriff?"

"I did," Jim said. "You, too?"

"That's right. The son of a bitch might as well have told me my place might burn down if I told the truth about that no-account brother of his."

"I got pretty much the same threat," Jim said. "How did he find out we were summoned by the army as witnesses to the shootin'? I didn't even know for sure that you got one, too, but I figured you likely did. I don't know how the army knew me and you were the only witnesses to the shootin'. Somebody had to tell 'em, and I don't know about you, but I'd just as soon they hadn't."

"Me, too," Homer said. "Tell you the truth, I'm scared to go, and scared not to. What do you reckon the army would do if we didn't show up for the trial?"

"They'd most likely send a detail of soldiers over here to get us."

"I expect you're right," Homer continued. "Maybe the safest thing is to do what Yeager told us and say Mace was bushwhacked. It's a helluva thing to do to Clint Cooper, but a man has to think about his own skin."

"At least you just have to worry about your skin," Duffy said. "That evil son of a bitch started tellin' me about how bad he would feel if something happened to my wife and little Jimmy. Then he started tellin' me how he was gonna protect them from men like Clint Cooper. Told me to make sure I didn't do anything that might put 'em in danger. Now, what is that, if it ain't nothing but a threat?"

The conversation was interrupted then by Floyd's return to that end of the bar to chat with them.

"Looks like we're in the same boat, don't it?" Curly James crowed to Clint when he was brought from the hospital to the guardhouse. "They're tryin' you for murder, and they're tryin' me for attempted murder. Only thing is, can't nobody prove it was me that shot that old coot ridin' with you, and I'm sayin' it was Blankenship that done it."

Clint didn't respond right away. At least the army had the forethought to place Curly in with the general population, and not in the small cell with him. Looking at the despicable cur, with his shoulder bandaged and his arm in a sling, Clint struggled to control his temper.

After a moment, when he felt he could keep from trying to grab Curly's bad arm through the bars that separated them and wringing it off, he replied, "You damn fool, it doesn't matter who shot Ben. You both tried to, so attempted murder oughta be enough to let you stretch a rope."

Curly laughed. "Yeah, maybe so, but they was in the hospital talkin' to me, them officers that are gonna try you in the mornin'. And guess what, I'm gonna be testifyin' that I was the deputy sheriff that put a bullet in you after you shot Mace Yeager. And since I'm willin' to testify, they said they'll go a little easier on me in my trial. Whaddaya think about that?"

Again, Clint hesitated to reply, the fury growing

inside him threatening to choke him. He forced himself to remain calm as he glared at the sneering miscreant. "Why the hell would anybody believe a liar like you, Curly? You'll hang. And if by some chance you don't, then you'll have to worry about me."

"I ain't gonna have to worry about you no more after your trial, except maybe gettin' a good seat to watch your hangin'," Curly taunted, emboldened by the bars between them.

His scornful boasts were not particularly bothersome to Clint, because he felt fairly confident that the panel of judges would hardly believe Curly's version over the testimonies of Jim Duffy and Homer Lewis.

Chapter 13

The day of Clint Cooper's trial began on a cold, gray morning. After breakfast, he was marched across the snow-covered parade ground by a detail of four armed guards and escorted into the headquarters building. Clint was surprised to see a wagon and several horses tied up outside.

Inside, the room had been cleared to set up a table at one end with three chairs behind it, and another one a few feet away, which he assumed was the witness stand. Clint was surprised a second time to find a modest group of spectators from Miles City, crowded into a space behind a row of five chairs, which was hardly adequate to accommodate that number. Most of the faces were familiar to Clint, and all stared at him as he was led over to sit in one of the five chairs. His eyes, however, were locked on those of Simon Yeager's, who sat in the end chair, glaring at him, his lip curled in a contemptuous sneer that seemed at home on his flat, brutal face.

In a few minutes, Justin Landry and Randolph Valentine entered the room and hurried over to sit on either side of Clint.

"How you doing, boy?" Valentine asked. "They treating you all right? I told that damn major they'd better, or I was going to complain to the territorial governor."

Clint smiled. "Yes, sir. I just wanna get this thing done."

He saw no point in complaining to the old man. He looked over then and nodded to Justin, who was busy reviewing some notes he had written on a sheet of paper. Before they could exchange words, a corporal at the door ordered, "All rise," and the panel of judges walked in.

Clint studied the faces of Lieutenant Grant, Lieutenant Sawyer, and Major Kinsey as they filed past him and sat down in the chairs behind the table. Following close behind them, Captain Rodgers came in and sat down in the chair next to Simon Yeager. Justin quickly explained to Clint that Rodgers would represent the prosecution, since he had been in temporary command when the sheriff made the initial murder charge against him. It was Rodgers who initiated the search for Clint when Yeager posted the wanted papers, even though he had been somewhat reluctant to do it. Since Rodger had worked with Clint in the battle with the Sioux war party that struck Zack Bristol's trading post on the Yellowstone, it was difficult to serve as prosecutor. He found it hard to believe Clint would murder anyone. He had no choice but to perform the job to the best of his ability, however.

Major Kinsey called the hearing to order and made a brief, but clear, statement of the charges against Clint.

"For the sake of expediency," he announced, "we

will dispense with usual courtroom decorum, this being a simple hearing. Since there is no question that a warrant for murder was issued against the defendant, Clint Cooper, and there is no doubt that the defendant is, in fact, Clint Cooper, we will hear any evidence supporting the charges. In other words, gentlemen, let's not drag this thing out. We'll hear from you first, Captain Rodgers. Make your case."

"Yes, sir," Rodgers said, and rose from his chair. "The facts are, the defendant, Clint Cooper, went into town seeking to kill Deputy Mace Yeager. He waited in ambush behind the barbershop, some fifty yards or more from the Trail's End Saloon. When Deputy Yeager walked out into the street, Cooper shot him with a rifle."

"What evidence do you have to support that accusation?" Kinsey asked.

"There were witnesses to the shooting," Rodgers replied.

"Call your first witness," Kinsey said.

"Prosecution calls Homer Lewis, owner of the barbershop behind which Cooper waited in ambush," Rodgers said. Justin immediately sat up, confused. He looked at Rodgers with a questioning look on his face. Homer Lewis was supposedly a witness for the defense. Justin held his tongue, however, as Rodgers turned and motioned Homer toward the empty chair.

Nervous as a cat, Homer pushed through the spectators and walked unsteadily over to the empty chair, and after a soldier with a Bible took his oath, he sank down heavily. Once he seemed settled, Captain Rodgers said, "You've heard the charges, and you say you witnessed the shooting?"

"Yes, sir," Homer replied meekly, trying not to make eye contact with Simon Yeager, who was glaring at him, a menacing frown threatening.

"Tell the court what you saw," Rodgers instructed.

Homer hesitated to speak for so long that Rodgers started to repeat his request, when Homer replied. "Cooper was hiding behind my shop, and shot Mace when he came out of the saloon." As soon as he said it, Yeager's frown relaxed and turned into a smug smile.

There was a reactionary murmur from the spectators. "Why, you lyin' . . ." Clint started to spring out of his chair but was held back by Valentine and Justin.

"Your witness," Rodgers said to Justin. The look on his face betrayed the fact that Justin was astonished by the witness's answer as well.

Totally disarmed by Homer's testimony, Justin was hard put to cross-examine him. "Mr. Lewis," he began, "are you sure that's what you witnessed?" Homer said that he was. "Were you not told to count to three before Mr. Cooper and Deputy Yeager drew their weapons in a duel?"

"I don't remember nothin' about that," Homer answered, and coughed, almost choking on the lie. "I couldn't see too well where I was standin', anyway." He glanced over at Yeager to see the menacing glare return to his face.

Justin was struck speechless, unable to think of what to say. He looked at Clint, silently questioning what Clint had told him, but saw that he was equally shocked by Homer's testimony. Barely able to respond when the major asked if he had any more questions for the witness, he said no and sat down. He had been assured that this man would clear Clint without doubt, but now his only hope was riding on the testimony of Jim Duffy.

"Call your next witness," Kinsey instructed Rodgers. When the murmuring among the group of spectators started to grow, Kinsey called for quiet.

Jim Duffy took a nervous glance at Homer before taking the stand. His decision was a tough one to make, and he hesitated for a long moment before answering Rodgers' question. "I reckon I saw it about the same way Homer did," he finally muttered.

Clint was stunned. The simple hearing that was supposed to quickly dismiss all charges against him had turned into a nightmare of lies. Valentine jumped to his feet and roared, "I demand a mistrial! These witnesses are obviously lying." He turned and pointed at Simon Yeager. "Intimidated by that man."

"I have to remind you, Mr. Valentine," Kinsey said to him. "You have no standing in this court. You are a spectator. One more outburst from you and I'll have you escorted out of this hearing." He turned to Justin then. "Lieutenant Landry, do you want to cross-examine the witness?"

"I don't think it would do any good, if he's going to stick to that story," Justin said, knowing that his case was lost. "But I have one question for this witness." He turned to face Duffy again. "How do you account for the fact that Mr. Cooper was wounded himself in the gunfight?"

Jim was afraid to answer, so he said, "I don't know."

"Wasn't Mr. Cooper struck in the side by a bullet from Mace Yeager's revolver?" Justin pressed.

"I don't know," Jim repeated.

Clearly shaken by the unexpected testimony of the witness, Justin asked, "Do I need to remind you that you're under oath? Do you want to change your testimony?"

"No, sir," Jim answered, his voice so soft that it could barely be heard. Defeated, Justin threw his hands up in disgust and returned to his chair.

"I have an answer to Lieutenant Landry's question, sir," Captain Rodgers said. "I call Walter James to the stand." Unfamiliar with the name, Clint and Justin exchanged puzzled glances. Then a guard brought Curly in from another room, a smug grin on his face as he winked at Yeager. "Mr. James," Rodgers asked, "what was your position in Miles City?"

"I was a deputy sheriff, after that feller there killed Mace," Curly said, smiling broadly.

"Where were you at the time when the defendant shot Mace Yeager?"

"I was comin' up from the stable."

"Did you see Cooper shoot Mace Yeager?" Rodgers asked.

"Yes, sir, I shore did. I saw Cooper bear down on Mace with a rifle from way up the street. Then he jumped on his horse and hightailed it outta town. I had just enough time to get off one shot, so I let her fly."

"So you're the one who shot Clint Cooper, and not Mace Yeager?" Rodgers asked.

"That's a fact," Curly said smugly. "It was a pretty good shot, too, even if I do say so myself."

"Thank you, Mr. James," Rodgers said.

"Do you wish to cross-examine?" Kinsey asked Justin.

"One question, sir," Justin answered. He turned to face Curly and asked, "How do you account for the fact that the defendant's wound is in the front of his body, and not in his back?"

Curly shrugged, unable to explain. "I don't know. I reckon he musta turned around to look at me."

"He turned around," Justin repeated. He turned to

Clint then and said, "I wonder if you wouldn't mind standing up and pulling out your shirttail so the panel can get a look at your wound." Clint stood up and pulled his shirt and underwear up so the judges could see the still fresh scar where the bullet entered. "Take a good look, gentlemen," Justin continued. "Now, Clint, turn around and show them your back." Clint obliged. "You will notice that there is no scar of any kind on Mr. Cooper's back, since the bullet didn't exit his body. Gentlemen, I submit that Mr. Cooper would have had to be sitting backward in the saddle when his horse galloped out of town in order to have been struck by a bullet from Mr. James' rifle." He fixed his attention on Curly again. "Was the defendant riding out of town backward, Mr. James?"

Completely flustered at this point, Curly wasn't sure what to say. "No, he weren't ridin' backward. Maybe I disremembered, and I was at the other end of town, and he was comin' at me when he hightailed it."

"But you've already testified that you were coming out of the stables, and you just had time for one shot before Mr. Cooper galloped out of town. If I remember correctly, the stables are at the north end of the street, and Mr. Cooper fled out the south end. In any case, if he was coming toward you, wouldn't you have had time for more than one shot? In fact, the closer he came, the easier it would be to hit him, wouldn't it?"

"Hell, I don't know," Curly said in frustration. "He ran and I shot him. That's all I got to say about it."

"Isn't it true that you're one of the biggest liars in the whole territory of Montana?" Justin asked.

"That'll do, Lieutenant!" Kinsey blurted. "You may step down, Mr. James. Now, Lieutenant Landry, do you have any witnesses?"

Before Justin could answer, a voice in the midst of the spectators called out, "Yes, he does." Everyone turned to see Horace Marshall declare, "I saw the shooting from the window of my store. It was a fair fight. They faced each other in the middle of the street. Homer there counted to three, but Mace cheated and pulled his pistol on two. He shot Cooper in the side. Then Cooper shot him."

It was a lie. Horace did not actually witness the shooting, but he knew that was the way it happened, because Frank Hudson told him as much. He and Pete Bender had seen the shooting from the window of his saloon. In the face of such deceit, something inside Horace had snapped, and he had to speak out in the name of justice, even if it set him up for an "accident" like the one that took Spence Snyder's life.

"I saw it, too," Lon Bessemer called out then. "It was just like Horace said. Mace pulled first, and Curly James wasn't even there."

"I saw it," Orville Johnson declared. "It was a fair fight."

"Me, too," Ed Taylor volunteered. "Mace had been trying to get Cooper to have it out with him for a long time. I saw the fight. It was a showdown, fair and square, except Mace tried to cheat and drew early."

Arthur O'Connor, the postmaster, pushed through to the front. "I wanna testify, too," he stated. Like the others, he had not witnessed the duel, but he was willing to lie about it to keep Yeager from having his way.

"All right, all right," Major Kinsey ordered as others pushed forward to testify. "I'm going to have all of you cleared out of here if I hear one more outburst." He turned his attention back to Justin. "Lieutenant, none of these people have been sworn in, so their testimony is irrelevant to the case."

"Well, swear them in!" Randolph Valentine exclaimed. What he saw in that courtroom was the emergence of a group of frightened citizens who had been shamed into striking back at a gunman who had intimidated them under a yoke of fear. He had wondered for some time what it was going to take to encourage these men to band together and take their town back. It looked now as if it was finally going to happen. "Seems to me that you should be trying Simon Yeager for perjury and false accusation," Valentine charged.

Major Kinsey was on the verge of losing control of his courtroom, and was clearly unsure of what he should do, so he sought to regain that control.

"Quiet!" he shouted. "Or so help me, I'll clear the lot of you out. I've already warned you, Valentine. Now sit down or I'll arrange for you to sample the accommodations of our guardhouse." He glared at Valentine until he reluctantly sat down. "I'll remind the prosecution and the defense that Sheriff Yeager is not on trial here." When the room quieted down again, he tried to decide what he should do about the overwhelming requests to testify on behalf of Clint.

Finally he decided to wash his hands of it. "It's my judgment that we've heard enough from the witnesses already sworn, so the panel of judges will decide on the verdict." There was at once a swell of grumbling among the spectators. "I'm warning you!" Kinsey threatened, and the room settled down again. He passed a sheet of paper to each of the officers seated at the table with him. "You have heard the testimony, gentlemen. The matter to be decided is whether the defendant, Clint

Cooper, is guilty of murder or not. You will write your verdict on the paper and hand it to me."

None of the five officers in attendance had ever seen a military hearing quite as out of hand as this one. It was obvious to everyone at this point that Kinsey just wanted to have it over with. The three officers on the panel dutifully wrote down their verdicts and Kinsey collected Grant's and Sawyer's to add to his own. He started to read them, then remembered to tell the defendant to stand while the verdict was being read.

When Clint and Justin got to their feet, Kinsey looked at the two papers handed him once, then looked at each again, as if to be certain. Finally he stated, "By unanimous vote, this panel finds the defendant not guilty."

Judging by the reaction shown by the town's citizens, it would have been difficult to have come up with any other verdict.

Amid a cheering group of citizens, one man stood scowling in bitter anger, but he knew there was nothing he could do about the verdict. Clint Cooper was a free man. *He might think he got away with killing my brother,* Yeager thought, *but he'll die by my hand. I swear it.* He started for the door, but he was stopped before he reached it by Horace Marshall.

"Hold on there a minute, Yeager," Marshall said. Normally a mild man, he had decided it was time to take a stand. He was tired of paying the menacing brute for protection when the only protection he needed was from Yeager himself. And he was tired of being afraid of the murdering outlaw, and tired of being too meek to stand up to him. Throwing all caution to the wind, for he didn't know if he was one man alone or not, he said what he should have said when the Yeagers and their two cronies first came to town. "The town of Miles City no longer needs your services. You're fired as sheriff, and we want you out of town by tomorrow morning."

The room, which had been noisily celebrating the panel's verdict, suddenly went dead silent. Simon Yeager's brutal face was transformed into an angry frown. "What did you say?" he demanded, his voice low and deadly.

Marshall immediately felt every nerve in his body go numb, but he had gone too far to crumble now before the sinister gunman. "You heard me," he managed.

"Who the hell is 'we'?" Yeager demanded. "Who's gonna back you up, Marshall?"

"The whole damn town," Lon Bessemer said, and stepped up beside Marshall. "That's who."

"That's right, Yeager," Orville Johnson said. "We want our town back, and that means you and your kind ain't welcome here." One by one, including Homer Lewis and Jim Duffy, every man in the gallery of spectators stepped up to show their support for Horace Marshall.

Enraged, Yeager lashed out at the revolting merchants. "You sorry bunch of sheep, you need me to keep the peace in that shit hole you call a town. You can't throw me out. I own a business there, I own the Trail's End. I got as much right there as any of you." He turned to Major Kinsey for support. "Tell 'em, Major."

Kinsey, watching the rebellious turmoil in fascination, replied, "Tell them what? It appears to me that the elders of the town are unanimous in voting for the termination of your services as sheriff. And speaking for the military, the army will support the town's elders."

Wildly frustrated, Yeager demanded, "What about

my saloon? I got as much right to do business there as anybody else."

"You don't own Trail's End," Ed Taylor said to him. "You've got no claim on that saloon just because Spence Snyder was killed." He looked at Major Kinsey then. "And there's some of us that have a pretty good idea who shot Spence."

"You've got a mouth that's gonna be too big for you to tote," Yeager threatened. "I wonder if you've got the guts to back it up."

"That's as far as this is going," Kinsey interrupted. "You've turned this hearing into a brawl, and I'll have a detail of guards bottle the whole lot of you up if you don't clear out of this building and off this post." He turned to address Yeager directly. "Sheriff, or should I say, *Mister* Yeager? My advice to you is to collect your personal property and move on to some other part of the territory. It's plain to see there's no place for you in Miles City. Let me be perfectly clear when I tell you that if trouble continues in that town, it can be taken under military control."

Yeager stood stone still, glaring defiantly at the major for almost a full minute before the rage inside him allowed him to speak. He shifted his gaze to Horace Marshall then and said, "You ain't seen the last of me." He turned then and started for the door, and the men of Miles City parted to allow him a clear path. Just before reaching the door, he paused to turn and fix Clint with an ominous stare. "I'm puttin' my mark on you," he threatened in a voice so low that only those standing near the door heard him.

Incredulous witnesses to the chaotic scene just finished, Clint, Justin, and Valentine stood to one side of the room, scarcely able to believe the rebellion of the merchants of the town. Once the door was closed behind the fuming gunman, the mood changed to one of celebration for Clint's release. Valentine suggested that it was also Independence Day for the little town, and recommended celebrating with a drink at Ernie's Saloon. Everyone was invited and the drinks were on him. To a man, they accepted his offer, especially since they all wanted to travel back as a group instead of as individuals. None of the merchants were keen to travel the trail back to town alone with the prospect of the ominous Simon Yeager lying in wait. It was common knowledge that Yeager's method of dealing with troublesome problems was usually by squeezing a trigger.

"I'll be over to join you at Ernie's in a little while," Clint said to Valentine. "I've got to go get my horse and my weapons."

"Maybe I'd better go with you," Valentine said. "Since your regular bodyguard isn't here to take care of you," he added, referring to Ben Hawkins.

Clint laughed. "I expect he's probably givin' Rena a hard time, tryin' to get outta that bunk before he's healed up proper. But you'd better go on to Ernie's with the crowd, else they're liable to think you're runnin' out on payin' the bill." Valentine still hesitated. So Clint, knowing what he was thinking, said, "Yeager ain't fool enough to try anything on the post."

"I suppose not," Valentine said. "Well, don't be too long." He went outside to join the town merchants for the short trip to Ernie's.

Major Kinsey walked over to talk to Clint then. "Well, congratulations, Cooper. I guess there wasn't much doubt that Yeager was just trying to get you hanged for outdueling his brother. Of course, you're free to go. Lieutenant Landry can go with you to get your weapons and your

horse. I'll see about having those wanted posters destroyed."

"I 'preciate it, Major," Clint said.

Justin waited until the major walked away before
saying what was on his mind. "I guess I wasn't much of
a lawyer, but I'm mighty glad you came out of this
thing all right. I got caught with my foot in my mouth
when our two witnesses sat down in that chair and lied.
I thought we'd lost it. According to what I was able to
find out before the hearing, Duffy and Lewis were the
only ones who really saw the shooting. I had no idea
that there were that many more who witnessed it, too."

Clint smiled. "There weren't," he said. "Those two
witnesses mighta thrown you for a loop, but you sure as
hell held Curly's feet to the fire. Let's go get my rifle."

The Miles City men were seated around two tables on
one side of the saloon when Clint found them. They
waved him over as soon as someone saw him walk in.
He went by the bar first to pick up a glass.

"Welcome back, Clint," Ernie Thigpen greeted him,
a great big grin on his face. "I heard they cleared your
name."

"Yep," Clint said. "I wasn't an outlaw for long, but I
sure didn't like it much while I was." He took the glass
Ernie slid over toward him and started over to join the
party, but Darcy Suggs intercepted him halfway.

"Where the hell have you been?" she demanded. "I
thought you were dead or something."

"Did you miss me?" he teased. "I was just stayin'
away to see if you'd forget me."

"Hell no, I didn't miss you," she said, pouting. "But
everybody knew you went into town and shot Mace

Yeager. I thought you had enough sense to walk around those Yeager brothers, just like you'd walk around a snake."

"Couldn't be helped," he said with a smile. "One of those snakes killed Pick Pickens, and you have to kill a snake that does things like that." He took her by the arm. "Come on and join the party. Maybe you can lead one of the town's leadin' citizens upstairs to ride the bronc."

"What about you?" she asked. "I know you ain't been riding the bronc, and that ain't natural for a man as young as you. If you don't, everything in you is gonna dry up and you'll start to look like Ernie over there."

He glanced back at the bar. "I believe I've got a few years yet before I get that bad." He gave her arm a little squeeze then. "I tell you, it's a mighty temptin' thought, but I don't reckon I'm up to it right now." He placed his hand on his side over his wound. "That snake we were just talkin' about, the one I killed, well, he bit me before I killed him. And I'm afraid I can't really move much without being in real pain, so I couldn't tend to you proper."

"Liar," she charged. "You've always got some cock-amamy excuse."

"No, I ain't, darlin'. It's just bad luck about my side. Anyway, I told you, I'm waitin' till you get wore out from your profession, so I can marry you and make an honest woman outta you." He reached over and placed his glass on the table. "Pour me a shot, Horace." Horace Marshall picked up one of the bottles on the table and filled the glass. "Much obliged," Clint said, and returned his attention to Darcy. "Anyway, I expect I'll be leavin' pretty soon now. I have to go back to the ranch with Mr. Valentine. He don't like to go back by himself—scared of the dark."

She shook her head, perplexed. "Clint Cooper, you're the biggest liar I've ever met. Aren't you afraid your tongue is gonna turn black one of these days?" She spun on her heel and went back to the table where she had been sitting with a couple of soldiers before Clint walked in.

Bringing his mind back to more serious matters, he took a chair from another table and pulled it in beside Horace Marshall. Horace looked as if he had had a real need for a drink after his bold confrontation with Simon Yeager.

"That took some guts to do what you did back there in that courtroom," Clint said to him. "It was mighty damn risky, but looks like the town stepped right up when you needed 'em. And I wanna thank you for doin' it, because it looked like I was gettin' ready to stretch some rope after the witnesses testified."

Sitting close by, Jim Duffy overheard Clint's remarks. "I know you ain't got no use for me, Clint, but Yeager came to see me before the trial. He threatened to harm my wife and kid if I didn't back his story about that shootin'. I hate like hell that I had to do what I did, but I couldn't take a chance on him hurtin' my family." He looked as if he expected Clint to challenge him.

"Jim, there ain't no doubt about it, I'da been mad as hell if you and Homer had sent me to the hangin' tree. But since the rest of the town stepped up to do the right thing, I ain't gonna waste my time carryin' a grudge against either one of you. Besides, I heard it was you who let Yeager's and those other two horses outta the corral to give me enough time to get away after Mace shot me. So let's call it even and forget about it."

"You're a fair and Christian man, Clint, and I wanna thank you for that," Jim replied, greatly relieved. He was afraid it was not going to be as easy to repair his reputation with the rest of the town.

After a short period of celebration, Randolph Valentine decided it was time to talk about some serious issues to come. Addressing Horace Marshall, he asked, "Have you men talked about the problem with Yeager before?"

"Well," Horace replied, not sure where Valentine was going with the question, "sure, we've all talked about the problem."

"But you haven't gotten a committee together to discuss what action to take to get rid of the problem before?" Horace said that they had not. Valentine continued. "Well, you've damn sure taken the first step today, so you'd best be sure that everybody who spoke up today is willing to back it up. There might still be some trouble from that man before he clears out, and I can guarantee it if he catches any one of you alone. So I suggest you take to patrolling your street in pairs. You've got to organize, so the next gunman who rides into town doesn't have a chance to get as far as Yeager did."

Just as Horace had, everyone there decided that it was time to defend the investment they had made in the future of their town. The first order of business was to organize a vigilance committee, and the first official meeting was held right then and there, in Ernie's saloon. Horace Marshall was voted in as head of the committee, as well as mayor of the town. It was decided that the committee would handle all civil disorders until they could find a sheriff. When that subject came up, many eyes were turned in Clint's direction, but he quickly told them that he had a job at the Double-V-Bar, and that was where his future lay.

It was the middle of the afternoon before the Miles City vigilance committee left Ernie's for the trip back to town. For a couple of the citizens, it was fortunate that Horace had driven his wagon, seeing as how it was questionable whether or not they could remain upright in the saddle. Such were the dangers of holding their meetings in a saloon.

Clint and his boss started for the door, only to be stopped by Darcy Suggs. Ignoring Valentine, she grabbed Clint's arm. "Sure you can't stay with me tonight? I won't see nobody else if you do."

"Oh, you know I'd like to, Darcy," Clint said. "But I've got to ride back with Mr. Valentine."

She cocked a disapproving eye at Valentine, then released Clint's arm. "You don't know what you're missing, Clint Cooper."

He gave her a smile, then walked outside with Valentine. When they were untying their horses from the hitching rail, Valentine said, "I don't know what you've got on your mind, but if you want to stay here tonight with that woman, it doesn't make any difference to me. I don't need anybody to ride back with me."

Clint had to laugh at that. "No, sir, that's the last thing I need tonight."

"Glad to hear it," Valentine said. "I hoped you had higher ambitions than tussling with a whore."

Clint felt compelled to defend Darcy's honor, what little she had. "Darcy's just a friend. She's rode a hard trail, I reckon, and it's put a lot of wear on her, but she's got a heart of gold inside."

As they left the saloon, they encountered Justin on his way to Ernie's. "Looks like my lawyer's a little late for the celebration," Clint joked.

"I just wanted to say again that I'm glad things

worked out," Justin said as he rode up to meet them. Directing his remarks to Valentine then, he said, "I guess I'll see you on Sunday, if that's all right with you—if I haven't worn out my welcome."

"I leave that up to Hope," Valentine said. "As far as I'm concerned, you're welcome as long as she welcomes you."

"Thank you, sir. I'll see you Sunday, then." He nodded to Clint and wheeled his horse to return to the post.

Clint had to admit that Justin's courtship of Hope still bothered him, even though he and the lieutenant had sort of declared a truce between them.

Chapter 14

While the merchants celebrated the liberation of their town at Ernie's, the target of their recent revolt was bitterly assessing his situation after the trial had gone so wrong.

That damn fool, he thought. *They'd have had to find Cooper guilty if Curly hadn't let his mouth run on.*

He couldn't blame Curly for all of it, however, for he knew all of the voluntary witnesses wanting to testify clinched the verdict for the three officers on the panel.

The more he thought about what he had lost, the madder he became—so much so that he was in a state of overpowering rage by the time he got back to the Trail's End. There were only a few customers inside, and he ordered them out, saying the saloon was closed. When Floyd asked what was going on, Simon ordered him out, too.

One look at the fury etched on the face of the enraged brute was enough to clear out the saloon immediately. Simon could feel the burning rise of bile in his innards when he replayed the scene of the trial. He felt the need to strike out at something, so he picked up a chair and threw it crashing through the window of the empty saloon. The sound of it brought one of the two prostitutes hurrying down the stairs to investigate.

Alice Birchfield stopped halfway down when she saw the result of Yeager's frustration. "Well, that was a dumb thing to do," she said. "Now it's gonna be cold as hell down here with that wind blowing in the window."

Without a thought, Yeager turned, drew his pistol, and fired, needing something more than a broken window to release his anger on. The shot caught the unfortunate woman in the breast, and she crumpled on the steps and slid almost to the bottom before lying still. Yeager looked up at the top of the stairs when Bonny Fry screamed. His lust for blood already out of control, he cocked the pistol and fired at her, but she had already fled to her room, screaming as she ran for her life.

Knowing that his plans to operate the saloon were destroyed, he had no need for the two whores, so he started after Bonny. The sight of Alice's body sprawled near the bottom of the stairs added fuel to his anger, so he grabbed her ankle and dragged her roughly down to the floor. With Alice out of the way, he stormed up the steps, but he was too late to stop Bonny from locking her door and going out the window. When he kicked her door in and found her gone, he calmed down enough to begin to think about what he was going to do, now that he was being forced out of town. He thought about Horace Marshall and Lon Bessemer, and the others who volunteered to witness.

"They had the gall to tell me to get outta town," he declared. Thinking of the lot of them, he refused to believe they had the stomach or the nerve to run him out of town. "By God, we'll see about that," he decided. "I'll plant myself behind this bar and shoot anybody that comes through the door."

The more he thought about it, the more he was convinced that there was not a hatful of courage in the whole town. And if they did try to storm him, he was confident that he could take out enough of the town's business owners to cause the collapse of the entire town. Then he would leave, after he had brought the town to its knees and it was too depleted of its leading citizens to survive.

When that was done, he would settle with Clint Cooper. His mind made up, he went about the business of making a fort out of the Trail's End.

The somber woman paused when she heard Hope exclaim from the parlor, "Papa's back! And Clint's with him! The trial must have come out all right." In a few seconds, the young lady appeared in the kitchen. "Better put the coffeepot on. Papa's gonna want a hot cup of coffee after riding from the fort."

"Coffee on," Rena said, and pushed the big gray pot over from the edge of the stove to the center so it would boil. She walked to the window then to see for herself, and to estimate how long it would take them to pull their saddles off and turn the horses out. The bread she was making would not be ready to put in the oven for another quarter of an hour or so. She shrugged and said to herself in her native tongue, "They wait." It was only a matter of minutes, however, before Valentine came in the kitchen door, having left his horse with Hank to take care of.

"Where's Clint?" Hope asked when her father stormed in, looking for coffee.

"He went in the bunkhouse to see how Ben's doing. I told him to come on up to the house after he sees Ben." He looked at Hope's expectant face, the girl obviously eager to hear what had happened. "Where's Clint?" he joked. "What about Papa? You don't seem so excited to see me back."

"Oh, Papa, we're always happy to see you come home. Look at Rena—she almost smiled. I declare." She glanced at the serious Crow woman and received a somber glance in return. It was what she expected. "Here, I'll take your coat. Now tell me all about the trial. What happened? Was Justin brilliant?"

"Yeah, he was brilliant," Valentine said, and brought to mind the helpless look on Justin's face when the witnesses sank his hopes. "Yep, he did all right," he added when he recalled the way he had handled Curly James. He looked toward the coffeepot on the stove then.

"Not yet," Rena said.

"Tell me some more about the trial," Hope pressed. "Is everything settled now? Is Clint a free man?" Valentine went on to give her more details about what had happened that day, including the townspeople's firing of Simon Yeager.

In the bunkhouse, several of the men were gathered around Ben Hawkins' bunk, where they got the news firsthand from the defendant. "So they finally got their backbones up and kicked Simon Yeager outta town," Shorty Black commented.

"By God, that'll be a gracious blessin'," Bobby Dees said.

"Maybe so," Ben said, looking directly at Clint when he spoke. "But a man like Simon Yeager ain't likely to just ride away and consider hisself lucky to get out alive, or without spendin' time in prison. You'd do well to keep your eyes and ears open for a good while after he's gone." He nodded at Clint and said, "Especially somebody who killed his brother."

"If he's got any sense at all," Clint said, "he'll get on his horse and ride way the hell away from Miles City." He got up from the bunk he was sitting on. "I gotta go now. Mr. Valentine told me to come up to the house as soon as I found out if you were dead or not. I'll be back soon as I see what he wants."

"I 'preciate your concern," Ben replied sarcastically.

Clint strode across the barnyard toward the house, feeling light and lively, a state he attributed to the court's decision, rather than to the alcohol he had consumed. He figured he should be damn near cold-stone sober after the frigid ride from Ernie's. Stepping up to the kitchen door, he rapped politely, and in a few seconds, Rena opened it. She held it open for him while Valentine invited him to come in and sit at the table with Hope and him.

"From the looks of it, 'pears like Rena's fixin' to put supper on the table," Clint said. "Maybe I'd better not stay long. Milt was gettin' pretty close to throwin' some grub on the table down at the bunkhouse." He turned then when Rena nudged his arm and found her holding a cup of coffee for him. "Why, thank you kindly, Rena," he said. She nodded, and looked for a brief second as if she was about to break out a smile for him.

It did not go unnoticed by Hope, and she told him so. "I do believe you are the only person that Rena comes close to smiling at. Isn't that right, Papa?"

Valentine smiled. "You might be right. I hadn't noticed."

"Rena appreciates what a fine gentleman I am," Clint said. "By the way, did your daddy tell you that your fine gentleman lieutenant said he's comin' to see you Sunday?"

"No, he didn't," Hope replied, "and I wish you'd stop calling him 'my lieutenant.' "

"Sorry. I forgot," he said facetiously. He turned to her father then. "What was it you wanted to talk to me about?"

"Nothing in particular, really," Valentine replied. "I just thought you might want to join us for supper instead of eating in the bunkhouse."

"Well, I figured I'd be eatin' with the men—" he started, but Hope interrupted.

"Oh, for goodness' sake, every time we invite you to eat with us, you say the same thing," she said. "You'll hurt Rena's feelings. She thinks you prefer Milt Futch's cooking to hers. And besides, I want to hear all about your time in jail at Fort Keogh."

"Well, Rena knows I don't think any such thing," Clint was quick to deny.

"I fix plenty, bake bread," Rena said.

"In that case, I'll be pleased to eat with you," he said. It had not escaped him that the table was already set with three plates, and he knew one of them was not intended for Rena. It wasn't long before he realized the real reason his boss invited him to supper.

"I expect you're feeling pretty good, now that this thing with the army is settled," Valentine began. "But I think it would be a sensible idea for you to stick close to the ranch for a while, at least until we have some kinda idea that Yeager has really cleared out."

Clint smiled. "I just got told that by Ben."

"Yeah? Well, I think you should take the advice seriously. That man is dangerous, especially now when he thought he was gonna own a saloon. He's gonna blame you for ruining his run in Miles City, because you killed his brother. That's why I want to be damn sure you realize how serious your situation is."

Clint shrugged, not really that concerned, even though very much aware of the potential harm that could come his way if he was not careful.

"I'll try to be careful," he said. Then, quick to change the subject, he said, "I'll tell you one thing, when it comes to makin' coffee, there ain't no contest. Milt's eatin' dust tryin' to catch up to Rena."

"Listen to what Papa's telling you," Hope said, concerned that Clint's usual carefree attitude might carry over to this matter. "You've already gotten yourself shot once. Isn't that enough?"

"I always listen to what your daddy tells me," Clint replied. "Don't you worry about that." He couldn't help wondering if she might really be worried about him. As soon as it came to his mind, he told himself to forget it. He might be having supper with the boss and his daughter, but he was still just the hired help. Once he rid his mind of hopeless thoughts, the rest of the supper went pleasantly enough, and the general discussion turned to matters of the ranch and the cattle.

When it was over, Clint said good night and headed for the door, where he was met by Rena with another thick slice of the fresh-baked bread—in case he got hungry later on, she told him. He thanked her and complimented her on the quality of the meal. Then as he opened the door, Hope said, "We're really glad to have you back safe and sound. Please take care of yourself from now on."

"I always do," he said casually.

Damn it, he thought, *I wish she'd stop saying things to start me wondering.*

Simon Yeager's mind was churning with all of the things that needed to be done in order to carry out his plan to barricade himself in the saloon. If the citizens of the town had, in fact, decided to band together against him, he would be ready. They would most likely come as a gang to see if he had left in the morning as Horace Marshall had ordered. If it happened the way he envisioned, he would gun down several of the posse's leaders. Then he would see how dedicated the others were to rallying around Marshall's call to rid the town of their sheriff. He would have a stronger grip than ever. As a precaution, however, he decided to bring his horse up from the stable and leave it in the shed behind the saloon where Spence had kept a buggy.

On his way down to the stable, he stopped to peer in the window of Marshall's general store. He saw Lucinda, Marshall's wife, but no sign of her husband. Seeing the fearsome bully staring at her, she instinctively turned away to quickly move behind the counter. Her obvious fright made him grin mischievously as he continued along toward the stable. Passing the blacksmith shop, he noticed that there was no sign of Lon Bessemer. When he reached the stable and found Jim Duffy gone, he realized that none of the group of merchants was back from Fort Keogh.

Maybe, he thought, *they're having a meeting somewhere, getting up their nerve to hold a necktie party.* It might have occurred to them that it would be the best way to make sure they were rid of him permanently. "We'll see about that," he promised.

After throwing his saddle on the big dun gelding, he

rode up the short street as far as the Frontier. He looped his reins over the hitching rail and walked in to confront Pete Bender behind the bar. "Where's Hudson?" Yeager asked bluntly.

"He ain't here," Pete answered. "He ain't back from Fort Keogh yet." It was no telling what the menacing brute wanted with Frank, but Pete figured it couldn't be good.

Saying nothing more, Yeager turned around and left the saloon, his suspicions confirmed in his mind. They were having some kind of meeting, maybe with the army, maybe not. It could be they were trying to work up the nerve to try to hang him that night, instead of waiting until morning. The cruel smile returned to his face as he thought of the reception he was preparing for them.

Then the thought occurred that it might be a good idea to have an escape plan in the event that things didn't go the way he hoped, so he rode back to the stable. In the absence of the owner, he helped himself not only to an extra horse, but to a packsaddle as well. There were enough supplies in the Trail's End storeroom in case he needed them. Satisfied that he was prepared for any circumstances to come, he took his horses to the shed behind the saloon. There was plenty of room for them both after he pulled Spence's buggy out. Back inside the saloon, he leaned his rifle against the back of the bar with two cartridge belts on the floor beside it.

From behind the bar, he could watch the front door, the back door, and the landing at the top of the stairs, in case someone climbed up on the porch and came in a window. That possibility caused him to get his saddlebags from upstairs and put them on the floor beside the ammunition. With the money he had found in the safes in his saddlebags, he felt secure in the knowledge that he was prepared for any outcome in the standoff with the merchants.

Private David Bostic and two of his friends, all three members of the Second Cavalry, pulled up to the hitching rail in front of the Trail's End. "Before we go in the saloon," Bostic said, "I need to go in the store across the street and get some tobacco. If I don't get it before we go in the Trail's End, I might not have any money left when I come out."

Bob Simpson laughed. "Especially if you see Bonny, right?"

"That's a fact," Bostic replied.

His two friends went into Ed Taylor's store with him and waited near the door while Bostic made his purchase. He was in the process of paying Lila Taylor when he was startled by a woman's voice calling him from the door of Taylor's stockroom. "Bonny?" Bostic asked. "Is that you? What in the world are you doing back there?"

"I'm so glad to see you!" Bonny cried out. "He killed Alice!" She ran to him and put her arms around him, desperate for someone's protection.

"What?" Bostic exclaimed. "Who killed Alice?"

"He was trying to kill me, too," Bonny sobbed, breaking down in the security of his embrace. "Mrs. Taylor let me hide here. I didn't know where else to go."

At once concerned, Bostic tried to calm the frightened woman as his friends by the door gathered around to lend support. "Just calm down," Bostic said, "and tell me what happened." Bonny gathered her composure enough to relate the sudden outburst of violence from Simon Yeager with the brutal slaying of her friend

Alice. "And he came after you, too?" Bostic asked. She told him then how she had run into her room and climbed out the window to escape.

"Did you go tell the sheriff?" Bob Simpson asked.

"He is the sheriff," Lila said.

"Damn," Bostic said. "That's right." He looked at his two friends for support. "Well, we'll just go over and have a little talk with the sheriff." He got nods of agreement from both.

"Maybe you'd better not," Bonny said. "He's the meanest man I've ever seen."

"She's telling you the truth, soldier," Lila said. "I heard the shot, but with most of our menfolk still out at the fort, I doubt anybody had the nerve to go see what it was about."

"Might be he needs a little of that meanness taken out of him," Bostic replied, confident in the belief that the three of them could overpower him. "You stay here with Mrs. Taylor," he told Bonny.

Simon Yeager laid his rifle across the bar and put one of the cartridge belts beside it. He turned to look at the clock on the wall behind the bar, wondering how long it would be before the vigilance committee showed up.

Maybe they won't show up till after dark, he thought, *trying to catch me when I'm not looking.* He snorted in disgust. *Won't make any difference, because I'll be waiting for them, no matter what time they come.*

Settling in for the wait, he had turned to pour himself a little glass of courage when he was startled by a voice from the door.

"Simon Yeager? We need to talk to you."

Already primed to explode, Simon spun around to see the three men walking in the door. Without pausing to think, he grabbed his rifle and cranked three rounds in rapid succession. Unarmed, the three men were dropped to the floor before they had time to back out. Simon remained where he was, using the bar for cover, watching the doorway in case there were others. When no one else came in, he cocked his rifle again and walked over to examine the bodies, realizing only then that he had shot three soldiers.

"Damn!" he cursed, knowing that he might now be in bigger trouble than he had first imagined. They had called out his name, so that meant they had come looking for him.

So they got the army into it, he thought. That put a different light on things. When these three failed to come back, a mounted patrol would most likely be next. He had no desire to hang alongside Curly James. It was time to cut his losses and run.

"To hell with this town," he exclaimed as he hurried to take what he could from the late Spence Snyder's saloon. There were other territories and other towns where a man with over sixteen thousand dollars in cash could make his mark. Colorado came to mind, because he was not wanted by the law there.

But before I head for Colorado, he thought, *there's a little matter with Clint Cooper I need to clean up.*

He pulled the bodies of the slain soldiers out of the doorway with only a curious thought as to why an arresting party came to get him unarmed. Too busy with his escape to stop and think it through, he closed and barred the door. Then he carried the plunder and supplies he had gathered out to the shed and loaded his packhorse, pleased with himself for having the foresight to prepare for such an emergency.

It occurred to him that he would like to burn the

Trail's End down to the ground, but he decided it would take too long to get a proper fire started. Besides, he thought, it was better not to attract attention as he slipped out of town. He stepped up into the saddle then and uttered a curse.

"To hell with the saloon, and to hell with the damn town."

Chapter 15

At Valentine's insistence, Clint's activities were confined pretty much to home base, a situation that he was not particularly pleased with, but it gave him an opportunity to keep Ben company more often. He found himself doing more of the chores around the barn, which pleased Hank. For the rest of the hands, it was back to the normal business of rounding up strays and riding the herd, on the lookout for coyotes and wolves.

On the day after Clint's trial at Fort Keogh, Charley Clark and Shorty Black came back from Miles City with a wagonload of supplies for Rena and Milt. They brought back the news that Simon Yeager had locked the doors at the Trail's End and left town. As a farewell gesture, however, he had murdered three soldiers and Alice Birchfield. A committee of five, headed by Horace Marshall, had broken into the saloon and found the bodies. It was an unfortunate conclusion to Simon Yeager's reign of terror, but the committee breathed a collective sigh of relief when it appeared they had seen the last of the brutal man.

After helping unload the wagon, Clint went to the house to give Valentine the news. Rena opened the kitchen door for him, then went to fetch her boss. "Thought you'd like to know that Yeager left town," Clint said when Valentine came into the kitchen behind Rena. "Accordin' to what Charley and Shorty say, he cleaned the saloon out of everything he could carry on a packhorse."

"I reckon it was worth it to get rid of him," Valentine said. He hesitated for a moment when another thought came to mind. "There's no telling how much cash Spence had when he was killed, so I guess Yeager's time in Miles City was worth it to him. It's a damn shame that killer got away with it. At least he's probably got enough to take him far away from this part of the country."

"That's what I figure," Clint said. "I know I'm ready to get back to ranchin'." He started to head for the door, but Hope came into the room then, so he paused while her father relayed the news to her.

"Well, thank goodness," Hope declared. "Maybe we can live a normal life for a change. There are no more Yeagers, Clint's no longer a wanted criminal, and Ben's healing up just fine, according to Rena."

Standing by the door, with one hand still on the doorknob, Clint gave her a grin. "I reckon the next big news around here will be a weddin'." He refrained from saying that it wouldn't necessarily be good news to everyone.

Hope flashed him a painful expression. "And just who might be getting married, Mr. Cooper?"

He was suddenly overcome by a feeling of awkwardness when he felt all eyes in the kitchen, including Rena's, were fixed on him. "Why, I figured . . . ," he stammered, puzzled by Hope's stern look.

"You figured what?" she demanded. When he seemed lost for a reply, she said, "You figured I'd marry Justin Landry, right?" He shrugged helplessly, his usual joking manner suddenly missing. "I declare, you're dumber than a rolling pin," she lambasted.

He felt extremely uncomfortable. He had not meant to make her angry. His little teases never bothered her before. Evidently she was not in the mood for playful gibes about her courtship with Justin Landry. Maybe it was the wrong time of the month to be teasing her.

"Yes, ma'am," he finally managed. "I'd best get back to work. Bobby Dees said that section close to the house is about grazed out. I wanna save as much of the hay we've got, in case we get a heavy snowfall and they can't get to the grass. I told him I'd ride out with him to pick a new spot."

"Why don't you give it one more day before you start ranging very far out from the house?" Valentine said.

"Do what Papa says," Hope told him, still looking irritated.

"You're the boss," Clint said to her father, then went out the door, mystified by the atmosphere he had just left in the kitchen.

Behind him in the house, Hope looked at her father and shook her head, exasperated. "Dumber than a rolling pin," she repeated.

"You can't very well blame him," her father said. "Isn't your relationship with Justin serious?"

She shook her head impatiently. "I can't think of anything worse than being married to a soldier."

"Why don't you tell him how you feel?" Valentine

asked. He already had plans for Clint's future, and it would make him happy if the two were married.

"I'm not going to tell him," Hope insisted. "If he can't decide on his own, then how can I be sure he really loves me?"

Standing just inside her bedroom door, the solemn Crow housekeeper listened to the conversation between the young woman and her father. She thought of the young man under discussion, and the many times she had seen the wistful look in his eyes. Rena knew long before this point that Hope did not desire to be the wife of the lieutenant. She was convinced that Hope would make Clint a good wife, if he had the nerve to ask her. Rena knew what was in his heart, but she also knew he was afraid to tell Hope, afraid she would reject him, and possibly be insulted. So he would forever keep silent.

Rena shook her head sadly. She cared about both young people.

Where is the son of a bitch? Simon Yeager wondered to himself, growing more angry and impatient as the hours passed without a trace of the man he hunted. It had been two days now since Yeager fled Miles City, and he had spent both of those days watching the comings and goings on the Double-V-Bar Ranch. So far, there had been no sign of Clint Cooper. He watched the crews going out into the prairie, and their return in the evenings. At night, he moved in closer so he could see the night-herders ride out. The longer he watched with no sighting, the more frustrated he became, and the closer he moved in. Soon it became so infuriating that he was almost driven to ride boldly into the ranch, shooting everyone in sight. Only the thought of all he could lose by doing so kept him from surrendering to the notion.

Finally his patience was exhausted, and he decided that if he didn't sight Clint riding out with the crew the next morning, he was going to risk working his way all the way into the ranch yard and finding him. It had become obvious to him that Clint was staying close to home, afraid that he might face an ambush. It would be risky, but Simon was confident that he would have the element of surprise working in his favor. His only regret was that the killing would have to be done quickly, and then he would have to run for it before anyone there had time to get after him. He would have much preferred to kill Clint slowly and painfully. Mace deserved that much at least.

Now with darkness setting in, there was nothing for him to do but to return to his camp, hidden in a deep gully at the base of a low ridge one half mile south of the ranch yard.

Morning brought low clouds, dark and heavy with moisture. It was Ben's guess that snow would be falling before noon. He said as much to Clint. "Nothing for you to worry about," Clint teased. "You'll be sittin' up here in the bunkhouse with a good fire goin' and Milt bringin' you coffee whenever you want it."

"Damn right," Ben replied. "What are you goin' to be doin' today?"

"Well . . ." Clint paused to reflect. "I had planned to ride out near the Parson's Nose to make sure Jody and Shorty rounded up those strays Charley said he saw on his way back from town." He shrugged. "But I made the mistake of tellin' Mr. Valentine I was gonna do that. He wants me to stay close to the house for at least a couple more days. So I reckon I'll give Hank a hand and clean out some of those stalls in the barn while he splits up some more firewood for Rena."

"You're doin' so much of Hank's work he'll be afraid you're takin' over his job, for certain," Ben said, laughing. "He's always worryin' about gettin' fired."

"If he knew nobody else wants his job, he might be askin' the boss for a raise." Clint got to his feet then. "Well, I ain't gettin' those stalls cleaned out sittin' around here, jawin' with you. I'll be back later on to see if you're dead yet." He pulled his coat on and started for the door.

"Strap that forty-four on," Ben told him.

"I ain't goin' anywhere but the barn," Clint said, "and it gets in the way when I'm ridin' a shovel or a pitchfork."

"You don't never know when you'll need a gun," Ben called after him as he went out the door.

"I might slip on some of that horse shit and accidentally shoot myself in the leg," Clint joked, "or shoot Hank."

"One of these days you're gonna learn to listen to me," Ben yelled, but Clint was already out the door and hurrying across the yard to the barn.

When he got to the barn, Hank had already gone behind the smokehouse, where a large mound of sawed lengths of wood was waiting to be split in sizes the stove could handle. Clint had to laugh when he saw a rake, a shovel, and a pitchfork propped conspicuously against the wall of the first stall, left there by Hank.

In case I forgot what I promised to do, Clint thought. He pulled his heavy coat off and laid it across the top of the stall, unaware of the dark figure standing in the shadows of the last stall.

A wicked smile spread slowly across the harsh face of Simon Yeager when he saw the man he hunted walk right into the barn where he was hiding. It could not have turned out any better. He had managed to sneak up behind the barn to find no one around except one man, and that one had gone off somewhere to chop wood. He had just started to move through to the front of the barn, with the thought of getting a better look at the house and bunkhouse, when Clint walked in. Afraid that he had been spotted, he ducked quickly into a back stall, his pistol drawn. But there was no reaction from Clint to indicate he had seen him. Instead he picked up the rake and went into the first stall.

Yeager could scarcely believe his luck. His victim was not even armed. He moved out of the stall and cautiously inched his way along the stalls, making his way to the first one. He could hear the sweep of the rake as Clint skimmed off the loose hay on top of the muck beneath. As Simon neared the first stall opening, he thought about his plan to strike quickly and make a run for it. Since there was no one else around, he saw an opportunity to take a little more time killing Cooper and to give himself the satisfaction of seeing him squirm before he finished him off. More than anything else, Simon wanted Clint to know who killed him and why.

Clint propped his rake against the side of the stall and had reached for the pitchfork when he heard a pistol cock and a voice behind him.

"Keep your hands offa that pitchfork." Clint froze. "Now you turn around real slowlike."

Clint recognized the voice at once. With no choice to do otherwise, he turned around to see the hulking form of Simon Yeager, his face fixed in a crooked smile as he gloated over his triumph. "You thought you was gonna get away with murderin' my brother, didn'tcha? Now you're gonna learn that nobody gets away with that."

"I didn't murder your worthless brother," Clint said. "You heard what the witnesses said, the ones that didn't lie. Your brother cheated and drew before the count went to three, but he's dead anyway."

Simon had total advantage over him; there was nothing Clint could do to save himself from being shot. But he had no intention of giving Yeager the satisfaction he obviously sought of seeing him grovel and beg for his life.

When am I going to learn to listen to Ben? he thought.

"You and your brother together aren't worth a shovelful of this muck I'm cleaning outta this stall."

"Why, you smart-mouth son of a bitch," Simon spat. "I'm fixin' to spatter your brains all over that wall behind you. Then let's see how big you talk."

Defiant to the end, Clint replied, "You'd better take good aim, 'cause I'm comin' after you, and I guarantee you, I'll be on you before you get off the second shot."

"Is that a fact?" Yeager responded, pleased by Clint's defiance. It made the execution more enjoyable. "Well, let's see if you're just blowin' hot air." Very deliberately, he aimed the .44 at Clint's forehead. Clint crouched, hoping to survive long enough to spring at his antagonist before he fired a second shot. Yeager's smile widened into a sneer.

Less than a second after, however, his eyes suddenly opened wide in shock and he recoiled with a startled grunt from the impact of the pitchfork in his back. In reflexive action, he squeezed the trigger, but the shot went into the loft floor above him. Stunned, he staggered backward, almost colliding with the determined Crow woman behind him. It was enough time for Clint to charge into him, planting a shoulder into his midsection. The force of Clint's attack was enough to send them both crashing against the side of the stall, causing the pitchfork to swing wildly back and forth as they struggled for possession of the gun. Impeded from deep penetration by the heavy coat Simon wore, the tines of the fork had not caused lethal damage.

Like the powerful bear he resembled, he fought ferociously to maintain possession of the pistol, but he wrestled with an antagonist who was just as powerful as he was. It appeared that the deadly contest could go either way until the Crow woman planted her feet solidly and swung the shovel in stoic determination, catching Yeager with the blade in the back of his neck. It was enough to cause him to lose his grip on the pistol, and Clint snatched it away from him. Yeager made a desperate lunge for it, only to be met with a bullet at point-blank range, dropping him dead on the barn floor with a black hole in his forehead.

It was over.

Still in a state of shock, he sat down on the floor and stared at the Indian woman smiling down at him. It didn't strike him until later that Rena was, in fact, actually smiling. After a few minutes, when not a word was passed between them, he finally regained control of his senses.

"You saved my life," he said earnestly. "If you hadn't stuck him with that pitchfork, I'd be dead now."

"Everything all right now," she replied.

"Yeah, thanks to you, everything's all right now," he

agreed. "Where did you come from? I didn't even know you were in the barn."

"Chickens make nest in barn. I look for eggs," she said. She didn't feel she should tell him that she believed that she was guided to the barn to look for eggs. She had found none when she had checked several days before that. "I go cook now," she said as Hank ran into the barn, having heard the shots.

"What was the shootin'?" Hank blurted. Then, before Clint could answer, he saw the body lying in the stall. "Lord have mercy! Who is that?"

"Simon Yeager," Clint said. "You'd best run up to the bunkhouse and tell them before Ben tries to strap his gun on and come staggering down here." He turned to Rena after Hank took off at a run. "Rena, I wanna thank you for what you did. I'll never forget it, I promise." As he gazed at her, the always stoic Crow woman quickly looked away when her eyes began to mist and a tear formed in the corner of her eye. Astonished, he wondered, could the always solemn woman have deep emotions after all? "Rena, what is it?"

"Dust from hay get in my eye," she lied. "I go tell Hope and Mr. Valentine what gunshots were."

"Good," he said. "I'm surprised Mr. Valentine isn't down here already. I'll stay here and help Hank when he comes back. Then we'll see if we can dig a big enough hole to bury that murderin' devil."

"Don't bury near garden," Rena said. "Make soil bad."

Clint couldn't help laughing. "It might at that," he replied.

The end of the threat from Simon Yeager was just one of several things on the Crow woman's mind as she started to leave. There was another issue that she had felt was not her concern, and she paused at the barn door to make up her mind whether or not she should speak. Deciding, she turned back toward him and said, "You must ask Hope to be your wife."

"What?" Clint exclaimed, hardly believing what he had just heard.

"You don't ask, she never say yes," Rena said, then turned on her heel and walked out of the barn, leaving a truly astonished young man. As she walked briskly back to the house, she questioned the wisdom of what she had just told him.

Every mother wants the best for her son, she told herself. *Hope will make a good wife when she stops acting like a silly girl.*

Thoughts of a wedding between Clint and Hope caused her to think back on the past, a past that was not always happy. She knew that Clint did not remember much about Clayton Cooper, his father—but she remembered Clayton Cooper very well. The tall, glib, white scout had charmed a young Indian girl into marrying him, then had abandoned her two years after the birth of a baby boy. He had left for Wyoming Territory, taking the child with him, for no reason she could think of. Perhaps it was because she adored the child, and he knew that she would be devastated by the loss.

Clayton Cooper was not capable of real affection for anyone other than himself, as evidenced by the small C-shaped scar he left on the boy's neck when he hurled a hot metal cup at him to stop him from crying. The child was barely a year old at the time.

It was years later when she happened to see a young man in Ogallala, where she worked as a housekeeper for a man named Nathan Wood, who owned a dry-goods store. He had come in to buy a bandanna, and when he removed the old one, she noticed a C-shaped scar just below his left ear. It struck her as an unusual coincidence, and when the store owner asked his name, she was virtually stunned. He left, unaware of the shocked Crow woman standing near the window.

When Mr. Wood's wife decided she didn't need a housekeeper anymore, he recommended Rena to Randolph Valentine, who was in town to purchase cattle. Her relationship with Valentine and his daughter, Hope, was a good one. But the miracle she often prayed for happened when Valentine decided to hire Clint and Ben in Ogallala, the place where she had discovered her son was alive. Now, as she started to open the kitchen door, she decided there was no point in telling her strange story to anyone. Who would believe it? Anyway, she had a feeling that she had a permanent place in Clint Cooper's life. He had promised her that.

Once again, things were back to normal on the Double-V-Bar. Ben was making amazing progress in coming back from his wound, a recovery he attributed to Rena's skills as a surgeon. The cattle looked to be in pretty good shape as the winter wore on, encouraging Valentine to estimate a high percentage of healthy cows come spring. Clint was content to be back in the saddle, overseeing the running of the ranch, so much so that he thought nothing of the fact that Sunday came with no visit by Justin Landry. It struck him as odd, however, when the next Sunday rolled around, and again there was no sign of the lieutenant. Finally his curiosity got the best of him and he decided to remark on the subject the next Sunday.

Valentine had sent for him to talk about the advisability of moving the cattle back up to the northeast

section where there was more shelter from the trees.
When the discussion was concluded, Rena was handy
with the cup of coffee she always had ready for him
whenever he came up to the house. Hope came in,
poured herself a cup, and sat down at the table with
him. Clint couldn't resist the opportunity to tease her.

"I don't know what it is," he began, "but something
don't seem right around here." She gazed at him, questioning, but did not reply. "It's like something's mis-
sin'." When she still was not interested enough to bite,
he asked, "Rena, today is Sunday, ain't it?" The stoic
woman paused, holding a large wooden spoon over a
pot of boiling potatoes. She looked at him but did not
answer.

"If you're talking about the fact that Justin Landry
doesn't call on me anymore," Hope said, finally rising
to the bait, "why didn't you just ask?"

Thinking that he had maybe touched a tender spot,
judging by her reaction, he immediately regretted his
attempt to tease. "I'm sorry, Hope. I reckon I shouldn't
have said anything." Ready to retreat then, he pushed
his chair back. "I guess I'd better get back to work."

Hope wasn't finished with the subject. "Since you
brought it up, Justin asked me to marry him three
weeks ago and I told him no."

"You told him no?" Clint asked. "But I thought you
two were goin' to get hitched."

"Well, you thought wrong," she said. "I'm not going
to marry someone I don't love. I'm fond of Justin—
he's a good friend—but I don't want to marry him." She
waited for that to sink in to see if he had any notion of
what she felt inside. When he just continued to stare at
her, she said, "I love someone else, but he hasn't asked

me, so I have to assume that he doesn't love me." This caught Rena's attention and she stopped what she was doing to hear Clint's response.

Clint was stunned. There wasn't anyone else that Hope had been seeing. He suddenly felt numb all over. Could she be possibly referring to him? In a moment of confused desperation, he forced himself to speak. "I reckon you know I've always had a hankerin' for you."

Hope looked at Rena and shook her head, perplexed. "You've always had a hankering for me?" She echoed. "You have a hankering for a piece of taffy! You have a hankering for a slice of pie!"

He was dumbfounded, knowing he had somehow said the wrong thing, and it seemed to have made her angry. There was no way he could undo what he had just blundered into. The only thing he could think of to do was to retreat, so he got to his feet and had started to head for the door when he was suddenly struck in the back. He whirled around to find Rena standing behind him, her wooden spoon poised for another blow.

"You ask!" she demanded.

He looked back at Hope, standing there with her hands on her hips, a challenging look in her eyes. It was an instant in time that would no doubt define the rest of his life, for if he was wrong, he was determined to pack his bedroll and his saddlebags and leave the Double-V-Bar for good. He spat it out as fast as he could say it. "I love you, and I wanna marry you!"

"Well, it took you long enough," Hope said.

"Is that a yes or no?" Clint asked nervously.

"Oh, I guess it's a yes. I've had a hankering, too."

Read on for a look at
the next thrilling adventure
from Charles G. West,

THE DEVIL'S POSSE

Available in March 2015 from Signet.

"Here you go, boys!" Oscar Bradley called out as he approached the group of men waiting at the corner of the corral, their saddles and other gear on the ground beside it. "It's payday." He picked a saddle to sit on and set the leather bag in which he kept his notebook on the ground in front of him. "Like I told you when you signed on back in Ogallala, this is gonna be my last drive, and I'd pay you a bonus if we made it here in less than twenty-three days." He paused to look around at the expectant faces. "Well, we made it in twenty-one, with the cattle in good shape. But the price for cattle is down, so I ain't gonna give you that bonus." He paused again to witness the looks of shock and disappointment, but unable to play the joke out any further, he cracked, "I'm just joshin' ya. I got top dollar for the cattle, but you oughta see the look on your faces." The silent void just struck over the drovers immediately erupted into a burst of cackling relief. "Like I said, you can each pick one horse outta this bunch in the corral, too. Now, who's first?"

"I reckon I am," Smokey Lewis volunteered, and stepped forward. The cook on the drive, Smokey owned his chuck wagon and the team of horses that pulled it. He had a separate arrangement with Oscar, since he had come along as an independent contractor to do the cooking. "You might not really be japin', so I'll get my money before you run out." His remark, made in jest, brought a few chuckles from the other men. Oscar Bradley was a fair man. Each of his drovers knew that he would lose money on the sale of the cattle before he would go back on his word to them. Their only regret was the fact that this was Oscar's last drive.

One by one, the men stepped up to receive their pay. Oscar marked each man's name off in his notebook with his pencil, then shook the man's hand. He paused briefly when the Cross brothers stepped up. Billy, the younger, was first. He and his brother, Logan, had been working for Oscar since they were teenage boys, and they had proven to be his most dependable drovers. "I'm sorry I don't have something else for you fellers, but like I told you, I'm headin' back to Omaha to sit in a rockin' chair on my daughter's front porch. I know I'd sure as hell give you a good recommendation, if anybody was to ask me."

"Thanks, Oscar," Logan replied.

"What are you plannin' to do, go back to Ogallala with the rest of the boys?" Oscar asked.

"I reckon so," Logan said. "We ain't talked about doin' anything else."

"Except gettin' a drink of whiskey first thing," Billy piped up. "That's about as long as I wanna stay around this place." He and Logan had already decided that there was no future for them in Fort Pierre. It seemed the only sensible thing for them to do was to return to Ogallala with the others in hopes of signing on with another cattleman. Herding cattle was all they knew.

"Hang around till I get everybody paid," Oscar said. "There's a little somethin' I'd like to run by you."

Billy glanced at his brother and Logan responded with a shrug. "Sure thing, Oscar," Logan said. "I'm gonna go throw my saddle on that flea-bitten gray standin' over by the fence before somebody else has the same idea." The gray had been his favorite and the one that he had most often ridden. It was the only one he had named, calling it Pepper. Having already set his sights on a buckskin, Billy followed him.

After every man had selected a horse and saddled it, Smokey Lewis motioned to Logan and said, "We're goin' over to the Cattleman's Saloon. You and Billy comin'?"

"You go ahead," Logan said. "We'll be along."

When the others had gone, Oscar put his notebook away and picked up his leather bag. "I was talkin' to a feller at the cattle sale, and he said he was lookin' to hire a couple of men to help him drive some horses over to Sturgis in the Black Hills. He's got two men who work for him, but he could use a couple more, since he wound up buyin' more than he planned." Oscar smiled and winked. "I sold him the rest of the horses here in the corral at such a good price, he couldn't pass it up." He paused for their reaction before continuing. "Anyway, I told him I knew two good men who might be interested. Whaddaya think? You wanna drive some horses over to the Black Hills? There's a helluva lot goin' on up that way ever since the government opened the hills up for prospectors. This feller said there's a heap of travel on the roads between here and Sturgis—mule trains, bull trains, wagons, and everything else that rolls or trots. Might be somethin' else over that way for you boys."

As usual, Billy looked at his older brother for his reaction. "How long a drive would it be?" Logan asked.

"He said it's about a hundred and fifty miles from here," Oscar said. "It'd take a week or more, I expect. I told him I'd see if you were interested."

Again, looking to Logan for his opinion, Billy shrugged and joked, "I don't recollect any appointments we've got. Whadda you think, Logan?"

"Wouldn't hurt to talk to the man," Logan replied. "Where do we find him?"

"He said he'll be in O'Malley's Place in about an hour from now. It's that little saloon down the street from the hotel. His name's Matt Morrison—seems like a reasonable feller."

"Okay, we'll go talk to him," Logan said. "That all right with you?" he asked Billy, knowing that his brother would agree. When his brother shrugged indifferently, he turned back to Bradley. "Much obliged, Oscar. We appreciate it." They shook hands again, and then he and Billy climbed into their saddles.

Oscar stood there and watched them as they rode off toward the town of Fort Pierre. *I wish I was as young as those two,* he thought. *I'd ride to the Black Hills with them.*

Fort Pierre was settled on the west bank of the Missouri River, on a level plain that provided easy access to the river. It was a pleasant setting for a town, but it held no attraction for the Cross brothers. They rode past the Cattleman's Saloon, even though there was plenty of time to have a drink or two with the rest of Oscar's crew before Mr. Morrison was supposed to be at O'Malley's. They both agreed that it might cause some resentment if the others found out that Oscar had favored them with his recommendation.

There were a few horses tied up in front of O'Malley's, though not as many as those at the larger saloon's hitching rail. Dismounting, they pulled their rifles from the saddle slings and walked through the doorway, the door having been left open to draw some air into the stuffy interior. They paused to let their eyes adjust to the darkness of the room, a sharp contrast to the bright summer sunshine outside. After a moment, they started toward a table against the opposite wall, thinking it a good place to watch the door and hope to spot Morrison when he walked in.

They had taken no more than a few steps when they were stopped by the bartender. "Howdy, gents," he greeted them cordially. "If you don't mind, I'd appreciate it if you'd leave those rifles on that table by the door." When both men balked for a second, he continued, "I reckon you fellers ain't ever been in here before. We ask every customer to do the same." He smiled then to show he meant nothing personal.

Logan looked back toward the door. Like his brother, he hadn't noticed the table with half a dozen pistols on it. "Sure," he said, "seems like a good idea." He and Billy went back and propped their rifles against the table and laid their pistols on top. Then they proceeded toward the table they had selected.

"What's your poison?" Roy, the bartender, asked as they passed by the bar.

"Whiskey," Billy answered. "Just whatever you got—rye, if I've got a choice." Neither he nor Logan was a heavy drinker, so it really didn't matter.

"I've got rye," Roy said. "And I've also got some smooth Kentucky bourbon, if you'd rather have it."

"Which is the cheapest?" Logan asked.

"Rye," Roy said.

"Then we'll have that, and a couple of glasses of beer to chase it," Logan said, and stopped to wait for it while Billy continued to the table.

"Well, here's to another cattle drive behind us," Logan said after they were seated. He raised his shot glass in a toast. Billy raised his glass to meet it, and they tossed the fiery whiskey down.

"Whew!" Billy coughed. "That stuff burns all the way down."

Logan laughed. "It makes a difference when it's been a long time between drinks."

Working slowly on the beer, they looked around them at the sparse crowd in the saloon. Only three other tables were occupied. And of the three, only one had more than two men quietly enjoying an afternoon drink of whiskey. That table, back in a corner of the room, was occupied by three men and a woman. The two brothers had sat there for only a few minutes before the woman got up to take an empty bottle to the bar to exchange for a full one. On her way past them, she openly eyed the two strangers, and on her way back, she favored Billy with a smile. It didn't surprise Logan. His younger brother had been blessed with the good looks of his mother, while he seemed to have inherited the brawn and strength of his father. It often amused Logan, because he wasn't sure that Billy's handsome features might better be called a curse. The thought had no sooner occurred to him than he began to hear a raising of the voices at the corner table. He turned to Billy and asked, "You smiled back at her, didn't you?"

"I don't know. I mighta," Billy answered. "Why?"

Logan gave his younger brother a tired sigh. "That's why," he said when the conversation at the corner table suddenly escalated into a loud argument.

"You don't own me!" the woman exclaimed indignantly, and rose to her feet.

"Set your ass back down!" one of the men demanded. "Countin' all the whiskey you drank, I sure as hell made a down payment on you." His remark brought a laugh from his two companions, who seemed to be enjoying the spat between the two.

"I'll set my ass where I damn well please," the woman replied. A large-framed, long-legged woman, who appeared to have many miles etched into a not unpleasant face, she seemed capable of handling the likes of her rough company. "I've wasted enough time on you and your friends. You coulda got drunk without me, if that's all you were interested in."

"Set down!" the man demanded again, and grabbed her wrist.

Logan glanced at the bartender. Seeing that he was now aware of the potential trouble brewing at the corner table, Logan was satisfied that the bartender would handle the situation before it became violent. As he had figured, Roy walked back to the table where the woman was still standing defiantly before the three men. "Hey, fellers," he began, "ain't no need to get your backs up. Gracie didn't mean nothin' by it. Right, Gracie?" Gracie didn't answer. She just continued to glare at the belligerent bully holding her wrist. Since Gracie was obviously not inclined to apologize, Roy attempted to appease the quarrelsome brute. "Let her go and we'll have the next round on the house. Whaddaya say?"

"I ain't takin' no sass from a broken-down old whore," the bully replied. He looked back at the woman and said, "I told you to set down." To enforce the order, he attempted to pull her down on the chair, but she fought against his efforts. The ensuing struggle knocked the chair over and landed Gracie on the floor, her wrist still captured in the brute's hand.

"Mister," Roy said, "I'm gonna have to ask you and your friends to leave now. I think you've had enough."

Fully agitated at that point, the bully clamped down as tight as he could on the woman's wrist while she strained to free herself. "I'll leave when I'm ready to leave," he roared, then threatened, "How'd you like it if I tore this whole damn place down?"

"Wouldn't like it," Roy replied.

To this point, the few other patrons of the saloon had watched in silence. Seeing that things had seemingly gotten out of hand, two of the men got up and made a hasty retreat out the door. "Damn," Logan cursed softly when it became obvious that Roy's efforts to defuse a situation already gone bad were not going to succeed, for Logan had no desire to get involved in the altercation. "You had to smile at her," he said wearily aside to Billy.

"Hell, I didn't know," Billy replied lamely.

By now, Gracie was desperate to free herself from the brute's clutches. When her struggles proved useless, she resorted to attacking his arm with her fingernails. "Yow!" her captor roared in pain, and struck her roughly with a backhand across her face.

That was as much as the Cross brothers could tolerate. Logan was the first to move. "That's far enough," he stated emphatically as he rose to his feet. "Billy, go over there by the door and take care of those weapons." He walked over to the corner table to confront the trouble-makers. "All right, the man here asked you politely to get outta his saloon. Now I'm tellin' you that it's time for you to turn the lady loose and do what he says."

His statement was enough to cause the bully to release his hold on Gracie, but he got to his feet and kicked his chair back. "And just who do you think you are, big mouth?"

"I'm the feller who's gonna whip your ass if you don't get outta here like I said," Logan told him.

"Huh," the brute snorted defiantly, "you gonna whip all three of us?"

"If I have to," Logan replied calmly. His assessment of the trio told him that they all appeared too drunk to put up much of a fight—that, and the fact that the man's two companions did not seem overly enthusiastic about joining in. And he was not discounting Billy's help after his brother finished emptying all the cartridges out of the weapons on the table by the door.

"He's talkin' mighty big, ain't he, boys?" the bully snarled with a sneer. "Let's see if he can back it up."

ALSO AVAILABLE FROM

Charles G. West
Crow Creek Crossing

Wyoming holds the promise of a bright future for
newlyweds Cole and Ann Bonner. The young couple
have braved the long, hard road across Nebraska in
hopes of building a new life for themselves on a
tract of land near Crow Creek Crossing. But their
dreams of a fresh start are quickly cut short. While
Cole is away in town, a gang of outlaws led by the
vicious Slade Corbett raids the family homestead,
leaving behind a smoking ruin and the mutilated
bodies of everyone Cole holds dear...

Also Available
Wrath of the Savage
Silver City Massacre
Mark of the Hunter
Long Road to Cheyenne
Way of the Gun
Black Horse Creek
Day of the Wolf
A Man Called Sunday
Death Is the Hunter
Outlaw Pass
Left Hand of the Law

Available wherever books are sold or at
penguin.com

National bestselling author
RALPH COMPTON

"A writer in the tradition of Louis L'Amour and Zane Grey!" —*Huntsville Times*

Available wherever books are sold or at
penguin.com

S543